The Palm Oil Stain

Nadia Maddy

Published in 2011 by New Generation Publishing

Copyright © Nadia Maddy 2011

First Edition

www.newgenerationpublishing.info

Nadia Maddy is the daughter of the Sierra Leonean playwright, Yulisa Amadu Maddy. She lives in London teaching Sociology and Health and Social Care 'A' Levels. *The Palm Oil Stain* is her first novel.

For my son, Akir who told me to remove all the unneccesary adverbs and continues to be my strength and inspiration.

Acknowlegments

Very special thanks are due to Mark Lewis, Maxine Gordon, Martin and Hannatu Gentles for reading the first draft in all its mistakes and encouraging me to push forward. Lisa Dean who taught me how to pitch and never faltered in her belief for my work and Julian Hall who did it before me then gave me the tools I needed to move forward. Fin Kennedy who loves his craft and shared that love with me with invaluable information and encouragement and Leslie Leigh for his advice and support since the early days.

Other thanks to the translators, Vamba Konneh who patiently translated the Mende language for me on a dull Saturday afternoon and Patrick Massaquoi, a student at Njala University, Sierra Leone who corrected all the written Mende.

Shalimar Zahra, my cousin whose tears of separation I never forgot in 1996, and whose name I use in this novel in admiration of her strength and perserverance to get through the worst.

Thanks for all your unwavering faith and support in me; Naseem Hudroge, Ramilke Kamarakeh, Jenneh Coker, Diane Smith, Ulisses jr, Tony Chidi, Shenis Kilkason and Amira Hudroge

Jacqueline Asafu-Adjaye and *The Voice* Newspaper for publishing an interview on *The Palm Oil Stain* for International Women's day.

Lastly my father, Yulisa Amadu Maddy for passing on his talent unwittingly and my mother, Harriette Williams for baby sitting while I attended dozens of evening writing courses after work.

Dedicated to the memory of:

Patrick Peter Brimah Kebbie (RIP) who was brutally killed on 25th December 1994 during the conflict.
Samuella Richards (RIP) (1970-2009). A friend who showed me how special Sierra Leone could be.

Despite conflicting accounts of the circumstances of the death of Patrick P. B. Kebbie, to this day no official inquiry into his death has been initiated.
Amnesty International News Service 167/95

Chapter 1

Shalimar carried the makeshift cardboard dustpan to the outside bin, ignoring the chickens flapping around her feet.

'No scraps for you!' she said with a smile, as the birds squawked and pecked around her.

Shalimar replaced the cover and looked up at the clear sky: 'Argh; another blistering day,' she said wearily. A bead of sweat trickled from her hairline, tracing a line down her cheek. She mopped her brow and stared up the dirt road that stretched out into the distance before her. As she shielded her eyes from the hot sun, she noticed the bent-over figure of old Mama Kaikai - the village gossip - walking slowly towards her. She lumbered past Shalimar, leaning heavily on her cane, and stopped by the cement steps of 'Long Life'- the local bar where Shalimar worked. Shalimar respectfully addressed the old lady.

'Good Afternoon, Mama KaiKai.'

'Bia na, kahui ye na?'

'Did you stop by to have a drink?' Shalimar asked.

'No of course not,' the old woman said abruptly, 'do I look like I can afford to drink here?'

As the old woman sneered, her single protruding white tooth became even more apparent against her bare black gums. She mumbled to herself, chewing the sides of her mouth. Her eyes narrowed as she snarled again.

'I drink my palm wine at home. I stopped by to ask you about your father's health and that sister of yours, the wild one *tee yae nah?*'

'Papa is fine, mah.'

The old lady cocked her head to one side, peering at Shalimar who had not responded to the enquiry after her sister. Mama KaiKai, unimpressed with both the attitude and the answer, scrutinised her for challenging the order of respect.

The two women eyed each other. Neither wanted to give ground, and so an awkward silence descended. A rolling ball of red dust appeared in the distance, announcing that a vehicle was coming their way. Shalimar noticed it first, and averted her gaze. A horrendous rattling, like nuts and bolts in an old paint tin emanated from its midst, as the engine complained of its exertions. The white Land Rover slowed as it neared them, and pulled up outside Long Life; the red dust it carried with it settling onto the cement building like a coat of fresh paint.

The bar's most frequent and affluent customer, Barrow, had arrived unexpectedly early with an entourage. His driver hooted at Shalimar in recognition as Barrow climbed out accompanied by two more white men.

'Excuse me, Madam,' Barrow said politely, moving past Mama KaiKai and ushering his guests into the bar, and out of the sun.

The old woman eyed the two men suspiciously; she recognised one of the men as a palm wine lover who sometimes caused mayhem in the small village with his irresponsible behaviour. She pursed her lips, sucking in as much air as she could, and then spat on the cement steps next to him. Shalimar stood speechless, shocked at the old woman's rudeness. The man stopped for a moment, first looking down at his feet, and then raising his gaze to study the old woman. A large scruffy beard hid the man's face. His clothes were unkempt, and because he wore 'Jesus sandals' that white men loved to wear so much, Shalimar noticed he had filthy toenails. She shuddered to herself and looked away. Shalimar regained her composure and snapped at Mama KaiKai,

'I've got work to do, Ma. If you pass by the house, I am sure you can find out what Baindu is up to!'

Without waiting for a response she stormed back into Long Life, where she noticed the bar supervisor - Salia - had already poured drinks for the new arrivals. He sensed her mood.

'Don't get upset with that stupid old woman; she is just bored and wants to be noticed. She does it to amuse herself.'

'Some people just live for bad news happening to others,' Shalimar sighed.

Salia shook his head. 'She will always be like that. She is miserable and you are not. Don't let her pass it on to you.'

Shalimar smiled faintly as Salia's fingers warmed the crease between her shoulder blades with soft, soothing strokes. Salia knew how to appease her no matter what the problem. She writhed like a cat under his expert touch, moving her head from side to side when he gently squeezed the nape of her neck.

'Ok, my mood is improved, Salia.' She said with a smile. 'You remember we have customers?'

Shalimar reached for the green bottle of Gin hovering in its own special corner, just for Barrow. Barrow and his crew sat next to the gaping shutters overlooking the open road, the only people in the bar. Ice cubes clinking in the now-empty bourbon glasses celebrated the arrival of the Gin bottle to their table. Barrow joked about the incident outside with Mama KaiKai when Shalimar served them. He told her he knew a few people that needed to be put in their place and, that maybe he should hire her, if her fee was not too unreasonable. Shalimar smirked at the thought of Barrow turning up for a business meeting with Mama KaiKai menacing at his side.

Barrow was an overweight white Nigerian in his 50's, Shalimar guessed. His permanently blotchy red skin and crooked yellow teeth always managed to hold the gaze of others. His rusty-coloured hair stuck to his scalp as though it had been glued on in a hurry, and dark patches of sweat covered his safari outfit. Barrow's overly thick Nigerian accent stunned Shalimar at times, leaving her to speculate whether it was at all exaggerated. He had been coming here for several months now, the Long Life Bar seemingly ideal for his needs, as he always dropped in with different unsavoury-looking characters, forever trying to impress them with the amount of drinks he bought.

Today looked like being one of those occasions, so it was no real surprise when Barrow got up from his table and headed towards Shalimar and Salia behind the bar. 'Probably checking if we have any more fancy spirits,' Shalimar mused to herself as Barrow approached them.

'I need a favour, good people. My friends are sick and it looks like they are getting worse.'

'No problem, they can sleep it off in one of the corners, it's a lot cooler further inside.' Shalimar replied, assuming the men were drunk.

'No, it's more than that. They have fever. I have to find Dr Banda and bring him here. I need them to stay here overnight until I come back.'

Salia nodded, 'I will keep them in the stock room. Shalimar, take them to the back while I talk to Mr Barrow.'

Salia's instruction caught her by surprise; why was he ordering her to take them to the stock room? Why not let them lay on the benches, here in the bar? Somewhere she could keep an eye on them – and more importantly – the stock! Salia beckoned to Barrow to join him outside, and the two men left the bar leaving Shalimar alone with the strangers.

Light showered into the stock room through the small window, gleaming on crates of beer that filled the shelves. The younger, clean-shaven man coughed violently as she helped him inside. He lay down on the wooden table, instantly curling into a ball, swearing in another language whenever he could catch his breath. The bearded, older man, shivered as Shalimar looked around for a sheet, knowing already that there were none.

9

Shalimar left the room to get some water. She could hear Barrow's voice getting louder as the conversation outside turned into argument. 'Salia must be demanding money for the inconvenience,' she thought. She carried the glasses full of water back to the sick men. The bearded palm wine lover was now seated. He looked up and nodded graciously as he took the glass from the tray and sipped slowly. The younger man seemed in worse shape than his friend, and struggled to drink. As Shalimar helped him raise the glass to his lips, she noticed there were spots of blood on his white shirt.

'*Nor to malaria dis.*' She said to no one in particular.

This was bad. White men brought money to the village, but never any good luck. The palm wine lover's only friends here were those involved in the process of fermenting the drink as well as themselves. He would appear in the village for a few days to sit with the local men, drinking and singing all night. A couple of times, when Shalimar had risen early in the morning to collect water, she had spotted him sprawled out half naked in the fields sleeping unashamedly. Such scandalous behaviour was unacceptable, especially around young children. He deserved to be robbed but no one ever bothered him. Shalimar believed this to be one of the reasons he returned to Blama. He could do whatever he pleased; left alone to wheel and deal, or whatever it was he did with any lawless rogue in and around the area. Shalimar walked out of the room informing Salia she was going home for lunch and would bring back medicine for the men.

'Why?' Salia asked, genuinely curious.

'Do you want them to die on us? They are white men and cannot handle our diseases. If they die, nobody will drink here again.'

Salia thought for a moment and laughed.

'That is very true! Tell Mama to make it properly and not poison them. I need to keep my job.'

Shalimar set off home, slipping and sliding in the mud that covered the roadside. This was the only remaining evidence of the sudden burst of torrential rain that had pounded the earth that morning, before the sun had burned through the clouds. The water had poured itself into the large misshapen pot holes that scarred the roads, leaving an assault course of muddy pools for Shalimar to negotiate. She kept to the side of the road, stopping whenever a car drove past so she would not get splashed. Most of the red earth had dried up, but the puddles remained, large and threatening. The midday sun warmed the back of her neck and arms as she quickly made her way home from Long Life. Despite the good intentions of getting medicine for the sick men, Shalimar also wanted to get home in time to help her Mama finish cooking the cassava leaves. The very thought of sweet palm oil poured over ground greens had her salivating as she hurried along.

Shalimar took the quick route through Blama Massaquoi, keeping to the narrow paths that separated the huge rice paddies that were full of people doing the backbreaking work of planting and seeding. The small town was home to the Mende and lay in the middle of the Southern District of Sierra Leone. The town was quiet as she hurried through; most of the elderly folk were sat outside gossiping, and the women were bent over large steaming pots, preparing lunch for the men in the fields. All greeted Shalimar as she passed through their domain.

'Shalimar, Bia na? Bi sieh.' An old woman said when she saw her.

'Ah wua na, ah woo sieh,' Shalimar replied waving. 'I think the men are making their way back for lunch.'

'Oh, thank you. Say hello to your family.'

'I will do. Goodbye.'

Shalimar finally reached her home, and headed straight for the coolness of her bedroom to take refuge from the sun. She found her sister folding her clothes. Baindu was tall and naked from the waist up. Her dark complexion and slim figure allowed her to appear magnificently regal. Cropped curly hair complemented her perfect aquiline features and heart-shaped lips. Baindu's beauty was the talk of the town; the local men constantly eyed her stately figure and perfect round bottom when she walked through the streets. Baindu picked up a packet of cigarettes from the floor and lit up.

'Ali has asked me to go with him to Koindu…today.'

This piece of news alarmed Shalimar. She straightened up and shook her head at her sister.

'Bi li loougor wa Baindu! He is an RUF Rebel, anything can happen. He is with dangerous soldiers.'

Baindu's expression remained neutral, not reacting to Shalimar's words. She stood up and wriggled her long fingers in Shalimar's face. A pure gold diamond encrusted ring fixed snugly on her wedding finger.

'We are engaged and getting married. You see….this is real. When they win the war, Ali and I will build a house for all of us to live in. We will have drivers and servants too, just like the Minister's children.'

Shalimar stared at the mineral wealth on her sister's finger before touching it cautiously as though it would fall apart. It felt cold and hard against her sister's warm skin. Baindu slipped her feet into her flip-flops and shook her head.

11

'I'm a woman of action, Shalimar; you know this. Our life will be even better soon. The Rebels have taken all the villages to the west and will be here soon.'

She patted down her curly cropped Afro, smiling into the mirror at her sister's horrified reflection. Baindu had made her decision yet again without consulting anyone.

'Ali is going to make sure nothing happens to Mama and Papa. When you come back from work tonight I won't be here. Don't tell Mama what I told you. She thinks I am going to Bo with friends.'

Shalimar stood up, looking petite and curvaceous next to her sister. Despite being four years older than Baindu she was often mistaken for the younger sister. At twenty-two years of age, Baindu asserted herself more than most in the village, career-wise. Unfortunately her immaturity shone through brightest when it came to men. Once again, Baindu was playing with fire; her impulsive behaviour drove Shalimar insane. She tried to stem the panic in her voice as she spoke.

'*Kone lay* Baindu, Mama will cry for days if she finds out the truth, and Papa is not well. Why would you be so selfish? You know I have to work. Why would you do this to Mama?'

Baindu knelt down, lifting up a corner of the mattress at the head of the bed, and pulled out a wad of notes. She stood up and shook the money in Shalimar's face.

'300,000 Leones, Shalimar. No man you ever meet will be able to give you this. I just did. I am going to change our lives. We can buy the medicine that Papa needs so he can get better. I am doing this for all of us.'

Shalimar stared at the money scattered on the bed. She could already imagine her parent's reaction to the money, and Baindu's outrageous behaviour. Mama would take the cane to Baindu as though she were a ten-year-old girl if she ever found out what her intentions were. Worse still, Baindu gave no thought to how her liaison with RUF Rebels could affect Papa. Shalimar's temples tightened with agitation. She grabbed the money from the bed and stuffed it back under the mattress; annoyed that Baindu would take this amount of money from an RUF soldier. She turned to reason with her sister, but Baindu had left the room. Mama's voice trailed through the shutters calling Shalimar's name. The food was ready and she did not like to be kept waiting.

The flawless cassava leaves had Shalimar savouring every morsel as she dipped her hand into the enamel bowl to scrape up the yellow stained rice. Mama listened to the story of the sick white men and suggested they enlist the help of the local boys playing football across the road. Shalimar interrupted their game by promising a few Leones for their troubles. Mama instructed the local boys to gather the herbal leaves from the forest. They listened intently to Mama's descriptions of shape, size and colour of plants and shrubs she needed. Once out of sight Mama aired her frustrations about the Long Life bar.

'Has Salia found an assistant yet?'

'No, mah. Not yet.'

'I will have a word with him tonight. Enough is enough. You are just supposed to be helping him out. I did not raise you to be a bar woman.'

Shalimar ate in silence as she listened to her mother. It seemed acceptable enough for Baindu to have unsavoury boyfriends, but not for her to help out in the local bar and bring money home. Shalimar turned as she heard a shuffling from behind, and smiled as Papa joined her and Mama to sit under the shade of the guava tree.

'Did you sleep well? Bi gaahu yea-na?' Mama asked as Papa slowly shifted his weight onto his hands, easing himself into his chair.

'I always sleep well. Kayii ngeiwo ma.'

'You want to eat now?'

'Later, later...' Papa mumbled, waving a hand dismissively, and then wiping his brow with a cotton cloth.

Mama nodded at no one in particular. Her eyes darted over the tall grass in front of them as though searching for a lost chicken in the bushes. She continued her earlier conversation with Shalimar.

'You are just doing them a favour, Shalimar. You are not going to work there next month.'

'Baindu started this Mama. She told Mr Foday that I was available.'

Shalimar felt the need to remind Mama that this had never been her idea. Her parents had the habit of forgetting details when it didn't suit them to remember; especially when they were Baindu's.

Mama mumbled something under her breath. A waft of cool air met their faces; there was silence as they savoured its generosity. Shalimar looked over at her Papa with a heavy heart. He was not very active these days. He complained of chest pains and always appeared short of breath. Baindu had taken him to see the doctor in Bandawo, but the medical fees proved to be too much even for her salary as a Supervisor at the local Coca Cola factory. The doctor advised them that he should stay at home and rest until they could raise funds to pay for his consultation, as well as medicine.

'Shalimar, you have to tell Salia to escort you home from now on,' Mama insisted

'Why, Ma?'

'Don't you know that the Rebels are everywhere? What is wrong with you?' Mama snapped; clearly irritated by Shalimar's casual attitude.

'Tell Salia he must escort you home today. Otherwise he will have to find somebody else from tomorrow. You hear all these stories about these Rebels waiting in the bushes jumping on women and even girls as young as twelve and raping them. It is not safe, although God has protected us all up to now.'

'Thank the Lord we are still alive,' Papa spoke aloud to himself.

'Yes Mama,' Shalimar asserted.

The boys reappeared with a heap of leaves and shrubs. Shalimar helped Mama prepare the herbs in the huge brewing pot, which was then placed on the fire to infuse the healing properties. Stirring and tasting, trying to get it just right took what felt like hours. Finally, Mama said it was ready, and so Shalimar poured the thick brown liquid from the pot into two coke bottles. She searched around and found an old sheet, grabbed it, and along with the medicine she hurried back to Long Life to see how the patients were doing.

*

The two men remained in the same position as she had left them. As she entered the stockroom, she found Salia taking money from the pocket of the younger man on the table, who was now deathly pale with sunken eyes. His body jerked when he coughed as if being prodded with electric shocks. The rasping sound of air fighting to exit his body made Shalimar wince. Salia gleefully waved the notes above his head in triumph.

'We will share this when they have gone with their doctor. They must pay for using the back room.'

She ignored his childish behaviour.

'I do not want their money. A hani weka gbi, they are sick men.'

'Don't feel sorry for them. There is plenty where this came from. They will not miss it. It's diamond money.'

Shalimar did not answer; instead she poured the first bottle of thick brown liquid into a glass and pushed it to the lips of the big and sturdy young man on the table.

'If you don't change your mind in the next ten minutes it will be too late,' Salia said leaving the room still waving the notes around as though he were selling them on a market stall.

Shalimar ignored him. She did not feel that sorry for the men, but she did not want their deaths to be on her conscience either. She thought that the bearded man should have been dead long ago. He often hung around the village with the local alcoholics; unwashed and stinking. But he never preyed on the village women like other foreigners - he would just drink, sing and swear all night with the local men, and then spend all day sleeping off his excesses under the nearest guava tree. There were many stories about how many diamonds he had acquired and how many men he had killed. It seemed strange that such a man, with rumoured wealth and power would live his life this way.

The palm wine lover remained silent as Shalimar covered him with the clean faded sheet. He gulped down the herbal medicine with ease and handed her the second empty bottle. That was when she noticed his savage emerald eyes. She stepped back, stunned that she had not spotted this before. Green eyes were the very source of evil and witchcraft. She was alone in the room with two complete strangers and there were no witnesses. Demons changed shape to disguise themselves, but they could not hide their eyes. It slowly dawned on her that this green eyed monster could be sucking the life out of the other man to receive and strengthen his own energy. Once he had finished with his friend, he would turn on her, suck out her energy and claim her spirit. She would be under his spell forever, soulless and without a home. Shalimar rushed out of the room, her heart pounding.

Salia finished cleaning up and stood outside waiting for her.

'I am closing for the evening. We cannot do business with sick people at the back. Barrow has compensated us well for our loss tonight.'

Shalimar nodded, enjoying the prospect of a paid night off.

'Barrow has gone to get the doctor. They should be gone by tomorrow.'

'That will be a relief, Salia. I don't like them being here.'

'Forget about them. Would you like some roast beef?' Salia asked with a glint in his eye. He nudged her playfully.

Shalimar smiled. 'I'm not that hungry, but I'll eat some roast beef with you.'

'Roast beef and *poyo*? That will set us up for the night. *Mek we sleep well!*'

He laughed aloud and slapped her on the back playfully. The muscles in her shoulders slackened as she felt the tension leave her slowly. It was second nature for Salia to relax women in his presence, and Shalimar knew his reputation as the local lady's man was well justified. His big brown eyes and sparkling white teeth warmed the hearts of many of the women in Blama.

They walked casually home together along the main road, greeting a few villagers on the way. The distant howling of dogs broke through the receding purple gaze of the evening, threatening to fuse with the skyline as sundown approached. It was a wise decision to close the bar early. This was their night to relax without the bother of putting up with the usual drunken louts in Long Life.

Mr and Mrs Foday had built the bar because of the diamond mines in the region. It was a good location as it was less than twenty minutes from town, and just set back from the main road that linked the mine to the highway. There was a constant flow of traffic passing one way or the other, with people either heading to the mine to buy a small plot or - if they had struck it lucky - heading off with their new-found wealth. Either way, Long Life was the only bar in a twenty mile radius, so business was always pretty good. The diamonds brought an influx of Lebanese, Indian, Nigerian and Chinese, all hoping to get a piece of the pie. Shalimar was used to the foreigners and their somewhat bizarre requests and occasional generous behaviour.

As they approached more of the familiar houses, a lone figure emerged from the darkness moving fast towards them. The figure became recognizable as it got closer.

'Mama?' Shalimar called out a little unsure.

Mama's pace did not change when she came into focus. Salia greeted her but she walked right past him grabbing Shalimar roughly. She shook her as though she was shaking dust out of a bed sheet.

'You knew your sister was going to leave with those RUF boys! You knew it, and you did nothing to stop her! What kind of a sister are you? What is wrong with you? Are you sleeping? You knew this, and did not think to tell me!' Mama shouted; beside herself with anger, her eyes filled with fire and hate.

Shalimar tried to pull away from her mother who grappled clumsily to re-seize her. The veins in Mama's neck jutted out against her skinny frame as she tried to reclaim her grip on Shalimar. This was the most shameful thing, for a parent to have to lay a hand on you when you were a grown woman.

Salia moved swiftly in between the women in an attempt to calm Mama down. Mama continued to roar, pointing accusingly at Shalimar.

'You better find your sister and bring her home. Do you hear me? She left because you allowed her to! You better bring your sister home if you know what is good for you!'

A mixture of shock and shame rose inside Shalimar. She put her hand to her burning cheeks. A small crowd of people appeared from nowhere gathering around them. Salia held Mama firmly by the shoulders in a futile attempt to calm her down. He turned to Shalimar.

'Go home. Go home now! I will sort this out. Let me talk to your mother.'

Mama slapped Salia's hands away as she tried to get at Shalimar.

'You let Baindu go. It is your fault!'

There were discontented mutters from the crowd when Baindu's name was mentioned.

'But Mama, I have nothing to do with Baindu leaving...'

'What kind of sister are you? Why would you allow her to leave? Why did you not tell us?'

Salia bellowed, 'Shalimar, Go home now!'

Shalimar stepped away; suddenly aware of the growing crowd behind her. Her face grew hotter. Blinded with shame she ran to her house and did not see Papa who grabbed her arm as she ran past him.

'Have you seen your mother? Bi bi nje loi lo?'

'Yes Papa, she is down there with Salia.' She said pointing in the direction she had come.

Papa gazed at her with sad weary eyes; patting her on the back in response.

'I see.' He said knowingly. 'Don't worry; you know how your mother is. Go to your room. We will talk in a minute.'

'Yes Papa.'

*

The lantern cast long shadows around the room. Mosquitoes buzzed and bumped haphazardly around the light. Shalimar wished the mosquitoes would just die and the floor would open up and swallow her. Baindu always created problems. Mama spent a lot of time beating Baindu as a child. She stressed that Baindu's behaviour had to be nipped in the bud immediately otherwise it would get out of hand. Shalimar spent a lot of time consoling her younger sister with hugs and coconut cakes. Baindu would cry a little then run off to play forgetting anything had ever happened. Minutes later the resonance of a slap on naked flesh and Baindu's shrill cry could be heard once again. Shalimar would shake her head and carry on with her household chores in disbelief. Now that they were adults, nothing had changed. To Shalimar, it seemed like she always received the blame for not taking

17

care of and protecting her sister, when in her own mind that was what she had always done.

Shalimar's finger trailed around her stomach, as she lay curled up on the bed. She often did this when upset. She traced the outline of the dark birthmark that covered her stomach area. The birthmark moulded itself around her belly, stretching and changing shape whenever she examined it. Baindu said it resembled the shape of a beautiful butterfly, whose wings moved as Shalimar flexed and moved her stomach. To Shalimar it was a disfigurement that detracted from her beauty, and the polar opposite of the smouldering dark chocolate complexion that covered Baindu's lean, curvaceous frame.

The sound of her name interrupted her thoughts. Salia appeared at the door, smiling that friendly smile of his.

'Shalimar – may I come in?'

Shalimar lay there without responding.

'Well I assume that's not a no,' he said, entering the room and sitting on the edge of the bed next to her. He patted her awkwardly on the back as she lay there motionless.

'Your mother has calmed down. She is just upset that Baindu left the way she did.'

Shalimar could not respond to her friend's consoling words, the shame too much to bear. Salia grinned as he pinched her cheek.

'Come early to work in the morning. We will have a drink together. Forget about this, it will all blow over. Your sister will be back tomorrow. Then you make sure you give *her* a good slap.'

The corners of Shalimar's mouth turned slightly. She turned to Salia just as Papa's worn out figure appeared in the doorway. Salia noticed too, and stood up and excused himself almost immediately.

The mattress sunk as Papa's large frame sat down. His fingers brushed against her neat cornrows affectionately. He sighed.

'Baindu left with an RUF man in a fancy car. We know he is RUF because they have no respect for anyone. They are a different breed. They are all taking *brown brown*, these disgusting creatures. Baindu showed no respect today; she ignored your mother and jumped into that animal's car. Your mother loves you, Shalimar, but she has no one else to take it out on. You know this don't you? She is just beside herself with worry.'

Papa always took her side against Mama's constant accusations. He had cradled her with soft comforting songs and folktales into many a starry night after Mama had broken the cane on her back and there was nothing left to beat her with. Papa had always been the appeaser. Shalimar always managed to find her voice when he was around.

'Baindu is a grown woman Papa; I cannot stop her from doing what she wants to do.'

'We all know this. Your mother just needs somebody to blame. I have sent her to bed. Don't worry anymore. She will be fine in the morning.'

Papa leaned over to kiss Shalimar's forehead, muttering something inaudible under his breath, he stood up and shuffled out of the room.

Chapter 2

The humidity made it hard to breathe outside the house. So far, not even the occasional gust of wind had graced the village with its presence through the entire day, and the mud block hut had provided the only relief from the torturous heat. Although cooler inside, Shalimar still slept naked with no covers.

When she awoke, she lay there a moment, looking down at her burnt caramel complexion. Her skin had always been fairly patchy, and she inspected her arms in dismay, hoping her skin troubles would disappear like dust, once she had her shower.

Born out of wedlock, Shalimar was always going to be different from the other local children. She stood out as half Fulani. The Fulanis were nomads who resembled the Berbers of the desert, and they hailed from Guinea, the neighbouring country to the North.

As a young girl, Mama had worked as a cook for a wealthy family in the capital; Freetown. She had begun an affair with the man of the house, and soon fell pregnant. The master of the house chose the name *Shalimar* before she was born; his instincts told him it would be a girl. He came across the name on a business expedition in a foreign land and so she was given a name that represented neither his tribe nor her mother's. The wife found out about the pregnancy, and when she caught her husband alone with the cook, she soon put two and two together, and Mama was thrown out of the house as a result. With nowhere to go she returned to live with her family, and soon after married Papa only to have another daughter, Baindu.

The other children called her 'Dirty Mulatto' during the dry season when the sun was unkind to her skin, and her tone was more patchy than usual. Shalimar was used to the teasing and never cried. When it was particularly bad, Mama scrubbed her neck raw, accusing Shalimar of shaming her to the other villagers - afraid when they saw Shalimar they would see her skin as some form of neglect.

Mama interrupted Shalimar's thoughts by popping her head through the door. Shalimar placed her arms back by her sides and watched her mother force the rest of her body through, as the door heaved forward slightly. Mama was in her seventies now, although nobody in the family knew her exact age. She was the colour of charcoal with even wrinkles defining both age and wisdom. She stood small and frail, wearing only a lapa tied tightly around her tiny waist. Everyone was feeling the heat.

'Shalimar you want to eat now? Before you go?'

'I will have just a little, Mama. I'm not very hungry.'

As usual Mama behaved as though nothing had happened the night before. This is how it was, and would always be. Shalimar dared to ask about the money Baindu had left behind.

'Did you put the money in a safe place Mama?'

Mama ignored her daughter's questions. 'It's white okra today.'

'I'll dish out the rice in a minute, Mama. Mama, did you put the money away?'

Mama snapped. 'Yes I did, *leff me*!'

'You put it somewhere safe?'

Shalimar knew she was walking a fine line, but pushed on anyway. 'Safe? '

'I dug a hole under my stool by the guava tree.'

'You hid the money outside? Mama!'

Irritated, Mama clapped her hands over her daughter's head in dismissal and raised her voice.

'Who will look there? Eh?'

Shalimar leant backwards to grab the bath towel laid out at the foot of the mattress. She knew better than to acknowledge her mother's frustration. She stood up and wrapped the blue towel around her chest. Mama interrupted this by cupping her daughter's left breast.

'They are drooping. You need to wear a brassier to sleep from now on.'

Mama's hand lifted Shalimar's left breast with the intention of having it point to the ceiling.

'Too much breasts. Your sister's breasts are still pointing straight; they are round like oranges. You have watermelon breasts. A brassier will stop your back from hurting.'

Shalimar turned her back to tie the worn blue bath towel around her waist, and walked out of the room to have her shower. When her mother compared her to Baindu she shut her ears. Words like bullets to the chest could not penetrate if you protected yourself and did not listen. On days like this she was glad to seek refuge at Long Life.

The washing area was positioned at the back of the house and surrounded by bamboo leaves to prevent the occasional passer-by from looking in. Shalimar covered the roof of the square area with her towel; a signal to others that it was in use. A large green bucket filled with water stood in the corner. A small plastic multicoloured bowl floated aimlessly inside the bucket. Shalimar filled the small bowl with water, crouched down and poured it over her naked body.

21

*

There were not many opportunities for work around Blama, except to help out in the rice fields. The money that Long Life brought in for the family allowed for small luxuries such as shoes, perfumed soap and - most important - Papa's medicine. Salia only required Shalimar during the busy periods from Thursday to Saturday, and this was perfect as it left plenty of time for Shalimar to help out at home. Her parents couldn't cope with the rice fields and their frailty was beginning to show. Shalimar treasured the time away from her family and the freedom it gave her. She enjoyed the strangers and frequent drunks that showed up with stories to tell and the generous tips that sometimes accompanied them. This Friday night was no exception as she counted her tips in the empty bar towards closing time. The busy bar was hotter than usual tonight, with the accumulated body heat of the many patrons. The big white fans that hung off the high ceiling spun round so fast that the wooden beams creaked and shook with their force. Throughout the evening, Shalimar had taken every opportunity to linger beneath them, as she served her customers. Anything to feel the vigour of the artificial wind blasting through her blue cotton dress. Baindu's supervisor role at the Coca Cola factory made it possible to occasionally buy decent second hand clothes, which Shalimar only wore to work. The cotton dress, though plain, showed off her hourglass figure. The tips counted and shared, Salia disappeared into the back room to tidy up the stock whilst Shalimar wiped the tables.

The unmistakable sound of a magazine being loaded into a gun caused her to swing around. Two men in casual clothes, both sporting red bandanas stood at the door, each brandishing an AK47. One pointed his weapon straight at her; he laughed when he saw her freeze then lowered the gun and walked to the corner of the room. Shalimar's heart sunk. She held onto the back of the wooden chair, her legs suddenly weak. A large round black figure in full military uniform stepped into the bar following behind the first soldier, and walked over to the table overlooking the dusty road. Barrow emerged from behind him, wearing the same safari suit with added patches of sweat. He looked around the bar. His eyes fell on Shalimar and he grinned.

'Shalimar, where is Salia?'

Shalimar was rooted to the spot, unable to respond. Salia emerged from the back room, the ubiquitous smile disappearing immediately from his face. His eyes searched the room in total panic, but he visibly relaxed when he saw Shalimar.

'Mr Barrow, Sah. Bi gahu yeana?'

Barrow sat with the military man and signalled for two of the usual to Salia. More undesirables filed into the bar, filling up the tables.

'Shalimar, why are you still standing over there? Come here,' Barrow demanded.

She heard Barrow beckon her, but invisible nails kept her feet pinned to the wooden floor with fear.

'Come on woman...over here!' Barrow said again; this time a lot less friendly than the first time.

Barrow's aggressive tone startled her back into reality. She walked across the room, every step feeling like her last. A light slap on her bottom surprised her.

'What are you doing?' Shalimar exclaimed.

'This is my faithful girl...' Barrow said to the men at his table. Ignoring her protestation, his hand trailed up to her arm and squeezed it gently. 'She is a good girl...'

The military man ogled Shalimar, who deliberately kept her gaze to the floor. A mixture of stale and fresh sweat seeped from his pores. The longer she stood there the worse the odour seemed to become. Shalimar's throat tightened. He was so black, the whites' of his eyes shone in contrast. The military uniform hugged him so tightly, the buttons looked ready to explode from his stomach.

'Go get me two bottles of gin,'

Barrow's tight grip on her arm turned into a short shove. Shalimar was glad to get away.

'You know my favourite drink. And don't forget the tonic,' Barrow called after her. 'Stay in the bar area...eh...don't go to the back.'

The entrance doors opened loudly and Mrs Foday, the boss's wife appeared wearing a magnificent green country cloth gown. The lapa that encircled her waist made the waistband clearly visible regardless of the large mass of her body, and her wide arms carried the sleeves over her gown effortlessly. She moved slowly and spoke loudly, unaware of the events unfolding in the bar. Shalimar stood wide-eyed as Mrs Foday approached the bar. How could she be so oblivious to the tension in the room? To Shalimar, it was thick enough to be visible, and heavy enough to reach out and grab. Mrs Foday walked straight up to the bar, calling Salia's name several times. The beer-bellied military man stood up automatically from his chair when she entered the room, and followed silently behind her. Mrs Foday chewed gum with her mouth open; she smiled at Shalimar and placed her Florida key ring holding several keys loudly on the counter. Chewing gum appeared to be her mark of importance as she continued to chew loudly, looking straight into Shalimar's eyes.

'Where is Salia?'

The military man now stood directly behind her. Mrs Foday squinted and sniffed before turning around to see the military man grinning at her.

'Hello Madam, how are you?'

Shalimar couldn't see Mrs Foday's reaction but heard the stern reply.

'It's Mrs Foday.'

The military man smiled.

'Mrs Foday, I see. Where is Mr Foday?'

Mrs Foday hesitated. 'He has gone to see his brother in Bo.'

The military man nodded, still smiling. Shalimar noticed two more white men entering the saloon and a very tipsy Barrow greeting them. She felt a surge of relief inside. Perhaps there would be no trouble tonight as there were so many foreigners. The military man took Mrs Foday's hand gently,

'I would like to discuss business with you...about this bar'

Mrs Foday looked taken aback. 'Business?'

The military man nodded. 'Yes Madam. Business. This is a good strategic place to make money; let's go somewhere quiet and discuss it. I have a proposition for you.'

Mrs Foday put her black handbag next to her keys and pushed them to the corner of the counter.

'Shalimar keep my bag for me now… I will be back soon.'

The military man pointed to the narrow hallway behind Shalimar that led to the back office. Shalimar nodded and pulled the bag from the top of the counter and placed it underneath as Mrs Foday and the military man walked to a back room. At this point Salia reappeared, and continued serving drinks to the remaining men in the bar. Shalimar left him to it, and remained seated on one of the stools behind the counter, wondering if the RUF Rebels were finally in town. She hoped and prayed they were just passing through and that her parents were okay.

There had been stories, terrible stories of unspeakable atrocities taking place in villages in the District. So far Blama had been insignificant and lucky. The RUF were said to be merciless killers and now they were here, perhaps to destroy the village and take the land. Salia came back from serving Barrow and told her to get a grip. Their survival depended on it. Barrow was definitely with the RUF and the fat military man.

'Shalimar, you have to look busy. Act normal and don't attract attention.'

Salia pushed the dirty glasses into her hand and pointed to the sink.

'Rambo is here.' He continued in a low voice staring straight ahead into the dirty sink water. 'He is the ugly one.'

'The one that smells?' Shalimar whispered.

'Yes,' Salia answered.

Shalimar looked at her friend more closely, and realised his calm demeanour barely masked his fear. The sides of his mouth quivered as he swallowed and coughed, and as he passed Shalimar another glass she saw how his hand shook.

'What are we going to do?'

'We just carry on as normal. Hopefully they will leave without any trouble. Mrs Foday is here and Chameleon is here so maybe they will leave soon.'

'Who is Chameleon?'

'The crazy white man who loves the palm wine.'

Salia shook his head and heaved a long sigh.

'His eyes change colour and shape. They say he used to be a woman-demon. She lived in the bush and changed her appearance because of the war. They disturbed her land, so she changed into a white man to fight the Rebels.'

Shalimar caught her breath and tried to block out the brilliant green eyes that had tugged fear into the hollow of her stomach. She dared to search the room for the demon white man.

'Don't raise your head Shalimar!' Salia hissed, making her jump. 'Don't draw attention to yourself and don't look any of them in the eye. Just start praying.'

Salia moved around the bar wiping glasses that didn't need to be wiped. He looked occupied, grinning at the group of men every time he glanced up. Shalimar left the dirty glasses in the sink and went around collecting empty beer bottles from the tables, deliberately keeping her gaze on the floor. She could hear the white men talking to the Rebels about land and money, and as she cleared the table next to Barrow she noticed he was counting out a thick wad of banknotes. A RUF soldier grabbed her arm as he spotted her looking at the money, and then laughed at her inability to look him in the eye. He seemed to take pleasure in her fear. She shrugged away from his grasp and carried on collecting the empty glasses and beer bottles

'Bring an ashtray!' An order shouted from across the room. Shalimar nodded, and returned to the counter.

At this point, Commander Rambo emerged from the back room, but without Mrs Foday. He sauntered across the barroom floor and joined Barrow and the Chameleon at their table. Shalimar picked up the ashtray and took it to the table. Rambo's deep voice rose above the others as Shalimar approached. He grabbed her arm, pulling her down to face him. The smell of Mrs Foday's perfume did not mask the gut-wrenching stench that seemed to surround him. A mixture of urine, sweat and blood encircled him. His enormous pink tongue appeared like a toads, only to lick the right side of her face. Shalimar yelped in disgust and pulled back. His response was simply to pull her roughly back to him.

'You're interrupting my conversation,' The accent was unmistakably South African.

Out of the corner of her eye, Shalimar saw the palm wine lover staring at Rambo with an undisguised look of disgust on his face.

Commander Rambo sucked his teeth, then yanked Shalimar so hard that she fell onto him. He immediately put his arms around her and squeezed as she struggled to get away from his grasp.

'I can't do business with you doing that shit.' The palm wine lover suddenly spat at them.

Shalimar felt like she would suffocate as Rambo crushed her with his thick arms. Her chest caved in when she tried to breathe. The more she struggled, the stronger his grip, the worse it became for her. A loud bang sounded in her ears, the ceiling above them rumbled, and pieces of wood fell to the floor. The strong grip around her suddenly slackened. Shalimar pulled herself away falling to the floor as she did so.

'I'll shoot one of your monkeys if you disturb my concentration again.' The palm wine lover sneered as he sat back in his chair. Barrow helped Shalimar off the floor.

'You're causing problems here, Shalimar. The men need to concentrate on business.'

'Gbay huay, I'm sorry.' Shalimar choked.

Rambo shrugged his shoulders and chuckled.

'No problem. I can take her away with me tonight. You finish your transaction.'

'She stays here,' was the calm reply. 'Non-negotiable.'

Shalimar blinked back the tears. The palm wine lover was not slurring or spitting. He was without fear; his voice calm, authoritative and clear. Knocking back his drink, his frosty grey green eyes touched on her momentarily as he slammed the empty glass on the table.

'She is with me now.'

Barrow laughed aloud. The all-too-familiar sound of gunfire suddenly filled the air outside the bar. A burning sensation filled the pit of Shalimar's stomach. She put her hand to where the pain was emerging from and trembled. The two white men were doing business with the RUF rebels. Commander Rambo's large frame pushed his chair back as he stood up.

'My boys are here... time to go. *Muaa lima.*'

A colossal sound of chairs scraping against the wooden floor filled the room, and the rebel soldier's filed slowly out of the bar. Against a backdrop of multiple engines starting up and revving loudly, Shalimar allowed herself to exhale deeply.

Barrow remained in the bar, calmly finishing his beer. Evenings such as these were obviously not uncommon to him. He raised a hand, gesturing the two workers over to him.

'Salia, you and Shalimar stay in here tonight. It is not safe to leave. Close all the windows and lock the doors.' He turned to Shalimar. 'If you try to leave, he will not hesitate to kill you.'

He pointed to the South African palm wine lover who was just leaving the bar with a loaded pistol in his hand. 'We will be back tomorrow. Keep safe huh...'

*

Shalimar did not move from the spot as Salia ran to bolt the door behind Barrow. He picked up the long piece of metal resting against the wall, and then slotted it into the makeshift groove behind the doors. As he moved to the shutters, the gunfire drew closer. He secured them quickly before pulling Shalimar towards the back, behind the counter. He killed the power. All the lights in the bar went out, and as they stood still for a second to allow their eyes to adjust to the sudden darkness, all they could hear was the gentle whoop-whoop of the fans as they slowed. No gunfire; no revving vehicles. Everyone had left. Shalimar followed him to the stock room to retrieve the torch. Salia slipped in front of her, arms flailing in the air.

'Oh dear, Salia. You are so clumsy,' she teased.

'Lord have mercy! Lord have mercy!' He scrambled to get up as quickly as he had fallen but with each effort, he slipped again.

'What is it? What do you see?'

'Lord have Mercy!'

'Salia what is it? You are scaring me!'

27

Salia finally gathered himself and stood up slowly, pausing to gain some sort of composure. Without responding to Shalimar, he tiptoed to the middle of the room chanting a prayer; his outline silhouetted by the moonlight that shone through the window. Shalimar stayed put, too scared to break the deathly silence between them.

'Shalimar.' He said softly. 'Return to the bar immediately.'

'What's wrong? Why...'

'I said go now!' Salia shouted, in a way he had never done before. Startled, Shalimar obeyed, leaving the room quickly. A few minutes later Salia rejoined her in the bar. Salia pointed the flashlight onto himself revealing the blood that now drenched his shirt and trousers. Shalimar covered her mouth in shock.

'Mrs Foday is dead?'

Salia nodded, slumping down next to her, turning the flashlight off. They were both numb with exhaustion and fear. Mrs Foday had been murdered in cold blood and they were trapped at the edge of town in the bar. Shalimar moved closer, laying her head on Salia's shoulder. There was nothing left to do but wait and pray that nobody would try to get inside or alternatively burn the building down. Gunfire suddenly erupted outside, followed by several explosions.

'Oh my God! How close is that, Salia?'

'It is Blama, I think.'

'But that is so close. My parents...' Shalimar struggled to get the words out, as tears formed in her eyes and began to trickle down her cheeks. Salia put his arm around her as she sobbed softly.

'Salia,' she finally said through the tears, 'if the Rebels are not around maybe... *Mua-li lo.*'

Salia shook his head. 'They are around. Just because you can't hear them doesn't mean they are not here.'

'But I have to check on Papa and Mama, what if the Rebels have gone to Blama?'

'If they went to Blama, someone would have managed to escape and come to tell us.'

Shalimar stood up urgently and looked around.

'I have to go and check on my parents.'

'Don't be stupid, Shalimar. We should wait for another couple of hours at least.'

'I can't wait,' she said, and shrugged Salia's arm from her shoulder.

'What are you doing?' Salia hissed as Shalimar headed for the back room.

The moon still shone through the window shedding a little light for her to see. Although she couldn't make out the body, the room felt eerily cold compared to the bar area, prompting goose bumps to spread briskly over her arms. She blocked out her uneasiness by focusing on the window whilst edging slowly towards it. Shalimar slowly lifted the handle, pushed the window outwards, and warily peered out into the blackness. The air was still, the smell of wet grass even now apparent after the early evening rain.

'This is why your mother wanted to slap you last night. You don't listen.' Salia breathed heavily beside her, as he too surveyed the outside. Shalimar turned to him.

'I have to know. I can't sit here all night worrying if my parents are all right.'

She clambered onto the crates of soft drinks and lifted herself up to climb out of the window.

'Wait!' Salia hissed, grabbing her dress with such force he ripped the bottom.

'What? What is it?'

'Shhhh be quiet!' The urgency in his voice heightened. 'There... Look over there.'

He pointed to the right of the building where the grass rose slightly higher. Shalimar peered with difficulty in the dark, unable to make out anything.

'I don't see anything,' she whispered.

Salia did not answer; his eyes remained transfixed. Shalimar turned back to observe the darkness before her. A few seconds passed before she saw a subtle movement. At first it came across as the shape of a dog or cat, but Shalimar gradually realised there were two people lying on the ground. Shalimar lowered herself back onto the floor.

'Do you see what I am saying? Those are Rebels just waiting to kill anyone they come across,' Salia reprimanded her.

'You think they are guarding this place?' Shalimar asked. Salia nodded. She had not stopped to think that the Rebels would want to enjoy themselves in a bar full of free alcohol before they destroyed it. They would definitely be back in the morning for their spoils.

'We have to stay here Shalimar. We have no choice.'

Chapter 3

Violent banging on the doors startled them both awake. The sun shone through the gaps in the shutters, allowing rays to filter over the counter. Salia jumped to his feet as the banging continued. Shalimar pulled the bottom of his dried bloodstained shirt to get him back down again.

'No. Salia! It's the Rebels, don't open the door.'

The banging got louder and heavier. Salia crouched down, desperately trying to think. The voices suddenly hushed in union. An abrupt direct order was shouted.

'You better open this door now if you want to stay alive.'

Salia stood up and ran over to unbolt the entrance.

'I'm coming! I'm opening the door. Don't shoot!'

Nausea rose from the pit of Shalimar's stomach, and she put a hand to her mouth as she thought she was about to be sick. Footsteps came through the door, men talking and shouting orders for the back to be searched. Two men with rifles walked past the bar area without spotting her. She wanted to show herself and get it over and done with but she couldn't move. More footsteps were heard entering the bar; more orders to search were being shouted. A shrill laugh above her head made her look up, a young boy leant over the bar pointing at Shalimar.

'Over here…a woman…she is hiding.'

Wide-eyed with terror, Shalimar saw two men approach the bar. Without a word, they reached under the counter, took an arm each, and she was dragged out and into the room. Long Life was full of men and boy soldiers, all standing around talking, joking and laughing. Shalimar's heart sunk to see Salia's small frame engulfed by the familiar Commander Rambo, who they now knew had murdered Mrs Foday. He smiled when he saw her; the gleeful smile of a child presented with a new toy.

'Stand up!' One of the two men holding her snapped.

She was becoming too heavy. She tried to lean on her legs but still she trembled violently. Salia did not look at her. Rambo stepped forward, instructing the two soldiers to hold her firmly. They tightened their grip on her small trembling body. The military man got down on one knee and forced his hand under her dress. Shalimar's face froze with terror.

'Open your legs,' Commando Rambo spoke softly, staring at her stomach.

She obeyed, crying openly. Salia stood away with his back to her staring at the floor. Rambo rammed his fingers inside her, causing her

30

to shriek in pain. A satisfied smile broke onto his face as though pleased with the reaction. He stood up tilting his head to one side slightly to observe her sobbing, before ordering Salia to serve the soldiers. A sudden shove towards the bar area made Shalimar scramble to safety. Salia gathered a stack of glasses and asked her to place them on all the tables. He still did not look at her. Shalimar blindly grabbed the tray and did as she was told.

Some of the men now reappeared from the stockroom, carrying crates of beer. After dumping their load on an empty table and ordering Salia to serve the other men, they disappeared back to the stockroom, seemingly intent on emptying it. It was becoming clear this was probably the last hurrah for Long Life.

Serving without eye contact was difficult. Shalimar ignored the Rebels attempting to slap her bottom and pull at her skirt and hair. She quickly wiped away the tears that blinded her vision, and dutifully poured the alcohol into the clear shimmering glasses. At the third table, a Rebel pulled her to him and placed his hands firmly on her behind. She could feel his long fingers invade the folds of her skin as he squeezed hard whilst the others cheered and whistled. He placed his hand under her chin so that she could look into his vacant junkie eyes. His tone full of lust edged on a threat,

'When Rambo is finished with you, I am coming for mine for a couple of weeks.'

She closed her eyes as the others clapped and hooted in anticipation for a possible peep show, but the Rebel pushed her away to finish serving. The Commander's table was the last to be served. She kept her head down, deliberately looking at the floor while making her way over to his table in the corner of the room. The bottle of brandy shook in her hands as she poured the drink; missing the glass and spilling some on the table.

'Why is she shaking like that?' The distinct South African accent surprised her. The usually dirt-smudged, bearded palm wine man had transformed into a clean-shaven businessman. He sat at the next table with two other men who both wore camouflage bandanas around their heads.

'Just pour.' Rambo snapped at her.

Then Chameleon got out of his chair and walked towards Shalimar as she poured out another glass, making an equal mess. Her head and body were now shaking uncontrollably, as though she was having an epileptic fit. A soldier at Rambo's table spoke up as the South African brushed past.

'Chameleon, go and sit down. This is not your war and this is not your woman. We are not like those yellow bellied South African blacks that you are used to. Mind your business.'

Chameleon stopped and turned to the soldier. He put one hand on the man's shoulder and appeared to whisper something into his ear. Almost immediately blood splattered across the table hitting Rambo and spraying Shalimar in the face. Commander Rambo jumped out of his chair pushing her over in the process.

Chameleon gently sat the man back in his place, and turned back to his table. In his bloodied hand he held a cutthroat razor. His grey green eyes cold, mouth set.

'Anyone else want to go swing on a tree in monkey heaven?' There was no emotion in his voice as he insulted the room.

The sound of bullets cocking in chambers rapidly spread around the room. Many of the Rebels shouted angrily, and several wielded their machetes, starting towards Chameleon. Shalimar knew they would gut him mercilessly in front of her and that she would probably be next. But to her astonishment Rambo stood up, bellowing at his men to sit down. Chameleon sauntered unaffected back to his seat. She noticed the automatic rifle lying on his table. He picked up a large padded brown envelope from his chair and threw it over to Rambo's table. One of the men he was seated with pulled the cigarette from his mouth and flicked it in the Commander's direction.

'Shalimar!' Salia called her to the bar.

She hurried back, confused and numb. Their eyes met for the first time since the men had arrived.

'Stay behind here. I will serve alone.'

She nodded automatically, and still shaking uncontrollably, she wiped the blood off her face with the bottom of her dress. There was nothing to do behind the bar so she tried to control her trembling by lifting up her hand to see if she could will the shaking to stop. It did not work. She had witnessed two murders. She couldn't feel or think properly, and she was too afraid to look in Rambo's direction to see if his man was alive. A tapping finger on the bar made her look up; Chameleon stood before her.

'Get what you have. *Mua-lima*, we are leaving.'

She stared at the man unable to respond. Salia rushed back to the counter to hear what Chameleon was saying to her. He nodded at Shalimar, and pointed to Mrs Foday's bag which was where it had been left the night before. She looked at the bag, then at Salia, and then back at Chameleon, who stood patiently waiting for her.

'Take the bag and go,' Salia instructed. 'C'mon, c'mon.'

He grabbed her arm roughly and shoved the black leather bag into her hands, pushing her away from behind the counter.

'*Ngii lima*, Salia... I can't leave you!'

'What do you think will happen if you stay, huh? Go now!'

She held on to Salia. Without him what would she do? Salia glanced over at Chameleon who impatiently walked out of the bar with his companions. Salia shoved Shalimar towards the entrance, and when she resisted he dragged her forcibly across the room, out the door and towards a silver Jeep. Chameleon was standing by it, shaking hands with the two men he had been seated with inside the bar. Salia tried to calm her down as Shalimar sobbed hysterically.

'I can't leave without you...'

'You have to go. You must not worry about me,' Salia reassured her. 'Go now and remain with him until it is safe to come back to Blama.'

'But what about you?'

'You get out of here and stay with him until it is SAFE!' Spit flew in all directions as he roared directly into her face. Shalimar flinched, responding with a quick nod. She squirmed at his forceful behaviour. His grip slackened as Shalimar's resistance waned. Shalimar turned to Chameleon.

'Can't he come? Please ...please allow him to come. He can work for you...'

Chameleon spat on the dusty red earth next to them.

'He is dead already. I'm not a fucking charity case.'

Salia opened the door of the Jeep pushing her inside. Shalimar wept as she held his hand.

'I will find your family. I am a survivor. I will come to Freetown, but you must wait for me. Don't come back here.' Salia said slamming the door shut.

Chameleon gunned the engine, reversed in a swinging arc, then accelerated away with a cloud of red dust in his wake. Shalimar turned in her seat and watched Salia's frail black figure grow smaller and smaller in the distance.

The scene that greeted them on the main highway shocked Shalimar. A sea of people swamped the road. Men, women and children ran in different directions falling over each other. Women held their heads wailing in despair. Children screamed. Many villagers had fled for their lives unaware that they were wounded. Shalimar scanned the crowd for a glimpse of her family amongst the confusion. People tried to climb

33

into the vehicle as they threaded their way through the molasses, but Chameleon pushed them off with one hand and steered like a man possessed with the other. He slammed repeatedly on the horn and swore at anyone who did not move out of the way fast enough. Shalimar shouted for Mama and Papa into the crowds but no one responded. Chameleon continued to speed through relentlessly, until gradually the crowds became smaller. Panic swept over Shalimar when she suddenly realised they were driving away from Blama, and her village lay on the other side of the crowd. She shouted at Chameleon to stop but he ignored her. Frantic, she grabbed the steering wheel catching Chameleon off guard. He swore at her throwing out an arm to block her advances, his elbow slamming into her Adam's apple. Shalimar gasped for air as blinding pain shot up into her head causing her to fall back onto her seat, clutching her throat.

The world suddenly fell silent around her. In her own little world for a few moments, Shalimar was vaguely aware of mumbling sounds around her. She opened her eyes and found Chameleon leaning over her, perspiration covering his forehead. He mumbled something, but she didn't catch it.

'It's dangerous out here. I didn't mean to hurt you. It was an accident.'

She could not answer him. He touched her throat then looked around hastily.

'Just stay lying down. Don't do anything stupid. Allow me to get us out of here.'

Shalimar remained listless. She felt as though she had been shot and left for dead. She closed her eyes once more waiting for the pain to go away.

*

The journey was a silent one. Shalimar stared out the window, looking at everything but seeing nothing. Her tears dried up, and the fear and the sadness had left her, leaving a vacuum with no space for feelings. The RUF Invasion had finally happened. Everyone had spoken about the possibility for weeks, but Shalimar never really believed it would happen. She looked in the side mirror, and saw the funnels of smoke that filled the air behind them; the tendrils rising high into the heavens, marking the spot where her town once lay. Shalimar looked away, trying desperately to shake the thought from her mind that the people of Blama were being wiped out. She reminded herself of the buried money. It was likely that Baindu had known of the imminent attack, and she would have warned her parents. They would have left immediately with enough money to pay their way to the nearest refugee camp. Shalimar blinked as she sat up and noticed the bloated bodies of civilians' sprawled out on stretches of the road. She closed her eyes again, too disturbed to look any further. Why did God allow this to happen? There was no answer, there hadn't been for years.

Evening drew near as the Jeep travelled through the difficult terrain. There were no street or road lights to guide them as they drove, only the reflection of the bright white crescent moon. The hazardous pot-holes created by hammering rain caused the vehicle to bump along incessantly. The speed of the Jeep generated enough wind around Shalimar to cool her down. Chameleon said nothing for the whole journey. He did not take his eyes off the road once, and he seemed to be familiar with the area as a whole. Every junction or crossroad they came to, he turned left or right, or carried on straight without barely a glance at any signposts. Exhaustion finally set in as Shalimar looked at the graceful form of the rolling mountains in the distance. Her body felt like dead weight. She leant her head back onto the head-rest and turned sideways to curl up into a ball, facing away from him.

A tap on the shoulder woke her up. A young soldier stood in front of her, rifle hanging off his shoulder. She turned to the driver's seat - it was empty.

'Are you driving with him?' The soldier asked her, nodding his head toward a group of men standing at what looked like a makeshift checkpoint. There were five huge boulders placed in the middle of the road, with soldiers swarming around them. Chameleon was standing amongst them, talking to one of the soldiers. Being around the Army was not a guarantee of safety, but these men appeared more organised and less sinister.

Shalimar poured out the day's events almost immediately. The soldiers would be able to help her; they could send more troops to Blama and recapture the village. Perhaps they had makeshift headquarters near the checkpoint. She would stay there and they could escort her back. She told the young man that she did not know where Chameleon was taking her or what he intended to do with her. That alone made her uneasy. The young soldier looked a little taken aback but chuckled in response.

'Don't be silly, that's Chameleon. Why would he kill you? You are lucky he helped you escape from the Rebels.'

Shalimar grabbed the soldier's arm.

'No, he is a murderer.' She lowered her voice, 'I saw him kill someone. You don't understand.'

The soldier pushed her back into the vehicle.

'I'm sure he is taking you to a better place. What is the point of him killing you? We are in the middle of a war and you are not safe. Get some money out of him and find yourself a job wherever you go. Make the most of it...'

Before Shalimar could respond to the young soldier's outburst the driver's door swung open, and Chameleon slid into the seat beside her. He opened the glove compartment to reveal a pistol lying amongst some CD's. Chameleon looked over at Shalimar.

'Go back to sleep. You are safe now, we are almost in Freetown.'

The Jeep engine burst into life once more and off they sped through the space created by the men pulling back the boulders. They were going to Freetown, the capital city and place where her biological father lived.

They turned off the main road, and Shalimar realised they were now following the coastal highway. Everyone in her village who had been to Freetown had spoken of Lumley Beach. The beach stretched for five kilometres, and had beautiful powdery sand that glittered in the dark. She could hear the waves crashing on the shore as they drove. The smell in the air was different; sharper and saltier. The Jeep turned right up a hill toward the bright lights of a six story hotel. As it slowed down the sound of the crickets broke the silence. They drove into a car park in front of what appeared to Shalimar to be a magnificent building. The car park was full of BMW's, Jeeps, Sport Utility Vehicles, and Mercedes Benz. Chameleon turned to her.

'We're here. Let's go inside,'

Shalimar clasped Mrs Foday's bag as she climbed out. The security staff held the glass doors open as they walked through, exchanging polite greetings. The bright lights inside made her squint after being in the dark for so long. She stepped onto the Persian rug and noticed the grand crystal chandeliers hanging from the ceiling. Men and women dressed in expensive western clothes moved graciously through the reception area.

Chameleon spoke to the well-presented lady behind the reception desk. Shalimar kept close behind and watched him counting a large sum of money into the receptionist's hands. The woman appeared to be in her mid twenties; her hair scraped back into a tight ponytail with a white rose pinned to the side. Her makeup and gloss lipstick were flawless. The precision of the black-pencilled outline that replaced her eyebrows was slightly unnerving. The receptionist eyed Chameleon curiously as he counted the wad of money into her hand. Her manner grew soft. She gave him lingering looks as he paused in his counting to clarify how much he had given her. She in turn licked her fingers and counted the notes fast, like an expert who was used to handling this amount of money. Shalimar had never seen so many notes before. Chameleon waited for the lady to finish then tipped her generously. The lady smiled and came out from behind the reception desk to escort them personally to their hotel room. They followed her up the stairs to the first floor. Tucked away in an obscure corner the receptionist stopped in front of a barely discernible door. She turned and faced Chameleon with hungry eyes scrutinizing him from head to toe in a seductive manner.

'Enjoy your stay,' she said skimming over Shalimar with contempt. 'I'm on duty most days. Don't hesitate to call me if you need anything at all.' She purred, before walking away swaying her hips deliberately from side to side for Chameleon's benefit.

Chameleon did not stop to watch the flirting receptionist. Instead, he opened the door to reveal a plush room fit for a visiting chief. An eighties black leather sofa with chrome handles and legs stood in the centre. Sliding glass doors leading onto a small veranda broke up the walls behind the sofa. Chameleon walked straight to the bar area and opened a bottle of Jack Daniels, pouring himself a generous glass.

Shalimar stood quietly in the middle of the room with Mrs Foday's bag against her chest, watching Chameleon nervously. He noticed her scrutiny and put the glass down.

'You have nothing to fear anymore. You will be safe with me; we are far away from any Rebels.'

Without waiting for a response he walked toward the closed door on the other side of the room, opened it and disappeared inside.

Shalimar remained still. This whole scenario had her thinking she was in a dream. The room was surreal. Far away from home in a strange place, she had never been exposed to this kind of wealth before. The furthest she had ventured was to Bo and Kenema to visit the markets. Everything here was alien to her. The same questions kept running through her mind. Why did he bring me here? What is he going to do to me? She wanted to believe the soldier's words but he seemed too casual about it. She remembered Salia had almost forced her to leave with Chameleon in the first place. Salia would not have deliberately put her in a bad situation so why did she not find this man's words remotely soothing?

Chameleon reappeared and beckoned her over, into the bedroom. A locally made king- sized bed filled the tiny space. Another small door to the right led to the bathroom. She noted there was no other bed in the room. He threw her a thick white towel that he picked up off the bed. Too slow to catch it, the towel fell to the floor. Shalimar bent down to pick it up and felt an ache in her muscles as she did so.

'Go have a shower.' It was more of a command than a request.

She pushed open the en suite door that led to the small bathroom. It was nothing like anything she had seen before. A rectangular white enamel bath with a fitted shower took up half the room space. Blue and white polka dotted tiles encased the walls from top to bottom. It was so clean it appeared to sparkle in Shalimar's eyes. She pushed the bathroom door shut behind her then leant over the bath to turn on the taps. The water fell straight from the shower and splashed all over her face and hair. She swerved out of the way to allow the spraying water hit the bath instead. Not having showered for two days this came as a welcome relief. Mrs Foday's dried blood had splattered all over the dress when Salia had grabbed her to stop himself from slipping. A bar of white soap lay in a soap dish next to the taps. She lifted her dress over her head and threw it to the floor then pulled the bra straps off her shoulders and twisted the bra around so she could unclasp it. Pulling off the rest of her clothes she stepped into the shower.

The cold water was welcoming as it was still hot and muggy. She loosened the two plaits in her hair and allowed the water to soak through the tight curls, soothing her scalp. Shalimar closed her eyes and soaped herself slowly. This could be the only bit of temporary peace for her, so there was no need to hurry. She was far away from familiar faces and in a strange place and had no idea what was in store. She remembered the soldier's words: 'Why would he want to kill you? That doesn't make any sense'. The refreshing feel of cold water against her skin soothed her soul as she continued to soap the rest of her body.

Shalimar pulled back from the running water to wipe the stream away from her eyes. The first thing she saw was Chameleon leaning with his back against the wall watching her intently. Muscular arms crossed over his chest revealed a large black tattoo. He didn't flinch when she opened her eyes. His sunburnt complexion and tousled brown hair contrasted with his glassy alien eyes. She hesitated, her heart pounding against her chest. He waved his hand slowly at her to finish off. Shalimar did not take her eyes off him as she rinsed the soap off quickly. She did not like this scenario one bit.

He picked up the thick white cotton towel hanging halfway off the sink and opened it up to receive her. She turned off the taps and climbed out of the bath uncertain of what to expect. In this instance she had to keep cool and play it smart. Her eyes darted around searching for a weapon as he patted her down gently, drying her shoulders and arms. Shalimar's heart raced as his hands moved the towel to her back, rubbing her gently. She bit her lip and squeezed her eyes shut. Dread crawled out of her heart pushing and pulsating through every vein in her body. He stopped abruptly handing over the towel.

'There's a white tank top on the bed for you to wear. I've put the air conditioner on so it should be cool in the bedroom now.'

She held the towel close to her body turning away quickly to leave the room.

'Hey!' He called to her, just as she stepped into the bedroom. 'You are going to have to learn to trust me. I'm all you've got right now. I would never hurt you. You are safe here with me.'

He turned his back to her and pulled his T-shirt over his head. Shalimar closed the bathroom door hastily.

Mrs Foday's leather bag was perched on the bedside table. She picked it up and searched through it hoping to find some money. There were a few notes in the side pocket totalling five thousand Leones. Five thousand Leones would buy her four bottles of Coke. That was nothing. Definitely not enough to pay for the bus trip back to Blama. There were a couple of blank papers with shopping lists on them for food and school books, but other than that the bag was empty apart from one photo of Mrs Foday's eight year old son. Shalimar looked at the back of the photo, scribbled in faded blue ink Shalimar could just about read the name: Charles. Charles was now motherless, that's if he was alive himself.

Sudden exhaustion consumed her as if rummaging through Mrs Foday's bag and finding nothing was the very climax to all the horrendous events of the day. She closed the bag and put it back on the bedside table. It was of no use to her now, even though she had clutched it tightly for the past four hours. The empty bag was the only physical reminder she had of her life, yet both its owner and the person who had shoved in her hands were now most likely dead. What was to become of her? Her weary body ached to lie down inside the soft white cotton sheets, but her mind wandered. By succumbing to the immediate comfort of the only bed in the room she would be accepting her fate.

A single white shirt lay neatly on the bed. The flow of water from the shower inside the bathroom stopped abruptly. Shalimar's heart rose to her throat as she listened to his movements with her eyes shut. She could hear him moving around the bathroom, brushing his teeth, opening and closing the cabinet door on the wall. She suddenly noticed her reflection in the large mirror against the wall opposite the bed. Her thick black hair contrasted with the expensive white towel now wrapped around her body. Baindu would have appreciated this situation but all of this was not without its consequences. If she didn't act quickly the mercenary would be out of the bathroom and all would be lost. Shalimar grabbed the shirt confusing the buttons as her fingers shook with fear and anticipation.

Shalimar scurried along the corridor and down the stairs. She ran in a blind panic, barefoot and wearing only the cotton shirt. The wind rushed through the oversized white shirt as she ran towards the main road, painfully aware that she was naked underneath. She followed the strange smell of salt water coming from the beach, as that was the way they had come. She didn't know where she was going and she didn't care. She needed to get back to Blama to find her parents, then she would search for Baindu and bring her back home. There was no pavement on the opposite side of the beach strip so she kept running with difficulty along the edge of the road. Cars whizzed past her hooting her out of their way. She could hear the waves crashing ferociously against the shore and wondered if anyone was drowning alone in the darkness. Although the sound of the endless water alarmed her she was determined to finish the strip in one piece. Music sauntered from the bars along the beach front but she knew she could not enter them. She wanted to stop and catch her breath but again this was not an option. With no end in sight she ran harder. The large shirt flapped angrily in the wind exposing her thighs but she did not care.

A searing pain shot up from underneath her foot, causing her to cry out and tumble onto the smooth black tarmac. Moaning with pain she held her leg and looked down. A piece of broken bottle jutted out from her foot. Shuddering, she tried to wrench it out but the pain was too much for her. Almost immediately screeching tyres reverberated alongside her. The Jeep pulled up abruptly and Chameleon jumped out bare-chested and feral as he slammed the door shut.

'What the fuck is your problem, woman?'

Shalimar tried to pull herself up to get away, clenching her teeth so as not to reveal her injury. He was upon her now and grabbed her arm but she pulled back and fell to the floor. The glass inched further into her foot causing her to shriek in agony.

'Don't touch me! You think I am one of those women who wants your money so that you can use me for sex?'

She sucked the air in with all her might then hurled and spat with such force that it flew over his shoulder and missed him.

'I know your kind. Going from village to village and flashing money around. I don't need your money. I don't want it. Go and satisfy your curiosity elsewhere!'

She bent over in agony as the throbbing in her foot overwhelmed her; blood seeped onto the tarmac. Chameleon knelt down beside her.

'What have you done to your foot?'

She pulled away from him, not wanting him to touch her but he yanked her foot roughly towards him. His eyes widened as he saw the cause of her pain. He shook his head, sighed and stood up.

'Now I have to take you to the hospital.'

He picked her up and carried her into the Jeep but she did not look at him, and refused to speak to him as he drove her to the hospital. The wait was thankfully brief in the hospital, as Chameleon knew one of the doctors personally, enabling them to jump the queue. A few people sat around openly discussing their problems. Shalimar wondered what they must be thinking of her clearly naked body underneath the white shirt.

The doctor ushered them into a small room. Framed certificates covered the dirt walls. He examined her foot before trying to remove the glass with a large pair of forceps. The sting marched through her leg like a school parade as the glass slowly pulled out. She moaned; clenching her teeth, fighting off the tears of anger and hurt that threatened to appear. After removing several tiny pieces of glass, the doctor administered an injection in her calf. He then made it clear that she would need stitches and asked how the injury came about.

'She was running down Lumley beach.' Chameleon answered gruffly.

'What are you doing running down Lumley Beach at this time of the night?'

'Trying to get away from him.' Shalimar blurted out before Chameleon could answer. 'My village was attacked by RUF today and I have to go back to find my family.'

The doctor looked at her suspiciously.

'How did you get to Freetown?'

'He brought me here, but I need to go back....my family...'

'Well, how are you going to get back?' The doctor said impatiently. 'Do you have any belongings or money to get there?'

Shalimar hesitated. She possessed nothing, not even any clothes. She pulled the shirt over her exposed thighs as the doctor eyed her over.

'Let's get these stitches done, my man. I have some things to attend to.' Chameleon said abruptly.

'What can I do? I need help. I cannot stay with him forever.'

The doctor snorted: 'Beggars can't be choosers, my dear. In this situation, you have no choice. There is a campsite for the displaced in the east end but I wouldn't advise you to go there. You seem like a nice girl....'

A knock on the door interrupted the conversation. A nurse entered the room greeting everyone with a warm smile. The doctor made it clear that Shalimar needed to be held down while he proceeded with the stitching. Shalimar looked away as she felt the prickle of the needle shoot up from her thigh to the rest of her body. She yelped as the stinging escalated, before writhing and struggling against the nurse. This unsettled the doctor. A quarrel swiftly erupted between Chameleon and the doctor regarding the previously administered injection. Chameleon demanded another be dispensed, but the doctor solemnly refused, seemingly unimpressed by Chameleon's reference to his livelihood as a 'cowboy operation'. Although painful, it was a swift procedure and the nurse was soon helping Shalimar to stand up. The ordeal was over. Chameleon said his goodbyes to a silent medical duo, leaving Shalimar to wonder whether they were scared of Chameleon, or merely tolerated him.

The silence between them in the Jeep heightened the severity of the ordeal that just taken place. The smarting in Shalimar's foot outweighed any further emotion of the day's events. She couldn't put the unnecessary tribulation out of her mind as she waited for the effect of the painkillers to kick in. Shalimar decided to break the silence as the Jeep zipped down the hill.

'Tomorrow you can take me to my father.' She told Chameleon matter-of-factly. It sounded like a statement, not a request. The mercenary raised a questioning eyebrow.

'I am not taking you to Blama.'

'My real father. His name is Abdulai Barrie and he lives in Lumley.'

Chameleon shrugged his shoulders. 'So be it.'

Back at the hotel Shalimar was helped up the stairs and Chameleon handed her another one of his T-shirts to change into. The off-coloured garment was far too large for her and she was not used to covering up her whole body during the night. At home she slept partially naked and only ever used blankets during the harmattan season.

'I'm just popping downstairs to make a phonecall and to pick up a couple of things. Let's not have a repeat of earlier.' Chameleon said. He left the room, leaving Shalimar to contemplate her position.

Shalimar cursed herself for not seeing the broken bottle. Such a simple stupid thing had stopped her from getting away. If things hadn't been so bad at the hospital she would have asked the staff for help, but the chaos that followed her injury proved too much for her.

Shalimar climbed into the soft cotton sheets, defeated and exhausted. The bandage felt extremely tight and her foot throbbed in time with her heartbeat. Chameleon knocked, before entering with a glass of water and some medicine. He pulled the sheet away from her face.

'Why do you cover yourself with the sheet like that? I am not going to hurt you. I'm going to the casino downstairs, and I'll be there all night. Get some sleep and I'll buy you some clothes tomorrow.'

The sheet crumbled delicately back over her head. Seconds later she heard the click of the bedroom door shutting quietly. Silence transpired and the stillness of the dark room allowed the memories of the day to come flooding back clear and bloody as they were.

Exhausted as she felt, her mind raced, conjuring up specifically the image of Salia's face as the Jeep sped away from Long Life. It was a mixture of defeat, fear and sadness at being left behind at the mercy of the blood thirsty RUF Soldiers. Tears welled up in Shalimar's eyes. She couldn't begin to imagine what they must have done to him. Then her mind returned once more to her parents. They were old and frail, with less chance of survival, but she had a notion they were safe. She couldn't think of them in any other way. When she failed to come home that night, they surely would have taken it for a sign, and would have left with the money that Mama had hidden under the guava tree long before the rebels would have arrived. Shalimar wiped her eyes and prayed. She did not know where God was right now, all she knew was that God needed to be there.

Chapter 4

Shalimar awoke when the sun streamed through the window. She lay still for a few moments, staring at the ornate ceiling and wondering where on earth she was. As the fog cleared, the previous day's events flooded her mind, and she turned to see Chameleon lying next to her. He was on top of the bed covers wearing only a pair of blue boxer shorts. Shalimar instantly shirked away at the sight of him half naked, this made her extremely uncomfortable as she had only ever been with one man. She looked around the fancy room, trying to find something - anything - to study instead of the white man. But she couldn't help herself. Soon her gaze returned to the sleeping form of Chameleon.

Chameleon stirred, turning in her direction and slowly opening his eyes, as if aware of Shalimar's scrutiny. Their eyes met in silence until she looked away. She could not run away this time to stop him from touching her but she would let him know throughout that she would put up a fight.

'Are you hungry?' he asked.

'You have to take me to my father's house today.' She replied, ignoring his question.

Chameleon picked up the bedside phone and asked for two set breakfasts to be sent up to the room. He rolled out of bed and stood up to stretch. His tanned muscular body was more of an athletic build. The sun had not managed to penetrate the top of his boxers. The creator coloured him in and forgot to do the bottom of his spine. He turned to face her, feeling her eyes on him. She looked away in embarrassment. He kneeled back onto the bed and leant over her, arms trembling from the weight of his body.

'You better get used to it.'

He pulled back and disappeared into the bathroom. Later that morning Shalimar emerged from the shower to find a pair of shorts and shirt on the bed. She wondered what her father would make of her dressed in the mercenary's clothes. The room smelt of baby powder and *plassas*. So much had happened in a short space of time and now she was in a strange place, separated from her family and friends with nowhere to go. She could hear Chameleon on the veranda listening to BBC World Service. She knew this because many of the elders listened to the radio in Blama. The smell of steamed rice and potato leaves suddenly overpowered the room reminding her of lunchtime at home. Shalimar would wait for Mama to leave the area before sneaking a peek inside the pot to savour the smell of steamed leaves in palm oil, closing

44

her eyes to inhale its aroma. Now her stomach responded to the smell saturating the bedroom with a desperate growl. A wave of fatigue consumed her as she entered the sitting room; it was as though they had just arrived in Freetown and she had been up all night.

Chameleon smiled and waved his hands at the food before excusing himself to the bedroom. Shalimar sat alone on the leather sofa and tucked into the food, all the time thinking that her mother's cooking far surpassed the hotel's attempt. The continual throbbing in her foot had her shifting about trying to get comfortable as she ate. She recalled the moment the bottled glass tore through her flesh and shuddered. All this bad luck that had befallen her in the last three days was simply incomprehensible. Shalimar's thoughts ran to her biological father. He was a wealthy man and lived here in the city. He could possibly assist her in finding her family. What father wouldn't be happy to welcome his child into his current family? Maybe he had only been blessed with sons? That could possibly work in her favour. Chameleon emerged from the bedroom with her medicine.

'If you don't take these your foot won't heal quickly.' He paused. 'It hurts doesn't it?'

She nodded. Chameleon knelt down and gently untied the bandages, raising her foot carefully to examine it. His hands were cold.

'The doctor did a good job,' He sounded surprised. 'You should be able to walk about properly in a couple of days. Then you can run away again faster this time, wearing my shoes.' He chuckled to himself, shaking his head incredulously.

Blood rushed to Shalimar's cheeks, she did not like being the butt of his joke.

'I don't think it's funny. You are not funny.'

'No?' Chameleon regarded her for a moment. 'If I had wanted to rape you I could have done it on the way down here and left you in the bushes for the RUF to find later. Why would I go all the way to Kono or Blama to pick up a woman when I can just pick up one around this area?'

'I don't know and I don't care.'

'You should have listened to your friend. He told you to stay put in Freetown till he comes to get you. I'm the least of your problems.'

'Well, he better hurry up because this situation doesn't suit me.'

Chameleon did not acknowledge her words. He silently re-arranged the bandage around her foot then pointed to the medicine wrapped in foil on the table.

'I'm ready to go to Lumley now.'

This was the place that Mama talked about - the green house on the long road in Lumley.

'Where in Lumley?' Chameleon asked.

Shalimar winced. She didn't know the answer to this.... surely they could just search the area and ask the locals.

'I don't know. He lives in a big green house on the main road. I told you, his name is Abdulai Barrie and the locals will know him. He is a business man.'

The mercenary looked at his watch without answering her but his response didn't faze Shalimar.

She continued. 'If you have things to do, I can go alone. It's not a problem.'

'Lumley is a very large area,' Chameleon finally said. 'It's not some village or small town like Blama.'

'I have to find him as soon as possible.'

Chameleon picked up the tablets, broke the seal and pushed the tablets into her hand.

'Take the medicine, you will feel better and later they will help you sleep.'

Shalimar stood up.

'I will sleep in my father's house tonight.'

'We'll see. Look, I have some things to sort out, but later I will drive you to Lumley.'

Chameleon was true to his word, and in the early afternoon Shalimar was once again in the Jeep, this time on the way to find her real father. Now in the light of day she could see the colour of the sea changed from blue to turquoise the further away it got from the shore. Shalimar gripped the car seat in terror, willing herself to concentrate on the melting tarmac in front of them. The noise of the ocean sounded like a million snakes hissing in the forest with trees breaking and falling around them. The short drive to Lumley meant they were soon on the main road leading away from the beach resort. Conscious of her ill-fitting clothes, Shalimar remained in the Jeep as she called out to locals enquiring about the *Fulani* businessman that lived in a green house. Most shook their heads or sent them on a wild goose chase; nobody seemed to know of the businessman, Abdulai Barrie. Chameleon stayed silent throughout the search slowing the vehicle down when instructed while Shalimar anxiously solicited pedestrians and fruit sellers. Magnolia, pink and yellow houses hid behind high concrete walls but there was no glimpse of a green house. She had not considered that her father might have chosen to move through the years. After all, her mother left Freetown over twenty years ago. He could even have left the country all together and gone back to Guinea or Mali.

'I don't think we will find Abdulai Barrie today.'

Chameleon's South African accent was suddenly detectable in the quiet of the car. His expressionless eyes followed a mango seller jumping over the potholes dotted on the road. Chameleon swung around and reversed the Jeep back the way they had come. The man's sense of direction was incredible. Despite the many twists and turns on their wild goose chase, after five minutes they were on the main road, heading back to the hotel. Shalimar knew she couldn't give up looking for her father or at least find out some news about him. She had no choice but to stay in the hotel with the mercenary until she figured something out. She swallowed to relieve the insides of her parched throat. Her eyelids grew heavy - the drowsiness that she had fought earlier threatened to resurface. Shalimar leant her head against the window glancing at the jagged mountaintops that separated her from her family. Something had to give but it would not be her.

Chapter 5

Shalimar sat on the veranda soaking up the early morning sun. For the past week she had been lethargic, nauseous and barely able to get out of bed. She managed to flush the white tablets down the toilet the previous night when Chameleon disappeared into the front room. Since then her energy had bounced back with a vengeance, confirming her suspicions that Chameleon was keeping her drugged up. There was still a slight discomfort in her foot, but that was all. Only her heart remained heavy; her eyes still swollen like golf balls from crying intermittently in the night.

Shalimar stared out at the palm trees and endless blue sky stretching out in front of the hotel. She searched the sky for the stories unfolding in the villages that the Rebels had usurped, but there were none. The sky remained clear and blue as though all that happened underneath it was an illusion. The many buildings sloping down the hill blocked the view of the ocean from the veranda. She didn't mind this obstruction as she was not sure she liked the idea of an endless mass of water surrounding them. She closed her eyes, trying to feel her parents' aura. Any sign from the ancestors would be welcoming.

Chameleon entered the veranda. A gust of wind blew his brown tresses over his face but he did not bother to brush it back in protest. She thought he looked stupid.

'I see you have finished the course of tablets. Well, since you're awake we need to get you some clothes so we better go into town.'

He held out his hand, gesturing for Shalimar to take it. As she reluctantly raised her hand expecting him to help her to her feet, Chameleon opened her palm and dropped a small foil package in it. Her eyes followed him as he moved past the glass doors and landed back onto the sofa. A surge of anger swelled inside Shalimar as she strode over to where he sat. He glanced up when she approached him.

'I am no longer in pain. I don't need your painkillers.'

He shrugged in response and looked at his watch. Shalimar opened her trembling hand to reveal the cracked foil.

'Put it on the table,' He replied flatly without looking at her.

He shook his arm to allow his watch to cradle itself neatly into the comfortable curve of his wrist. Shalimar moved in and almost managed to slap the silver foil onto his mouth. He was much faster than her; his fingers instantly curled and tightened around her wrist. The pain that followed prompted the foil to fall to the floor.

'You want to drug me? Why don't you swallow them and see how it works for you!' Shalimar snapped.

This man needed to know she was not some stupid village girl. Chameleon was up on his feet now; his grip on her was firm and strong. She stopped struggling. She was no match for him, but it didn't change her resentment. He let go, pushing her well away from him.

'What did you just try to do?' he asked.

'You take some tablets too, since you feel so good giving them to me. You think I don't know your game?'

He stared at her for a minute. The pits of her arms were damp from the heat of her fury. She wanted to harm him.

'You were acting crazy, what else was I supposed to do?'

Shalimar closed her eyes. Her impulse was to lash out and the urge grew irresistible as Chameleon kept talking.

'You run down the beach strip with no clothes on. What do you expect me to do? You end up with a glass in your foot and you still won't behave.'

'I have lost my family and I don't know you.' She exhaled slowly. The trembling in her body slowed. She opened her eyes. Chameleon's face gave nothing away as he continued to stare at her.

'You haven't lost your family. Your friend knows where to find us.'

He paused as if not sure whether he was about to say the right thing in such a volatile moment.

'I just wanted you to calm down that's all. You already hurt yourself. There was no need for another incident. Just be patient.'

Shalimar listened. She was not aware of any form of arrangement between Salia and this man. She did not even know how well Salia knew him. She would have to wait for a while to give Salia the benefit of the doubt.

'Why are you doing this?'

'We should go to town and get you some clothes. I don't have any T-shirts left to share.' Chameleon answered abruptly.

*

Freetown was spellbinding. Shalimar had never experienced a place so noisy and bustling with so many people. The wares of traders spilled over the pavements making it virtually impossible to walk anywhere other than the road. Women sauntered through the traffic slow enough to be noticed. Men moved briskly with greetings as they passed each other.

49

They arrived at the famous King Jimmy Market situated by the wharf. Shalimar felt awkward wearing Chameleon's shorts and t-shirt but nobody seemed to notice. The stalls were full of vibrant coloured items red, yellow, green, purple, blue that reflected off the glaring sun. The coloured garments reminded Shalimar of the wrapped foreign sweets given to her as gifts by the customers from Long Life. She couldn't wait to shed the beige outfits that stifled her personality and dimmed her spirit. The pale outfits suited their characterless owner who lived nowhere and wandered everywhere.

King Jimmy turned out to be just an extremely overcrowded market with people pushing and shoving in a hurry to get to their destination. There were endless stalls overflowing with goods from clothes, trainers, shoes, portable radios, cotton cloth and Gara Materials. Traders haggled under extreme conditions in the dusty open air market. They pushed items from shoes to materials in Shalimar's face, swarming around her knowing that her choices would influence Chameleon. They all shouted together shoving their wares under her nose. An overwhelmed Shalimar tried pushing them away. The traders ignored her; instead they placed items in her hand as though she had agreed a sale. Chameleon bartered expertly in Krio. The surprised traders turned their focus on him when hearing the main language spoken in the capital city. He asked for her opinion occasionally as he picked out several items of clothing and shoes.

Shalimar was glad when Chameleon finished his shopping. Her bandaged foot did not allow her to move quickly. The people that swarmed around her had no sense of direction as they bumped into her and then shoved her out of their way. Chameleon moved around effortlessly pushing mobs out of his way with complete disregard. Some of the traders laughed at his roguish methods taken to avoid the rabble, throwing out questions like 'where did you get him from?' to Shalimar. She ignored the gags but understood the undertone of their jibes. They were not the only ones who were in the dark about Chameleon's intentions towards her. So far he had made no advances and remained civil most of the time.

On the way back to the hotel Shalimar insisted on slowing down in Lumley to continue asking locals about the whereabouts of her father. They stopped outside crudely built shops with pockets of children in starched uniforms buying bottles of water for their walk home from school. Their curious stares and wide-eyed contemplation frustrated Shalimar's efforts as they pondered and discussed the green house's whereabouts. No one remembered seeing a green house.

Shalimar made her way to the bathroom as soon as they arrived back at the hotel. Chameleon called out that they were going out to dinner as she locked the bathroom door securely behind her. She placed the toilet seat down so that she could sit and quietly go over the day's activities alone. She much preferred the serenity of the hotel after all the mayhem and chaos of the city. She knew she needed money to leave and the mercenary had plenty from what she could see. If she asked Chameleon for this favour he would probably want something in return. Baindu would have handled this situation effortlessly. She would have tried to please Chameleon without a hint of denial. Baindu's appreciation of the finer things in life dictated her emotions. They had always been so different. Shalimar knew she must muster some of Baindu's fearlessness to get through this. She took a deep breath and got up to have a shower.

Shalimar emerged from the bathroom with her hair pinned up; wearing a modish purple wrap dress that Chameleon had bought for her that day. He was slouched on the sofa as she entered the main room, but opened his eyes at the sound of her new, white open-toe shoes clicking against the tiles as she walked towards him. The room smelt of aftershave. Chameleon stood up buttoning the rest of his striped blue shirt and shoving the tails into his jeans.

'The dress looks very pretty on you. *You* look very pretty.'

'Thank you. Did I hear you mention food?'

The restaurant was barely five minutes away. The air grew pleasantly cooler as they drove down the beach strip. Shalimar's stomach churned as she heard the slamming of water against the shoreline, the sound in the darkness rendered far worse than the sight of it. She thought of how vulnerable she had been, running by the ocean with nothing but a shirt on. Chameleon noticed her discomfort.

'The ocean is a beautiful creature to have by your side. To live within walking distance of the beach brings a piece of mind...it's not something to be afraid of, it's something to treasure.'

Shalimar did not answer.

The Atlantic Restaurant stood right at the end of the beach strip. Melodic Jazz sneaked through the windows as they approached the entrance, gently enticing any casual passers-by. A waiter in starched shirt and pressed trousers showed them to the reserved table, pulling out Shalimar's chair for her much to her amusement. Chameleon ordered for them both: grilled garlic prawns on skewers with chiffon rice, roasted vegetables and a glass of red wine each. Shalimar stared at the fancy glasses. Nobody ever asked for wine in Long Life - in fact she was certain there had never been a bottle in the stockroom.

Chameleon made no attempt to make conversation as they waited for their food. Instead he read a newspaper that he had brought with him. It was hard to work out what this man's plans were. So far he had bought dresses and shoes as though he intended to keep her for a short while. She was well aware that he was holding her captive in his own strange way. The dimmed lights and soft music had an almost hypnotic effect, allowing Shalimar's mind to drift into an almost dreamlike state. Visions of her mother and father fleeing their home plagued her imagination. Her parents were old and Baindu would not have been there to assist them. She wondered if they were still hiding in the bushes while she was sat in a restaurant in Freetown with a mercenary. Papa's chest pains prevented him from moving very fast, and Mama would not survive if Papa died. She hoped that the villagers fled together. Tears clouded her vision as she looked across the table at Chameleon calmly reading the paper, oblivious to her pain. Salia had pleaded with her to stay away until Blama was safe but she could not wait too long. As soon as the right time arose she would leave. She would steal the necessary money if she had to. The food arrived, interrupting her thought process. She did not want Chameleon to see her misery so she kept her head down as she ate. A tear landed on the large seasoned red pepper, slightly blackened from the barbeque grill. She picked up her fork to eat but every morsel that entered her mouth tasted like the stones that were scattered on the long dusty stretch of road to Freetown.

*

Chameleon requested a bottle of Jack Daniels at the Hotel Reception. He dutifully checked her foot, after which Shalimar quickly limped to the bedroom. The idea of night time with this man had lurked in her mind throughout the day and made her uneasy. So far he did not want to touch her while her foot was bandaged. She wasn't sure. Maybe if she fell asleep he wouldn't bother her. She climbed into bed and hid underneath the covers. Shalimar prayed that God would allow her to get through the night alive.

Baindu appeared at the bottom of the Long Life's steps in Shalimar's dream. Her hands were outstretched clasping onto notes that occasionally fluttered to the ground. The diamond-encrusted ring sparkled against the light gleaming all around them. Baindu's soundless lips moved anxiously. Shalimar climbed down the stairs to listen to the silent words coming from her frustrated sister. As she moved closer, Baindu nodded, beckoning Shalimar to come closer but the ground beneath them suddenly shook violently. The stairs between them formed a sizable crack and Baindu lost her balance. Baindu fell through the large hole, her eyes wide with fear and regret.

Shalimar awoke with a start in the darkness. What did the dream mean? What message was being given to her? Shalimar closed her eyes again, desperate to recapture the dream and understand her sister's visit. Baindu was still wearing the ring; this must mean she was still with the Rebels. She felt a sudden movement and turned to see Chameleon sleeping next to her. He had not spent all night in the casino this time. The bed was vibrating. Shalimar peered closer at the sleeping Chameleon only to realise he was shaking violently. His long arms stretched out as though he were a soldier called to attention. The cover sheet hung halfway off the bed. Baffled by his appearance Shalimar called out softly,

'Are you alright?'

There was no response. Groans emerged from his slightly parted lips.

'Are you alright?'

She raised her voice this time, placing her hands on his arms to wake him. They felt hard as rock when she squeezed them.

Chameleon moved unexpectedly, grabbing her with a vice-like grip. His eyes remained closed. She gasped, trying to move away but he was too strong. She shrieked in terror; Chameleons eyes shot open to find her staring at him in horror. Beads of sweat trickled from his hairline, down his forehead, and his wet hair stuck to his face and neck. He glanced around the room before releasing her and slumped back onto the bed, covering his face with his hands. Shalimar gaped at him. He took a deep breath.

'Did I scare you?'

Shalimar did not answer. This man remained as dangerous in his sleep as he was when he was awake.

He touched the nape of her neck and trailed his finger down to the small of her back. Her spine tingled from his touch.

'I am a man that doesn't sleep well. Sometimes I just avoid it all together. You don't have to fear me in or out of bed. I will not hurt you.'

He gestured for her to lay down closer to him, kissing her forehead in a reassuring manner. She lay still and silent for a while before stealing a quick glance. He had fallen asleep almost instantly, his face suddenly peaceful. She turned her back and pulled the covers over her head. What kind of a man was this? Her heart ached for her family. She prayed that Salia would soon arrive in Freetown soon to free her from this situation.

Chapter 6

Pedestrians swarmed around the entrance to the government building, like rats to a garbage dump. Chameleon had woken Shalimar early explaining that he had important business to attend to, and she was going with him. She supposed he did not trust her enough to leave her alone in the hotel room. When he told her his meetings included government officials she rushed to get dressed. She could speak to a minister or government official and formally request something be done for her village. She imagined the faces of the officials upon hearing her story with Chameleon as a witness.

Annoyance and frustration filled the air and rung through the corridors, as civilians leaned against walls arguing with others blocking the pathways. The third floor entertained a crowd of people sitting on benches facing several closed doors. A young gentleman paced up and down the corridor impatiently barking a name from the clipboard he was holding. No one stood up. He smiled when he spotted Chameleon as though he had just caught wind of a cash reward. Chameleon instructed Shalimar to wait as the young man hastily ushered him away.

'I want to meet the minister and tell them what happened in Blama. Your story alone is not enough.' Shalimar protested. He could not leave her to sit with the others and miss this golden opportunity.

Chameleon's grey eyes widened and his jaw moved as though he was thinking of something to say. His long fingers quickly slid through his brown hair stopping it from falling into his face.

'They already know about Blama.'

'But they need to send more soldiers to capture the Rebels. I can tell them about the area and what happened.' Shalimar protested.

'Lots of villages have been destroyed; Blama is not the only place. The government is working on it. Wait for me, I will be back soon.'

'But....'

'Wait!'

Chameleon was gone before she could argue. He followed the young gentlemen to the end of the drab hallway and disappeared into one of the rooms. The dreary office corridor was crammed with sweaty people fanning themselves as they lingered around in hopes of getting an appointment. Shalimar sat on the wooden bench and closed her eyes to shut out the ugly new world she found herself in. She wanted to remember better times. Within minutes her subconscious mind carried her back home to reminisce of times before...

The local alcoholic, Mohammed stood at the door of Long Life talking to no one in particular. Barefoot; his frayed white string vest and torn blue shorts looked comical against the feather stuck in his hair. Salia stood outside sweeping the front of the building. Shalimar washed some of the dirty glasses from behind the bar in a large bucket. Mohammed boogied to the local music playing on the tape machine. She laughed as he danced and reminisced about his ex wife who had left him for another man. Mohammed demonstrated the way the 'witch' used to move. He pouted his lips and swayed his hips like a woman with his hands outstretched as if trying to perfect the memory. Shalimar's laughs grew louder; Salia entered the bar with his broom, eyeing Mohammed suspiciously. He walked to where Shalimar was standing and placed the broom against the wall. Salia watched Mohammed for a few moments, then shouted over the music: 'Hey my friend, it's time to go!'

Shalimar rinsed the last glass and placed it upside down on the counter. She picked up the bucket filled with soap suds and carried it outside. Salia followed her with the intention of ushering Mohammed out of the bar.

There was nothing but a stretch of bushes outside the Bar. Long Life was stuck in the middle of nowhere with an equally barren feel. In the daytime, with the mineworkers hard at work, only the occasional car would zoom past without so much as a flicker to observe its structure. They welcomed infrequent visits by orange or mango sellers depending on the season. Mohammed was always a welcome relief even when he had no money. The only reason Salia encouraged Mohammed to leave was because he knew Mr Foday would be passing through this afternoon. Salia slipped his arm into Mohammed's escorting him slowly to the door.

'She came back to me but I did not take her back. I told her she was a barren whore. That is why she could not have any children. I threw her out.' Mohammed said as Salia encouraged him outside.

Salia nodded his head. 'Go on go home. Go home and sleep.'

A woman in her early thirties appeared at the foot of the steps smiling broadly. She wore a purple lapa around her waist with a matching scarf tied around her head. Shalimar noticed that her bottom rolled as she mounted the stairs in slow motion. It appeared to have a mind of its own bouncing with enthusiasm as if a separate entity to her body. Salia's face broke into a wide smile and he clapped gleefully, greeting the woman with a kiss on the cheek. His hand roamed from her arm to the large mass behind her closing his eyes as he squeezed it; a look of sheer satisfaction moved across his face. The woman giggled and slapped his hand away.

'Stop nuh! I've come to visit you like I promised.'

Salia pulled her up the remaining steps into the bar. Mohammed scoffed loudly; he too stood watching the scene unfold. He shouted out to the couple.

'Hey is that why you were trying to get rid of me!'

Shalimar moved to the side of the bar and poured the bucket of soapy water onto the grass; the effort of carrying the heavy plastic bucket brought a line of sweat to brow, which she wiped away with the bar towel she carried in her pocket. She watched Mohammed stumble off into the distance. Glancing back inside, Shalimar noticed that Salia was nowhere to be seen, he must have disappeared out the back with his visitor.

A car horn beeping in the distance distracted Shalimar from her musings. She moved forward to peek through the open window and noticed the slow moving white BMW that manoeuvred leisurely around the pot hole ridden road. A flash of recognition went through her face as she quickly bolted towards the corridor behind the bar.

'Salia, Salia! Mr Foday is coming!'

She continued to shout as she ran through the back towards the stock room door.

'Salia, Mr Foday is coming!' She banged on the closed door once with her fist then opened it hastily without waiting for permission.

Salia stood at the end of the table zipping his trousers hastily as his lady friend jumped onto the floor to quickly readjust her lapa. Shalimar's eyes widened. Her suspicions about what Salia did with his female admirers in the stockroom finally confirmed. She spoke in earnest. 'Mr Foday is here, he just drove up!'

Without lifting up his head from fixing his trousers Salia replied.

'Don't worry, I'm coming.'

He turned to the young woman who stood watching him and pointed to the half-opened window above the table they had just fornicated on.

'You have to climb out that way,' he said grabbing the woman's arm. Leaning over, he pushed the window open. 'Go on.'

'Well when am I going to see you?' the woman asked, fixing her head tie back in place.

'Don't worry you will see me soon.'

'When?'

Shalimar could hear the engine roar up to the front of the bar. Salia spoke to the woman in a low voice as he continued to push her out of the window with one hand on each cheek of her wide round bottom. The woman got stuck and giggled. Mr Foday's footsteps could now be heard approaching the back, calling out Salia's name as he came.

'Bi wua Mr Foday, I am just putting some beer in the fridge,' Shalimar called out.

Mr Foday would want to know why the front had been left unattended by the two of them. Salia now rammed the woman's bottom with both hands as well as his shoulder.

Shalimar left the room closing the door behind her, only to find Mr Foday standing in front of her. He was a large man; over six foot tall, coffee coloured with pink lips. He gave Shalimar a quizzical look,

'Shalimar? Why have you and Salia left the front unattended? What is going on?'

'I was mopping, Sah. I heard a loud noise and I thought that Salia had dropped something.'

Mr Foday's perplexed look did not go away. He took one last look at her before opening the door.

Salia spoke as the door opened. 'Bi wua Sah, a bird flew in here. I was trying to get it out.'

'A bird?'

'Yes Sah,'

Shalimar left the back office quickly. She did not wish to continue the sad lie nor be a witness to further untruths. She walked through the corridor shaking her head.

Shalimar filled up the bucket with fresh water and went outside to wash down the steps. Mr Foday suddenly appeared behind her, making her jump. He waited for her to empty the bucket, smiling a friendly smile as he observed her.

'How have you been Shalimar?'

'Hinda nyamu gbii na.'

'How are your parents?'

'They are fine Sah.'

'Give them my regards would you?' She nodded.

Mr Foday always asked after her parents. When Mrs Foday was ill, Mama cooked some cassava leaves and krane krane for the family. He never forgot that. Salia suddenly appeared on the steps, a wide grin on his face. He must have convinced the boss there was nothing untoward going on.

58

Just before climbing into the car, without warning Mr Foday gave her that *'I know you two are sleeping together'* look. This caught Shalimar by surprise. She glowered watching the car crawl slowly into the distance. Salia walked over to her grinning like a schoolboy. He winked at Shalimar who sucked her teeth in response and warned him.

'Don't involve me in your foolishness again.'

*

Shalimar opened her eyes and looked around her. Memories of Long Life and Blama helped nullify the musty smell of body odour that filled the corridor as she waited for Chameleon. She opened the newspaper Chameleon handed her in the Jeep to pass the time, but could not read it. It was too advanced for her reading level. She wondered if he did this on purpose to humiliate her.

A passing cleaner in a light blue overall uniform walked down the hall slowly, with his mop and empty bucket. He smiled at her as though she reminded him of someone. Shalimar stopped him as he passed, and asked after the location of the bus station that took commuters to the countryside. The man kindly told her the name of the road and tried to describe how to get there, but Shalimar found it hard to memorise all the roads and turnings in a big city that she was unfamiliar with. Still, if she got the chance, at least she now knew the name of the station she would head for at the first opportunity.

'Thank you for your help. Do you have an idea of the fare to Bo? It is the biggest town near to my village.'

'Ah, I have a friend who visits family in a village near there. He takes the bus to Bo. I think he paid forty thousand Leones last time he went. Yes, that is right. He was complaining about another rise in prices, as I recall.'

The price of the fare stunned her - forty thousand Leones! She was not sure how it would be possible to raise that kind of money quickly. She thanked the frail old man quickly, eager to usher him away before Chameleon reappeared and asked what they were talking about. The man nodded his farewell, and shuffled away slowly. Shalimar sat back in her seat and repeated the name of the bus station and the road it stood on, quietly under her breath.

Shalimar was now biding her time with her own plans. She had felt a good sensation taking the money from Chameleon's pockets that morning. He left her midway through breakfast to take a shower. Shalimar listened carefully until she could hear the hiss of water splattering on the walls, before she scurried into the bedroom to search through his pockets. There was no wallet; instead a dozen loose notes were folded up neatly in each trouser pocket. Shalimar slipped out three notes from each wad and stuffed them under the mattress on her side of the bed. She was surprised that she felt no guilt or remorse. She did not know how long it would take before he would start to expect something from her, but it was getting to a point where she was willing to sacrifice herself, if it could get her back to Blama in one piece. Nothing mattered to her more than being able to make that journey home. All she needed was the money. She would find out where he kept his wallet, take what she needed, and then split.

'They are working on it.' Chameleon said when he appeared from the far away room, beckoning for them to leave. There was no time to respond or ask him to expand on that statement as they walked along the corridors, down the stairs and back out onto the crowded city streets. There were those that recognised and greeted Chameleon warmly. Many shook his hand and acknowledged Shalimar with a nod. The stationary heat in the city was so heavy it made Shalimar conscious of her own breathing. Chameleon appeared unaffected. He merely wiped the sweat off his brow with the back of his hand then smeared it on his trousers. Taxis constantly beeped at pedestrians walking in the middle of the road, traders called out their wares hoping to attract customers, and people shouted to one another across the street in conversation. Shalimar continuously scanned through the crowd, wondering if anyone from Blama had made it to Freetown. A familiar walk or greeting would cause her heart to leap, but every time she scanned the crowd the faces were unrecognisable. Traders approached them trying to sell anything from toothbrushes to mangoes. Chameleon did not acknowledge their existence. Child traders turned to her with imploring eyes. They were thinner than the children that lived in her district. She shook her head politely turning away from them, trying desperately not to see the chaos unfolding all around her. There was no warmth in this place.

'Can you swim?'

'I am sorry?' Shalimar was distracted, and not certain she had heard correctly.

'I said can you swim?' Chameleon asked again, as they walked through the crowded streets.

Shalimar tried to place her feet in an appropriate place, away from the many gutters as they walked to the Jeep. She shook her head in reply.

'Well today you will learn a little.'

Swimming was not something she had given much thought to. Many people at home swam in the streams. Some would talk about the beaches far away. Now that she had finally come face to face with the ocean, it scared her. She kept silent, unsure whether exposing her fear would allow him to use it against her.

Chameleon drove back to the hotel, but instead of going up to their room he led her through an undiscovered dining area of the hotel. Most of the dining area remained unoccupied with one or two scattered diners eating in isolation. Staff in black and white uniforms stood in attendance, chatting to each other whilst tugging at the white lace tablecloths and endlessly straightening the cutlery or adjusting the empty seats. Chameleon led her through some doors and out into an open garden area. They walked across the patio to another small building, set to the side of a large swimming pool. A surprised Shalimar realised she had not taken advantage of exploring the hotel and its amenities as she was far too caught up in trying to leave. Chameleon placed his Puma travel bag on the table in the changing room and threw a white bikini set at Shalimar. She managed to catch it this time and held it up in front of her; she had never seen a bikini before. It looked like underwear. She couldn't believe he expected her to walk around the hotel in underwear. As if reading her thoughts he spoke without looking up.

'It's called a bikini, that's what women wear to swim. There will be other women in the pool wearing the same.'

'*We nor deh go beach*?' She tried not to show her fear.

Chameleon gave her a questioning look.

'I can't teach you anything in the ocean; it would be too rough for you. I don't want to have to answer to your mother.'

She thought she heard a slight sarcasm to his tone but couldn't comprehend why he would say such a thing. He turned away to undress and barked impatiently: 'Change your clothes.'

Shalimar stared at him in disbelief. Nobody had ever spoken to her this way. He was abrupt and rude.

'I'm not a dog.'

'What?' He looked up as though she asked him a question.

'You speak to me like I am a dog. I am not a dog...'

'I never said you were,' he answered walking past her towards the door that led to the pool.

'Just wait outside. I will be there in a minute.' Shalimar answered in an annoyed tone.

Chameleon turned back and smiled at her, then left the room, closing the door behind him. She shook her head. This man didn't even seem to know when he was being rude. The bikini totally threw her off and had her wondering for the first time whether Chameleon was accustomed to buying outfits for women.

*

The pool was a square box filled with water. Shalimar wrinkled her nose dubiously from the strong smell of chlorine. She could not fathom the smell in the swimming pool. Surely they would not be immersing themselves in some kind of bleach?

There were only two families lounging around. One family was much lighter in colour - they were Lebanese, Chameleon pointed out. He had chatted with the husband in the casino a couple of nights previously. The man swum in the pool alone as the relatives lay on deck chairs catching the sun. The women wore bikinis just as Chameleon said they would, with all their bodies exposed to the sun as well as the eyes of others. Their children ran around the edges of the pool screaming and laughing. The ground felt quite slippery underneath Shalimar's bare feet so she followed Chameleon with careful steps to avoid slipping. The other family looked like wealthy locals. As Shalimar and Chameleon walked by them, they stopped talking and just stared. Their expressions a mixture of contempt and wonder: was she his lover or a prostitute? Whatever the scenario, money was surely crossing hands. Shalimar squirmed inside at being exposed to strangers like this who did not care to hide their leering eyes. She had never been judged or thought of in this manner before. Chameleon held her hand, leading the way. He was either oblivious to the reception or he didn't care. When they reached the edge, he suddenly let go and jumped in. The water splashed at her feet as she watched him disappear.

He surfaced from the bottom slowly, the water glistening on his skin and his wet hair plastered to his scalp. The black tattoo marking on Chameleon's arm was clearer to read, but still she could not make out the words. His lean brown torso appeared almost as dark as hers when he emerged from under the water. He walked slowly to the stairs leading down into the pool where she stood waiting, and led her gently down the stairs. The water was surprisingly cold; she stopped as it reached her thighs.

'Come on,' he motioned.

The water covered her just below her chest. Chameleon stood tall in the water as it came up above his waist. He bent down under her,

'The water will feel warmer once you start moving. Stop trying to fold your arms, woman.'

Shalimar trembled. Partly through fear and partly because of the cold. Chameleon pulled her folded arms down and took her to the railings to teach her how to paddle. She was not sure how useful this session would be in her life but he seemed determined to teach her and have some fun whilst doing it. She attempted to paddle. Her legs beat at the water as though she was kicking her mortal enemy - the RUF Rebel. She would have liked to drown Rambo. Watch the water engulf his very existence and take away the life of the man responsible for bringing hers into disrepute. She concentrated so hard she forgot about her injured foot.

After a while, Chameleon asked her to let go of the bars and move further into the pool where he proceeded to hold her as she tried to float. The Lebanese man swam towards the edge of the pool and climbed out. Shalimar choked from swallowing water, finding it hard to concentrate as she coughed and spluttered. Unable to control herself, Shalimar started hyperventilating. Chameleon's orders for her to calm down fell on deaf ears as the water was now in her system. Shalimar tried to return to the rails alone but the water rose above her chest and petrified her.

'I want to get out of the water. Please let me get out of the water.'

The water now entered Shalimar's nose and she coughed ferociously.

'Go ahead if that's what you want.'

Shalimar jumped over the rippling water so that it would ripple under her but the more she jumped, the higher the water seemed to rise.

'I want to get out of the water. Get me out of the water,' she repeated almost shouting. Chameleon was not there. She looked around for the Lebanese man, but he had gone. The Sierra Leonean family were deep in conversation, walking away from the pool with their children running around their legs. They couldn't hear her and she was in imminent danger of drowning. The water now became an endless wave surmounting her. Shalimar panicked and screamed. Almost immediately, Chameleon appeared from underneath her.

'What are you screaming for? I just went under.'

He pulled her close and held her trembling body to his.

'I did not leave you in Long Life to die, so why would I do that here?'

63

Shalimar closed her eyes and clung to his neck tightly. His arms wrapped around her as she coughed profusely. She could feel them move slowly through the water. She hated her helplessness.

'Open your eyes.'

His warm lips and breath brushed against her ear when he spoke. Her eyes stung as she tried to open them. Chameleon surveyed her curiously as though he had just laid eyes on her for the first time. Shalimar could feel how pressed they were against each other. He winked.

'Is that better now? You're not going to freak out on me again, are you?'

Shalimar shook her head in response.

'I want to get out,' she said; softly this time.

She hated the water. The whole experience made her feel sick and helpless. Chameleon loosened his grip and pushed her up the stairs, and out of the pool.

Chapter 7

'Is Salia working this afternoon?' Baindu asked as she perched herself under the shade of the magnificent palm trees. She stretched her long legs so that the tips of her toes stroked the top of the running stream. The moving water rippled over the jutting rocks to form heart shaped wrinkles, before dissipating downstream.

Shalimar's hand moved against the tide as she waded through the torrent. The multi-coloured country cloth clung onto her legs. Shalimar lowered herself into the water to wash away the salty sweat that had hugged her body throughout the night.

'Is Salia working with you later today?' Baindu repeated, jumping into the stream. She waded slowly towards Shalimar.

'Yes. Mr Foday is coming today. He wants us to carry out a stock check.'

Baindu splashed Shalimar as she spoke. Shalimar laughed and pushed Baindu in response. The sisters wrestled playfully, allowing time to stand still. The cool stream always brought welcome relief to the heat-infested afternoons in Blama. Baindu helped Shalimar back onto her feet after toppling her. Her grip tightened as her eyes widened with surprise.

'What is that?' she asked pointing to Shalimar's arm.

Shalimar pulled away. Mama's nails had dug into her during an argument about Papa's condition that morning, leaving scratch marks. Shalimar turned away and climbed out of the stream. She did not want to discuss it with her sister; it would only create more resentment between her and Mama. The parched grass felt like straw under her feet. She took off the sopping lapa and allowed the sun's rays to envelop her body.

'You keep fighting with Mama, instead of finding yourself a boyfriend,' Baindu called out.

'That is supposed to solve my problems?'

'No. But several will.' Baindu added with a huge grin on her face. 'One of them will marry you and take you away...'

Shalimar lay down and closed her eyes, ignoring her sister's taunting and childish philosophies, which never made any sense to her. Instead she blocked out the incessant chatter, focussing on the many birds chirping in the trees above her. The dry grass poked against her skin through the thin material of her lapa causing some discomfort. Shalimar opened her eyes again as she heard Baindu striding against the torrent to join her.

'It is time to go home, Shalimar. We both have things to do.'

Shalimar tied the damp lapa around her waist. It would not dry off until they reached the village. She lent her sister a hand as she stepped over the rocks onto the banks. Baindu pushed her finger affectionately against the bruised cuts on Shalimar's arm causing her to smile. Holding hands the sisters strolled casually through the forest back to the village.

*

Shalimar counted one hundred and five Leones on the floor of the bathroom as she reminisced about her family. This was nowhere near enough money for the bus ride back to Blama, which she now knew would cost around forty thousand Leones. A month had passed, and still the money she managed to acquire was nowhere near enough.

She stood up and flushed the toilet to account for her time spent in the bathroom. Chameleon listened to the radio most afternoons and never paid her much attention. She was beginning to think he liked boys, the way Barrow did. That suited her down to the ground as long as she did not have to witness him in action.

Chameleon listened to a debate on the BBC's 'Focus on Africa' about Foday Sankoh; the leader of the RUF. He shouted at the radio as he listened to the different viewpoints, clearly unimpressed by the British radio stations assessment of the rebel leader.

Chameleon eyed her as she entered the front room. The radio blared so loudly, she put her hands up to her ears. He stood up and stomped towards her; the look on his face was one of fury, and Shalimar flinched as he neared her. He walked past her and grabbed the Jack Daniels bottle from the table.

'We can finish this war without any fucking interference!' His earlobes reddened as he shouted at the radio. 'The biggest exploiter is the native himself. He invites exploiters into the country, you stupid people!'

Chameleon paused to knock back a large shot, immediately pouring another large measure into the glass.

'These Europeans want to stop my cash flow in the name of human rights. I'd like to see them come out here and try. Have a glass...' He offered as he poured himself yet another.

Shalimar shook her head and looked towards the veranda. Salia's decision to send her away with this man confused her. How much did he know about Chameleon? What if Salia was gone?

Shalimar sighed. No, this could never be; he made a promise. Salia was resilient, and he always kept his promises.

Sudden clattering and crashing interrupted her thoughts. The radio lay broken on the tiled floor, its aerial several feet away from the wreckage. Chameleon ranted as he stormed into the bedroom. Shalimar walked over to the broken radio and picked it up. She proceeded to fix the Arial but the bottom had snapped off. She understood this display of behaviour from working in Long Life and knew the best thing to do was to just ignore Chameleon until he calmed down. Shalimar looked up to see Chameleon watching her from the bedroom entrance.

'I have a dinner meeting in ten minutes. Don't worry about the radio; I will get a new one.' He sounded almost apologetic.

*

Late afternoon was the best time to wash clothes in Blama, in the cool shadows of the trees. Shalimar half listened as Mahawa twisted the material allowing droplets of water to trickle out while she complained about her husband, Sallah. A large ceramic bowl full of colourful fabric sat on the banks of the river baking in the sunlight. Shalimar smashed her sopping clothes against the rock in rhythmic motion, only stopping to wipe the beads of sweat that appeared on her forehead. Sallah was not working long enough hours in the rice fields and Mahawa was pregnant. Shalimar listened respectfully, nodding appropriately, and giving only sparse advice. Unless you were a relative it was never advisable to give out advice to a married couple, and her friend had only been married six months. Mahawa waded out of the stream and placed the last set of clothes into the ceramic bowl. She waved goodbye to Shalimar, thanked her for listening, and moved off effortlessly through the grass with her load.

Shalimar continued to beat the clothes with vigour, slapping the gara against the rock ferociously as she thought about her mother's nails digging into her arm that morning. All she had requested was to take a trip to Bo to find out how much another doctor would charge for Papa's consultation. Mama did not want her to go, and argued that Baindu could make the journey instead. Shalimar turned her back on her mother who managed to grab her and swing her around again. Turning your back on your parents when they were talking to you was disrespectful but this was her way of showing that she had had enough of her mother's biased decisions. This display infuriated her mother who in turn flung hurtful abuse at Shalimar reminding her of her illegitimacy. It was those words that had Shalimar pounding her parent's clothes against the rock with such ferocity. It seemed as though the rock would shatter into pebbles and disappear into the rolling stream.

Shalimar spread the clothes out on the grass under the sun and returned to the shade of the trees. She loved to sit here all alone and peaceful, just listening to the noises of the forest, such as the familiar sounds of the chattering of chimpanzees. When she was younger, Shalimar always thought that if she listened and observed them long enough she would begin to understand their way of communication. Shalimar picked at the long blades of grass around her. Mama hardly ever allowed Shalimar out of her sight. She held a tight rein on her more than Baindu, who was the baby of the family. The words that her mother had uttered in the heat of anger had wounded her greatly. Shalimar secretly believed Mama thought her capable of being more promiscuous than Baindu because of the environment in which she was conceived. One day she would leave and show Mama that she was not a worthless bastard. She would no longer exist as a constant reminder of the mistake her mother made in her youth. Memories of her one and only lover, John, flickered into her thought process. Her fear had not allowed her to take up his offer to leave with him. Those memories remained painful because in times of despair, Shalimar regretted her decision.

*

John was an engineer from Freetown. He was a Krio: a descendant of returned slaves, many of whom resided in the capital city. John spotted her buying vegetables in the local market and approached her. He attempted to speak Mende, but was so bad at it she couldn't help but laugh at him. She understood Krio and reassured him that she did not mind conversing with him this way. He told her he couldn't help but notice her as she stood out from the crowd.

John was tall, dark and muscular. His short neat hair trickled into a stylish goatee to complement his full shapely lips. He walked her home that afternoon and introduced himself to Papa as though he were a long term family friend. There were not many places to go in the area so John whisked her away to Bo - the neighbouring big city. They spent much of their time in the restaurants and wine bars there.

One day he took her to the new hotel called Hotel Sir Milton in Bo, which had been named in honour of the first Prime Minister of Sierra

Leone. He guided her to the self-contained single room where he was residing whilst completing his project. Once alone in the room, his hands moved around her body with excitement. Anticipation mounted as he pushed her on to the bed pulling off her clothes. He grabbed her hips pulling her into him, sliding into her roughly. She yelped in pain, but his lips covered hers. Fingers poking in all the wrong places, Shalimar dried up while he pounded her. The pain was unreal.

They only met up twice after the incident. He arrived unannounced in Long Life, and sat alone in the corner. Shalimar served him, both surprised and happy for the visit. This educated man took the time out to see where she worked and who she really was. He was not a man of many words but he had many convictions, just like Papa. He made her insides flutter eyeing her as he sipped on his beer. She smiled and twirled while she worked, knowing his full attention was on her. At the end of the night he gave her a lift home. On the way, John pulled over and told her he was leaving and wanted her to go back with him to Freetown. The cold chill that ran through her body confused her. He was offering to take her away and marry her. This was what women dreamed of yet Shalimar couldn't understand the panic and dread that now consumed her emotions. When he touched her she flinched, surprising herself as well as him. Without another word he started the car and drove her home in silence, dropping her off with a swift peck on the cheek. The next day John passed by the house to say goodbye without even getting out of the car. Dust flurried around her as she watched the car turn into a speck in the distance. From then on she made a conscious decision to keep away from the enquiring looks of young men.

*

Shalimar used her time alone to plan for her future. What she really wanted was to be a market trader; a legitimate businesswoman. She admired these women who were so obviously in control of their lives. They bought and sold items through negotiation, always counting and managing money. They contributed towards the upkeep of their families and had their own lives. Often they would take their children to work with them and pass on their expertise. This was who she wanted to be. Shalimar fingered the clothes to see if they were dry – the fresh wind filtering through the humidity usually dried them out quicker at that time of the day. She would share her thoughts with Salia and learn how to take the next step towards a better future for herself. She folded the half dry clothes and placed them in her plastic bowl to begin her journey through the forest.

A faint sound disrupted the peaceful ebb of rustling leaves and manic crickets as Shalimar walked slowly through the grass. She stopped to listen, carefully moving towards the unfamiliar sound that was coming from deeper inside the forest. The sound was similar to that of the wild pigs that occasionally wandered around the vicinity. She moved slowly and carefully, well aware that they were dangerous creatures who did not hesitate to attack humans. As she moved nearer, the sounds grew louder but she could not make out if it was conversation or chimpanzee chatter. Her eyes flit about until she spotted a movement between some trees. She crept forward cautiously. If she could just get closer she would be able to make out what was going on. Filled with curiosity, Shalimar hid between the branches; crouching down, she concealed her washing in the tall grass. She stepped in closer to take a peak. What she saw caused her heart to drop into her stomach and suck the wind out of her lungs.

Baindu had her arms around Salia's neck and was laughing hysterically at something he said. Salia rubbed his forehead against Baindu's affectionately while pulling himself away from her clutches.

'We will leave this place and live in Bo.'

'When I see the money then I will know you are serious,' Baindu retorted; trailing her finger along his smooth facial skin.

'You don't believe me?' Salia chortled.

Baindu's hands moved seductively from his face to his chest before grabbing him and kissing him full on the mouth. Paralysed, Shalimar could not take her eyes off the grotesque image before her. Her sister had managed to seduce Salia with her charms. A surge of emotion engulfed Shalimar. The feeling of betrayal swarmed around her insides making her nauseous. How could Salia work with her and not mention anything about her sister? She had confided in Salia countless times on Baindu's behaviour and her mother's ongoing favouritism. He was supposed to be her friend. Shalimar let out a sob but she was too far away for them to hear. A rustle in the opposite direction made her swing around in defence. There was another spectator in the bushes. It was the palm wine lover. He sat leaning against the tree with a plastic jug of palm wine in his hand watching her emotions spill onto the grass. Their eyes met, and Shalimar's disappointment turned into anger and shame. Shalimar turned and fled. She ran through the village till she reached home.

*

Chameleon barely ate at all during dinner. His fork picked through the seeds of rice as though performing a dance ritual on the plate. The two Government ministers called him Jamie. This revelation surprised Shalimar, as she had never contemplated the possibility of Chameleon having an ordinary name like everyone else. Jamie was not the name she would have guessed for him either. Dutch names were unfamiliar to her and she imagined that his would be as strange sounding. He noticed her struggling with the noodles and handed her a fork. Chameleon conversed with the government officials in fluent Mende, showing that he had spent a lot of time in the country. Who was he and how did he manage to stay here this long? Salia had told her Barrow could not return to Nigeria because he was a wanted man, as was the case for many of the foreign men who lived in Sierra Leone willing to hustle for the rest of their lives.

'Jamie is your real name?' Shalimar asked as the Jeep bounced through the potholed road.

'Yes.'

'Why doesn't anyone call you that anymore?'

He took his eyes of the road for a split second.

'The people I do business with call me Jamie. The locals call me Chameleon. I didn't give myself that name.'

'Do you like being called Chameleon?'

He shrugged: 'They can call me Satan for all I care. As long as it doesn't interfere with me making money...'

Chameleon's foot slammed on the brake in mid sentence. Shalimar shot forward, her face dangerously close to smashing into the windscreen. He jumped out of the car and dashed across the road towards a young man walking with a chimpanzee, hurling abuse at him as he went.

Once Shalimar could catch her breath, she climbed out of the car to see what had caused Chameleon's unexpected behaviour. The two men seemed to be having trouble communicating with each other properly, and the voices were increasing in both volume and aggression. A chimpanzee paced about between them, clearly agitated, taking long puffs on a cigarette before blowing smoke through its nose. Chameleon slapped the cigarette out of the chimpanzee's hand; this infuriated the young man who roughly grabbed Chameleon's shirt ready to fight. This sudden physical aggression alarmed Shalimar and she hurried towards the two men, calling for them to stop. The familiar dull pain resurfaced in her foot slowing her down as she limped towards them.

'What's going on?'

The young man spoke first.

'This idiot is trying to tell me I should let the chimp go. As if I am going to listen to him? Ah go beat you!' he said, staring daggers at Chameleon.

Shalimar panicked. She didn't want any harm coming to Chameleon. If anything happened to him now, she would not be able to get her money.

'He won't touch you again.' She spoke calmly and reassuringly, as though she had the upper hand in their relationship.

Chameleon stared at her in disbelief. She could not tell if it was because she interrupted him or because of what she had just promised his adversary. He turned back to face the young man, ignoring Shalimar's words:

'Release the chimp before I snap your stupid head off your useless shoulders,' Chameleon shouted, ignoring her attempt to ease the situation.

Shalimar stepped between the two men and turned to face the young man.

'This chimpanzee is creating a racket. All this fuss over a simple creature? How much do you want for it?'

The young man gave her a questioning look.

'Why do you think I want to sell it?'

'Oh come on, how much do you want for it? Don't worry; you will get a good price.'

She turned to Chameleon for quick reassurance, and noticed a change in his demeanour. His grey eyes softened to her bartering.

'Forty thousand.'

The young man spoke defiantly. Forty thousand was one month's wages. Shalimar knew if she had forty thousand she would be off to Blama in less than a minute.

'I have trained him to do all sorts of tricks. You won't get any better, that's my price take it or leave it.'

Shalimar turned to see Chameleon already counting out the money. The young man stood triumphant, sneering at his rival. The chimpanzee, as if sensing what was going on, moved towards the young man waiting to be picked up.

'His name is Sam. He smokes Marlborough and drinks Star beer. His favourite food is cassava leave.'

Shalimar laughed hysterically at this revelation. Chameleon threw the money on the floor and grabbed the chain from the young man's hands.

'Money is money whether you throw it on the ground or not.' The young man sneered, bending to pick up the notes.

Chameleon ignored him and tried to cajole the chimpanzee into climbing on his shoulders, but the chimp grabbed the young man's leg and whimpered. The young man laughed and picked up the chimp affectionately.

'You see he doesn't want to leave me. I am like his Father.'

Chameleon snapped back 'I'm going to take him to a friend down the road. You better shut your mouth while I drive you there. I don't want to hear any more shit.'

Chameleon pointed to the Jeep.

'Get in the back, and keep him calm.'

Chameleon's friend lived only five minutes drive away from the beach. The young man and his chimp sat quietly in the back, much to Shalimar's relief. She had seen what damage an angry chimp could do, and did not want to be trapped in a car if the animal suddenly freaked out.

Chameleon pulled up outside a set of huge black gates, wound down his window, and shouted through the gates. A security guarded suddenly appeared and opened the gates for them and Chameleon slowly drove up the manicured drive, which led to a continental-styled house. A middle-aged Indian man appeared at the front door to greet them as they pulled up. Shalimar stayed in the Jeep and marvelled at the spectacle of the three men discussing in depth the fate of the wild animal. The whole ordeal was completely bizarre to her.

When Chameleon finally said his goodbyes, the young man called after him: 'Hey white man, aren't you going to give me a lift back to where you found me?'

'Fuck off.' Chameleon answered venomously. He sped off not even waiting for the security guard to open the gates properly.

Shalimar couldn't wait to get back to the hotel room and slumped down on the sofa exhausted as soon as she was through the door. She rubbed her temples, closed her eyes, and lay back into the soft cushions. The familiar sound of the whisky bottle clinking against a glass brought her out of her slouch. Chameleon gulped it down, and poured himself a second drink. She decided to say what was on her mind:

'Why are you so angry about the monkey?'

'Chimpanzee...'

'Why are you so angry about it? He fed that chimpanzee and took care of it...'

Chameleon turned to face her.

'You call that looking after? Would you allow your child to be looked after like that?'

Shalimar did not understand this man's logic. She spoke slowly so that he would comprehend her reasoning.

'It is an animal, not a human being.'

'So, what's your point?'

'You think it's right to give a chimpanzee alcohol and cigarettes? You believe that is a good thing?'

Shalimar sat up straight as he approached her. He clearly did not understand what she was getting at.

'No, but it is an animal. My concern is for human beings; not for animals.'

Chameleon took another swig from his glass,

'That's why this place is so fucked up.'

Shalimar laughed in disbelief at his conclusion. He justified the war down to the way animals were being treated. She put her index finger to the side of her head and twisted it to indicate his insanity.

'Children are dying, and you are worried about a monkey. People's hands and feet are being chopped off and you want to fight over a monkey? I will never understand this logic. I see all the time in the magazine pictures your people trying to turn their pets into human beings, dressing them in clothes and shoes. I really don't understand how you can value animal life over human life? Or maybe you value animal life over black Africans? In your country you used to treat animals better than you treat blacks so which one is it?'

Chameleon did not respond at first. He looked straight past her as if gathering his thoughts.

'Most human beings can try to defend themselves when the time comes, but that is not the case with animals. A lot of animals cannot defend themselves against humans. They certainly don't stand a chance against idiots with weapons.' He spoke softly as though trying to implant a lasting impression in her brain.

She sighed and slumped back lazily into the sofa. He obviously preferred animals to humans which is why he took human life without remorse. She nodded to humour him.

'How long do you think Salia will take to come to Freetown?'

Chameleon watched her as he sipped on his whisky. The brown liquid swished around when he shook the glass and swallowed the last mouthful.

'Six months is the maximum. If he doesn't turn up then I will assume he is dead.'

He placed the glass on the coffee table, as he walked towards the door.

'I am going to the Casino. Have a good evening.'

Shalimar stiffened. It was not the kind of answer she had expected. She had tried to shut the possibilities of anything unfortunate happening to Salia out of her mind. She wiped her sweaty palms on the sofa and pondered in disbelief. The stillness of the room engulfed her. Her toes curled against each other protecting themselves against the suddenly cool ceramic tiles. She now knew there was no option but to continue to steal as though her life depended on it. Her moralistic upbringing counted for nothing in the face of survival.

Shalimar exhaled. A sensation sauntered through her body slowly allowing exhilaration to set in. She was alone to do as she pleased. Quickly she ran to the bedroom, frantically opening every one of Chameleon's drawers to look for money. She searched his trouser and shirt pockets but only managed to find ten Leones. Although disappointed, she would put it with the rest. Note by stolen note she could soon be equipped to leave the city. With slight disenchantment, she wondered what Baindu would have done in this situation. Her sister was a calculating and sly woman. She would probably have gone to dinner with him and then excused herself to the toilet and disappeared with his wallet. Shalimar laughed at the idea. Baindu was so strong and clever. She was a fighter unlike her.

'Salia! You want to fight me and keep me here, don't you?' Shalimar shouted at the ceiling.

Tears continued to roll down her face as she forced a smile. She could almost hear her friend reprimanding her for trying to disobey him. He was protecting her by forcing her to stay. She closed her eyes, briefly hoping to feel his presence.

The half-empty bottle of Jack Daniels on the coffee table suddenly caught her eye. She grabbed the bottle and took a mouthful, cringing as she swallowed. Salia was the only man who understood her and cared for her as a real friend. He was the rock that made things bearable through her family's conflicts. She was certain he was still alive, as her spirit couldn't feel his death. He was somewhere out there - he had to be. The bitter taste of alcohol soon disappeared as the laughter of memories drowned her thought process. She stumbled to the bedroom with Salia guiding her footsteps and reminding her of better days.

*

The bushes block Shalimar's view. The voices sound familiar but there are so many bushes in the way making it impossible to see who is speaking. The big green leaves keep springing back up, making it harder to push down bush after bush to get nearer to the voices. There are people in the distance and Shalimar runs towards them, shoving the branches away even when they spring back, slapping her face. A low-lying branch is broken away easily and gives way to the sight of Commando Rambo standing over Mama. His gun is placed on the side of Mama's head. He looks up at the sound of the branch snapping and sticks out his pink tongue in response. He looks at Shalimar. He smiles and fires the gun.

Shalimar woke in the darkness, sweating profusely. Her head spun as her heart pounded irregularly inside her fragile ribcage. She looked around the room, disorientated and breathing heavily. The bedroom door opened almost immediately. Chameleon turned on the light.

'What happened? What was that noise?'

Her ears were still ringing from the sound of the gun blast. Mama's face was so clear and real. The familiar strong smell of palm oil filled the room. That smell surrounded her mother during and after every meal that she cooked with love for the family. The detail in the dream felt so intense. She wanted to go back to sleep again so her mother could visit her. So she could touch and talk to her. Just to be with her one more time.

Chameleon stood in the middle of the room trying to read her thoughts. Shalimar looked up at him. He was the reality of her situation. It was in the middle of the night and she remained alone in Freetown with a complete stranger. No Mama, Papa or Baindu. No Blama. Her bottom lip quivered uncontrollably and Shalimar burst into tears. The dream had strangely brought about a certain amount of relief, but to have Mama taken away in such a brutal manner filled her with horror. Chameleon's long arms circled her; he pressed her head against his chest, his hands gently massaging her back in much the same way as Salia used to. Her tears created a damp patch in the middle of his shirt. No words were exchanged as he quietly comforted her. After what felt like a lifetime, Shalimar regained her composure and moved awkwardly away from him.

'Finally having nightmares like me huh? That's what happens in war. Just don't end up like me.' He laughed softly at his own joke.

She couldn't look at him; the anguish she had tried to control was taking over. She wanted her life back. Chameleon stood up, aware there was no longer any need for him.

'Do you want the light on?'

She shook her head.

'Sleep. I'll take you to see Miatta in the morning.'

Chapter 8

The alarm clock on the bedside table showed eleven thirty. Haunted by the dream of her mother, Shalimar had woken up many times during the night, staring into the darkness as Chameleon slept soundly next to her.

The next morning, sapped of energy from her fitful sleep, Shalimar stayed in bed until her hunger pains reached an agonising level. She slowly dragged herself out of bed and checked the other room. Two plates of prepared food were covered up carefully with paper towels to protect them from the flies. Even as she ate, she marvelled at the power of her dream experience. Her present anguish felt like being at the bottom of a mortar with a pestle pounding her stomach. The force of the impact twisted her insides. Shalimar winced. Chameleon sat in the veranda unusually silent. He looked up from his paper as she crossed the room, but made no effort to talk to her. The dull headache at the back of her head had moved slowly to her temples while she ate, ruining her appetite. Shalimar left most of her breakfast untouched and now sought painkillers in the bedroom.

'I'm taking you to meet Miatta.' Chameleon said when Shalimar joined him on the veranda.

Shalimar nodded and swallowed the medicine with water.

*

Chameleon parked the silver Jeep on the sand in front of the Paradise Bar. The thatched-roof beach bar imitated the mud huts from the countryside. The staff greeted Chameleon with cheers, and waved at Shalimar. An array of empty hammocks hovered over the powdery white sand at the back of the bar, with the overhang from the thatched roof serving as some protection from the unforgiving sun. Chameleon climbed into the nearest available hammock, put his hands behind his head and smiled.

'This is the life, hey Shalimar?'

Shalimar searched for an empty chair, and dragged it next to the hammock, making sure her back faced the ocean.

'Perks of the job. I can enjoy my life and work when I want to. I'm not stuck in some office building with a piece of paper to my name calling some jackass a boss.'

His hand impatiently brushed the wisps of brown tresses on his sweaty brow fluttering under the sea's gentle breeze.

A slender woman holding a round silver tray sauntered towards Chameleon, her bare long legs pushed against the slit in her mini skirt. They gave each other a high five. Chameleon sat up to give her his undivided attention and Shalimar watched the woman's eyes sparkle at the sight of him. The silver tray held two bottles of Star beer. She leant forward and casually placed the bottles and glasses onto the table as she spoke.

'Nothing has been happening here, but that is better than something happening, I suppose.'

'Is it?' Chameleon retorted sarcastically.

Her laugher displayed brilliant white teeth. The black bob wig fitted perfectly over her heart shaped face and glistened under the rays of the sun.

Chameleon placed one leg out of the hammock, trying to maintain a balance. He leant over, grabbing the beer bottle and took a gulp before asking Miatta to share her story of fleeing from the RUF Rebels to Shalimar.

The young woman suddenly pretended to notice Shalimar. She smiled warmly looking back and forth at them as if trying to work out their relationship. Chameleon climbed out of the hammock to stretch.

'Don't worry I've spoken to Faruq. The bar isn't busy so will allow you some time off. Miatta nodded; clearly pleased with the way her day was turning out. Chameleon pulled out some notes from his pocket and handed them to Shalimar.

'I'm going to Casino Leone for the rest of the afternoon. Help yourself to whatever.'

Shalimar stood open-mouthed in shock, not daring to look at the wad of notes just yet.

'Talk to her for me heh?' he said in Miatta's direction. 'She needs to lighten up,' he added, winking at Shalimar before disappearing back into the bar area.

For the first time Shalimar wasn't sure if she liked the idea of Chameleon leaving her alone with unfamiliar faces. At least she knew what to expect from him. Miatta grabbed an empty chair, clearly eager to talk, and asked several personal questions almost immediately. Shalimar smiled and gave a vague account of how she found herself in Freetown. She omitted any real information, unsure of the relationship between the locals and Chameleon.

Miatta relayed her own story without hesitation. She arrived in Freetown two years ago. She had been washing clothes in the stream near her village, when her cousin had come running to bring the news that the RUF were heading straight towards them. They fled immediately, and her family had sought refuge in one of the many refugee camps along the way. However Rebels infiltrated many such camps posing as refugees and systematically raped the women. The family decided to leave after only a month and headed for Freetown; the general consensus being that nobody would dare attack the capital city. Miatta recited appalling incidences of mutilations to babies and child rape with shockingly vivid details.

Shalimar covered her face. She could not bear to hear anymore. The thought that such atrocities could have befallen her family made her nauseous.

Shalimar felt her shoulders being squeezed reassuringly as Miatta carried on with her story. As luck would have it, they had been able to contact a relative in Freetown who had welcomed them with open arms and helped them get their lives back together. Her father had found work as a security guard and her mother as a cook. Her two sisters attended the local primary school, and she had managed to keep her job in the bar for almost a year. The hospitality trade was always in need of employees because people loved to party. Miatta found work in the night clubs at first, and then had found this job on offer at Paradise Bar, which was more suitable for her than the sleazy club scene.

'Look at me now. I survived. I am making money and living my life.'

Shalimar couldn't smile at this friendly warm character, her mind still raced with the possibility that her family had been harmed. Miatta trailed her fingers on the neat partings that separated Shalimar's plaits in the manner of an older sibling. She hugged Shalimar with promises of future friendship, then paused and smiled mischievously.

'Now, how did you meet Chameleon?'

Suspecting all along that her newfound friend was curious about her relationship with Chameleon, she remained silent.

Miatta giggled and nudged her affectionately.

'Come on how did you meet him? He is a nice man once you get to know him, and he has a lot of money. Do you know how many women would want to be in your position? Life is so hard. If you waste time with him there are a dozen that will take your place.'

Miatta's humour, combined with the alcohol, allowed her to relax. The loud music from the bar pumped ferociously. A familiar light-headedness engulfed her consciousness. Shalimar found herself recounting the RUF's visit to the Long Life bar. It was the first time she had talked about what happened since leaving Blama, and she was surprised she could recount the story without falling apart emotionally. Time was beginning to play its part in healing without her realising it. Miatta grabbed the bottle of Star beer and shoved it in Shalimar's hands.

'Titi, leh we enjoy we life. Nar one life we get for live, yah.'

The women bought fried fish from the local fishermen's wives who trailed the beach in search of customers. They necked another beer and continued to chat about their hometowns and way of life. Shalimar could feel the muscles in her neck and shoulders begin to loosen up. Her new friend's soothing words and carefree attitude, along with a few drinks finally allowed her to unwind and it felt good. Hope fostered itself inside Miatta's slightly more secure world. Life would get better; it was not false hope to believe in such sentiments. Miatta recalled the refugee camps and numerous charities that were involved in helping the displaced thousands that were entering the city by the truckload every week. The war would dwindle away and all would be at peace, it was only a matter of time.

Shalimar wondered whether her friend was home-sick. She noticed Miatta talked of peace and hope but with no mention of going back to her town to pick up the pieces and build a new life. Miatta shrugged her shoulders.

'Go back to what? The town was burnt down, and there is nothing left for my family there. How would I earn a living?'

'We can work on the land. Go back to farming and feed ourselves like we did before.'

Miatta shook her head and chuckled: 'How can we go back after living in Freetown? It will never be the same again, look at all the action here. Why would I go back to a village?'

This attitude alarmed Shalimar. How could this woman just discard her home in this manner? As if its existence had no relevance in her new life. Shalimar became indignant.

'Because our life has better quality there, what is so good about this place? Yes there is money but there is stress and nobody has time for anyone. I want to go back. I don't care about fast cars and all this wealth. As soon as I get the chance I will go home.'

Miatta picked apart the head of her fried fish and sucked her fingers. She looked at Shalimar, nodding to acknowledge her point of view. She grabbed the lone white napkin from the table and wiped her hands

'You are with a rich man Shalimar, and live in luxury. You can't compare the way you used to live to the way you live now. You have forgotten what life is really like out of here. Of course you will romanticize about Blama.'

'Well I want to go home, and you can tell Chameleon I said so!' Shalimar interrupted impatiently. It seemed her friend did not share the same sentiment and she couldn't comprehend why.

Shalimar noticed a slight envy in Miatta's tone when referring to Chameleon. To avert displaying any emotion regarding Chameleon she found herself mimicking his accent and mannerisms in jest: a sure sign that the alcohol had settled into her system. It brought back sweet reminders of sitting outside with the family, drinking palm wine with the neighbours as they talked about their lives and those of the other villagers.

The temperature dropped as a strong wind blew the sand around their feet. The brightness of the sun was now visible from a distance as the shadow hours crept in unannounced. The ocean's waves that Shalimar had managed to ignore all this time could be heard crashing ferociously against the rocks in the distance. The bar area suddenly came alive with drunk customers passing through on their way to the hotels that harboured the nightclubs.

Miatta was the first to spot Chameleon's arrival. She jumped out of her chair and rushed over, throwing her arms around his neck causing them both to topple.

'Whoah! What are you people doing drinking so much if you can't handle it?'

He dislodged Miatta's arms from around his neck, trying to see where Shalimar was seated. Shalimar stiffened. For some reason, Miatta's actions annoyed her. She did not know how they both knew each other but it didn't warrant her greeting Chameleon in that manner. Chameleon successfully pushed Miatta away and smirked at Shalimar.

'It's time to go.'

She avoided his eyes, not wanting him to see how aggravated she was nor how tipsy she had become.

'Did she cheer you up then?' he said, tipping his head in Miatta's direction.

'Of course I did.' Miatta interjected causing Shalimar to look at both of them. 'I am good for a lot of things you know.'

Chameleon replied with a wide smile. 'I'm sure you are. You did a good job, you even got her tipsy!'

Miatta put her arm around Chameleon's neck once more. For a second, Shalimar noticed the two of them gazing into each other's eyes.

Resentment swelled up inside her. All potential trust with Miatta abandoned.

'You give me a job to do and I do it. Look at her, she is better now. What would you do without me? I even got her drunk.'

'I am not drunk!' Shalimar snapped.

She shot out of her chair and stormed past the bemused pair. Chameleon would have to follow her and leave Miatta behind. The sand flew in and out of her slippers as Shalimar marched towards the Jeep, not daring to look behind to see if Chameleon was coming. She stood there wondering why she felt so angry. A set of keys jangled behind her.

'You can't get in if I don't open the door.'

She said nothing, clearly wound up from the evening's unfolding events. A whiff of cologne streamed past her as he leant forward to open her door.

Chameleon got in the driver's side, and started the engine. He reversed carefully, the previously empty car park now almost full of vehicles parked in a haphazard way.

'Is Miatta one of your girlfriends?' Shalimar asked candidly, trying not to show any form of emotion in her voice.

He laughed as they joined the trail of traffic on the strip, stealing a quick glance at Shalimar who now felt stupid for asking.

'Is that what she told you? Does it matter if she is?'

'No'

'*You nor lek am*?'

Shalimar remained silent.

'If you really want to know, my last girlfriend was Kenyan and she looked nothing like Miatta.'

'I don't want to know.'

'Miatta nah fine oman.'

Shalimar couldn't help herself as she guffawed in disagreement.

'I think she has a pretty face and a good body,' Chameleon retorted.

Shalimar fell silent as they parked the Jeep in the usual spot at the Hotel. Chameleon's flirting with Miatta had brought about a dejected feeling inside her. He had been around her in a way most other men had not, but still had not made a move on her. Her skin did not resemble the smooth dark even complexion of most and then there was the large misshapen birthmark that disfigured her. It dawned on her that he didn't favour boys; it was her that he did not find attractive.

It felt unusually cold inside the hotel room, and Shalimar wondered if they had forgotten to switch the air conditioner off before leaving.

Chameleon religiously poured himself a shot of whisky. In his usual manner he swung the drink back, gurgling in an ungainly mouth washing fashion. He called out to Shalimar who turned around haughtily. Sometimes he behaved like a bushman and it was annoying to watch.

Chameleon moved in close to cup her face with his hands. He searched her face for something. Shalimar could feel her heart beating wildly in anticipation. He leant forward, kissing her gently, and then pulled back. This was the moment that she had been dreading. Her heart continued to pummel but not through fear. His lips were much softer than she had imagined.

Leaning forward he kissed her again, much harder this time. His stubble grazed her skin as he pushed his tongue into her mouth. His hands moved to the small of her back to pull her closer into him, kissing her harder and harder. His hands slipped under her knees and he lifted her gently and carried her effortlessly to the bedroom.

A wave of pleasure consumed her as he gently kissed her repeatedly. His warm hands lifted her white chiffon dress over her head. She found herself responding to his kiss, running her fingers through his hair and searching his back. Millions of tingling sensations invaded her whole body and she closed her eyes helplessly. Never once had she imagined she would be feeling this way in this situation. In her head a voice was shouting at her. It was not supposed to happen this way and this was definitely not how it was supposed to feel.

Chameleon outlined her birthmark with kisses. At that moment her heart leapt, her surprise was so great. He sensed her emotion and stopped to smile.

His hands moved under her pulling her into him, and it was then that she felt the pain. Sharp, tearing, powerful, overwhelming: she gasped as the blood rushed to her face. He kissed her neck and whispered softly,

'It's okay, it's okay. Relax.'

Slowly he pulled her in closer despite her efforts to push his shoulders and body away from her. The pain was so intense she felt it would surely kill her.

'It's okay.'

He repeated the words over and over, taking her hands and clasping them above her head. He whispered into her ears that she was safe with him. He told her she was beautiful and she had nothing to be afraid of. She kept her eyes clamped shut, trying desperately to focus on anything but the pain she felt inside. From nowhere she felt her body relax and start to move slowly with the bucking motion of his hips. She was wet between the legs, and Chameleon slid slowly and easily into her. The pain subsided, overtaken by another, more powerful sensation; something she had never experienced before...

As they lay together in silence, Shalimar noticed Chameleons hair soaked in sweat. She touched it curiously. It appeared flat and felt somewhat stringy, offering no protection to his scalp unlike her springy curls. Chameleon kissed her passionately before doling out an affectionate slap on her bottom. He climbed out of bed and headed toward the bathroom.

Shalimar awoke to find Chameleon fully clothed in a white short-sleeved shirt and black jeans. He grabbed the car keys noisily from the bedside table and flicked off some dirt from his jeans. He appeared to be in a hurry.

'You awake? I'm out of town for a couple of days. There's some money on the table and the food has already been paid for, so order what you want.'

Chapter 9

Chameleon walked out of the room without looking back. The sound of the front door closing left her feeling a little bewildered. Left alone, the first thing that entered her mind was escape. She turned to the bedside table, staring at the wad of money he had left her. She jumped out of bed and started to count it. There were fifty thousand Leones, plus the three hundred Leones she had saved so far; more than enough to pay for the bus fare to Blama and food for a couple of months. Fifty thousand Leones might as well be fifty million. She could do so much with this kind of money, but first she would rebuild the family home if the Rebels had burnt it down.

Shalimar took a quick shower and got dressed. She grabbed the black plastic bag left on the floor and stuffed her new clothes into it. The next couple of minutes were spent running around the room to make sure nothing had been forgotten. Nobody here would miss a damn thing. She spotted Mrs Foday's leather handbag and added it to her collection.

Shalimar hurried out of the hotel room. There was no sign of life as she sauntered through the hallway, smiling cheerfully at anyone who passed her by. She clicked down the tiled stairs gracefully and spotted the busy receptionist that did not like her. She moved toward the entrance quietly unnoticed.

The merciless heat outside contrasted enormously with the cool air-conditioned room she and Chameleon had shared. She ignored it, as there would be plenty of taxis on the long stretch of road to take her to the bus station. Petty traders of leather slippers and tie dye dresses approached her as she walked. They assumed she had money, some called out to her.

'Yellow woman....Look I get fine tings for you!'

She smiled in response but did not answer. Excitement swirled around inside her as she arrived at Aberdeen Junction. Now she had made it this far, she was free to leave the city behind, and Chameleon with it. She stopped at the junction and looked around for a taxi but there were none in sight. A quick decision had to be made, so she decided to head to Lumley beach and just hail one down on the strip. The road stretched out so far ahead of her she could not see the end. When she finally arrived at the beginning of the beach road and turned onto the strip, she had to catch her breath as she gazed upon the mass of clear blue sea. The vastness of the ocean stood out before her in all its grandeur, its endlessness given character by the small boats in the distance glimmering in the sunlight.

A thin dog with tufts of hair hanging off its pink skin settled onto the tarmac and licked itself. It was as though this was the last comfort before willing death to end its obvious suffering. A car rolled up in the distance but the dog did not flinch. Shalimar crossed the road and as the speeding car approached her she turned to witness the fate of the dog that still remained in the middle of the road, watching and waiting unperturbed. The car swerved slightly to avoid it and continued to speed off down the road. For a split second her eyes met with the miserable animal and both were unable to mask their disappointment.

Sweat trickled down her back as she walked along the strip in the unbearable heat with no refuge from the sun. Thoughts of Chameleon surfaced as she slowed down. She could almost feel his warm hands on her skin and his cool soft lips caressing her body. Those lips were softer than the feathers that managed to push through the cotton fabric of her pillow brushing delicately against her skin. She had experienced something no-one had ever told her to expect. Baindu had always professed that the day a man made love a woman she would instantly know. She declared it easy to fall in love with a man that knew how to make love to a woman. Now she thought about him whispering into her ear: 'It's okay.'

He did not want to hurt her; he had wanted her to relax. He did not force himself onto her as she had always anticipated he would, and he certainly did not prefer boys like Barrow. The intimacy she had experienced was almost like some sort of release. She had been in the city close to seven months and her yearning for some type of physical comfort had been satisfied in a way she had not expected. A yellow taxi approached in the distance, and with a smile of relief she put her hand out to hail it down. The taxi approached and stopped. Gregory Isaac's *Night Nurse* played from within the car. The young taxi driver smiled and asked, 'Where to Lady?'

'Bus station...for go up country.'

The taxi driver nodded. She opened the front door and climbed in, clutching her possessions tightly to her stomach.

The car sped off down the stretch of empty road. Children playing in the sand, fishermen landing their canoes with fish, jazz flowing out of the empty beach bars all made the sea front appear peaceful and friendly. The taxi turned into a road where traffic was at a standstill. There had been an accident with a poda poda, a small bus and a large black Hummer. The taxi driver explained to Shalimar he intended to reverse back the way they came and drive through the Aberdeen Bridge instead. She nodded with no idea of what he was talking about. They drove back up the beach front and turned back into the driveway of the hotel.

Shalimar shouted, 'What are you doing? I need to go to town! I need to go to the bus station!'

The young driver did not answer as he parked up. An elderly man stood alone waiting for them. The young taxi driver remained unperturbed by her hysterics and shrugged his shoulders.

'Madam, Boss man said if you leave we must find you.'

'What Boss man? What are you talking about?'

'*Go insiye*. At least there is someone to take care of you. You should be grateful.'

Shalimar slammed the dashboard with her fist.

'Grateful? Grateful! Grateful for what?! For bringing me to a hotel like a prostitute! Everybody thinks I'm a prostitute! I'm not a prostitute...he took me away! I am a prisoner!' Shalimar's pumping heart was out of control as anger swelled within her and hampered her breathing.

The elderly man's voice travelled through the open window.

'You don bring am back? Wetin nah deh problem?'

'Eh well Sah, eh say we deh look am lekke prostitute....'

The elderly man gently patted Shalimar's shoulder.

'No, no we don't view you in that way at all. Mr Jamie told us that the RUF destroyed your town and that's why he took you away. You will go home when it is safe but for now just enjoy this fortunate situation.'

Shalimar looked sharply at him as he spoke about her circumstances. A mass of white hair contrasted with his dark skin giving him a somewhat stately look. His peaceful demeanour and kind eyes calmed her down. He smiled at her.

'Yes Madam, he told us that you don't know where your family is and you have nowhere to go...of course you will get upset and try to go back. But you can't go back yet. Don't you know how many coaches have been ambushed? Don't you listen to the news on the radio? They are killing people like flies.'

The taxi driver backed up the elderly man's concerns,

'Freetown is the safest place you can be. You should know that by now.'

Shalimar said nothing. It was clear everything was against her, including fate and God.

88

'Come,' the elderly man beckoned, opening the taxi door. 'Come inside. Have a drink and relax on your veranda. You can visit places around here. Mr Jamie just does not want you to back to the countryside that's all.'

He leant forward and offered his arm to help her out of the vehicle. Shalimar accepted. The young taxi driver cheered as though she were a child cajoled into taking her first steps. The sound of clicking heels echoed around the empty dining area as Shalimar followed Mohammed towards the bar area. A slight draught caused the heavy curtains on the windows to flutter slightly. Mohammed pulled out a cold bottle of Star beer from the fridge and handed it to Shalimar with a smile. The open doorway leading to the pool slammed unexpectedly from the growing breeze outside. The whistling wind announced the arrival of a storm, as crackling thunder surrounded the dining area. Shalimar grimaced wondering if the severity of the storm would have affected her coach ride towards Blama. Mohammed hurried over to the rattling doorway dodging the throng of swimmers and sunbathers running from the rain. Shalimar called out her goodbyes and helped herself to roasted peanuts on the bar counter.

The room remained just as she had left it, with the veranda doors wide open. Chameleon had a habit of leaving papers strewn all over the coffee table, and some of those papers now fluttered around the room, whipped up by the storm. The rain splattered against Shalimar's face as she struggled to close the doors almost slipping over on the wet tile floor in the process.

She pressed a soft clean towel against her face to smell the sunshine freshness and wipe off the rain. She longed to wash clothes, light a fire, visit friends and cook like a normal human being, but the hotel life robbed her off any type of normality as she knew it. Seven months felt like a lifetime, and this existence was wearing her down. Chameleon probably assumed that this life was what the poor wished for, but it just left her feeling frustrated and restless. She sat on the toilet seat pulling at the loops of the cotton fabric in frustration. Chameleon had the staff watching her every move. She remembered what Mohammed said about listening to the radio. This was something she had left to Chameleon to do while she planned her escape, unaware of what was really happening around the country. Salia had not arrived and her sister was still somewhere out there in precarious surroundings. She felt so helpless, and to be helpless was to be useless. Mama called her useless many times and still she was unable to prove otherwise. Deflated, and resigned to being stuck in Freetown despite having the money to get home, Shalimar returned to the front room and slumped onto the sofa. She walked over to the radio and flicked it on. A couple of minutes knob turning discovered only a boring debate about national budget deficits, and some classical music she didn't like. Shalimar sat back down in a huff, angry at herself for wondering when Chameleon would be back.

*

It was a lonely experience for Shalimar - trying to occupy her time with no knowledge of when Chameleon would return. She would stroll down to the beach every day, keeping to the opposite side of the road to the beach, as far as possible away from the waves that crashed onto the rocks at the beginning of the strip. She strode under the blistering heat biding her time till the busy road offered up an opportunity to dash across and feel the sand between her toes.

The first couple of days Shalimar just sat alone on the veranda, watching the tourists, but eventually she willed herself to visit the Paradise Bar to see Miatta. As much as Miatta had annoyed her previously, she had no one else to talk to. A surprised Miatta was unable to conceal her enthusiasm as Shalimar entered the bar, and squealed with delight; rushing over and hugging her tightly. Shalimar offered to buy lunch and the two women sat in the neighbouring restaurant - Shalimar discussing hotel staff behaviour and Miatta gossiping about various characters that worked on Lumley beach. Miatta's streetwise manner made Shalimar acutely aware that she had a lot to learn about people and what they were capable of. Shalimar watched as Miatta flirted easily with the male diner's in order to acquire free drinks from them. Miatta sipped her Fanta from a straw reminding Shalimar, '*you are being taken care of, the rest of us are out here on our own.*'

After lunch, the two women ambled along the beach, and Miatta introduced Shalimar to the local traders. They sat outside poorly built shacks and sold anything from mangoes to matches. They all smiled and waved at Miatta, who was a regular customer with most of them. Shalimar still harboured the ambition of setting up her own business, and maybe now with the money Chameleon left for her, and the realisation that she would not be leaving Freetown any time soon, there may be an opportunity to realise her dream. Some of the trader's already recognised her from the times she had wandered along the strip alone. Next time they invited her to sit with them she would take up the offer, hopefully receiving some of the invaluable tips and information they no doubt possessed.

Shalimar had hoped Salia would turn up while Chameleon was away but he didn't. It would have been much easier to have just left with him. Almost eight months had flown by with no word or sight of her friend. Shalimar found it difficult to believe that he could be stuck in a displaced camp somewhere between Bo and Freetown. She had needed something to cling on to during these past months, and it had been the eventual arrival of Salia. But as the weeks, and then months passed with still no sign, Shalimar was starting to fear that something had happened to him. It was difficult to talk about her fears with the Hotel staff, because they had been paid off by Chameleon, and naturally took his side. They talked to her about her own safety, insisting on her being patient. But how patient could you be when your whole family could be in danger? When your sister was engaged to a RUF Rebel and hiding somewhere in the bush? How patient could you be with a sick father and an ageing mother who were probably in a displaced camp somewhere under the impression that their children were dead?

The nights were tougher to get through. Shalimar tried to hold on to the memories of her loved ones but sometimes their faces were blank. She traced the border of her birthmark repeatedly. Her heart grew heavy like the bundle of clothes she would take to the stream to wash every other day. She forced smiles to the staff as she passed them, but her world felt empty; devoid of the love she had once known.

Most evenings Shalimar listened to the radio reports, but they generally just left her puzzled. They were full of rumours and speculation and contradictory reports of what was going on. Some would have sightings of RUF and detail their intentions; other reports would describe successful E.C.O.M.O.G tactics. None of this mattered if her family was gone. If that were the case then what was there to live for?

The news was just depressing, and Shalimar felt bad enough already. She twisted the knob until she found some gentle jazz music, and settled back into the sofa. She wondered if some of her depression was a result of her being intimate with Chameleon. He had been gone for over two weeks now, and in her loneliness she yearned for him to hurry back. How had this happened? Shalimar shook her head: 'No; I will not allow myself to feel so defeated,' she said to herself. Tomorrow she would head to the beach instead of festering all day in her room.

*

Shalimar took breakfast out on the veranda, pleased that the sky was a brilliant blue with barely a cloud in sight. A gentle breeze fluttered around her, just enough to take the edge off the blistering heat. Shalimar headed downstairs determined to be positive and happy. Mohammed smiled at her as she passed, making her feel safe in a strange way. Somehow he reminded her of an older Salia. She had made a decision. She would bide her time and accumulate more money. She was finally learning the basics of trading from the beach vendors, and she sat with them any time her friend was busy. When the lunchtime rush was over, Miatta would walk along the beach to find Shalimar, who could be sitting by any one of the shacks. They would have a Fanta and gossip about the waitresses or barmen, and generally have a good time. Shalimar told Miatta about the haughty receptionist who always greeted her with a false smile and looked down her nose at her.

'I know of this woman,' Miatta said. 'She has no reason to think she is above anyone.'

'Why do you say that?' Shalimar replied, barely containing her excitement.

'Everyone knows she sleeps with any rich man who shows an interest in her. The people call her '*Lumley Mattress*' behind her back.'

Shalimar was almost in hysterics: 'How can you call someone that name?'

'I know everyone and everything that goes on in this area.' Miatta exclaimed. 'I know all about people in Lumley, ask me anything.'

Shalimar's laugh suddenly dried up at Miatta's declaration. She dared to think of her father again.

'You can't possibly know everyone....'

'Why not? I work and live here. I talk to everyone, so there is no one that doesn't know me.'

'Do you know Mr Abdualai Barrie?' Shalimar blurted out.

'The businessman? The Barrie that owns several farms?'

Shalimar's heart leapt into her throat. Mama had mentioned the farms. She felt the heat rush through her body in exhilaration.

'He lives in Lumley. Do you know him?'

'I have seen the wife many times. They live opposite the police station...'

'A green house?'

'No. It's yellow.'

Shalimar twitched. It was simple. It had always been simple, but she had gone about things in the most complicated way. Her father's house was in Lumley, he had not moved to Guinea or Mali. The house he had lived in for over twenty years had been repainted. Shalimar smiled and quickly changed the subject marvelling at the revelation of her father's whereabouts. She shouted her thanks out to God as she ran back to the hotel room punching the air. To be reunited with her father would make her life complete. The birds chirped louder and the heat seemed more endurable the next day as Shalimar headed off to Paradise Bar to see Miatta, unfortunately she was absent today. The bar staff described what were malaria-like symptoms that had befallen her during the evening shift, the night before. A disappointed Shalimar gave the bar staff money for Miatta's medical bills then went on to the neighbouring snack bar that sold different flavoured ice-cream, something unobtainable in Blama. She ordered strawberry, appreciating a single moment with some of the finer things in life. After indulging in several cones the walk back to the hotel seemed just about tolerable.

Shalimar's heart missed a beat at the sight of the pair of blue Adidas trainers in the front room. She checked the bedroom and found Chameleon fast asleep in his white tank top, sprawled out on the bed. She tiptoed carefully into the room and could hear his breathing as she moved closer. He did not stir but slept peacefully; chest rising and falling with the face of an innocent young man. She wondered what type of family and childhood he had, and how had he ended up a mercenary. Shalimar marvelled at how Chameleon managed to be on his own for so long in such an unnatural way. She could not live alone. It was the only possible explanation as to why he had such a strange manner. She left the room and headed for the veranda to sit quietly and wait for him, looking over the spectacular vista of mountains, beach and ocean.

An hour passed before the glass doors to the veranda opened. Chameleon emerged bare-chested, wearing a pair of khaki trousers. He sat down on the straw chair beside her and put his feet up on the stool. There was black residue in between his finger and toe nails. Shalimar noticed a faint purple bruise and several cuts on his right arm. He caught her looking and shrugged his shoulders.

'When I am working and someone doesn't understand me, I try to make myself very clear.'

'I didn't ask you anything...'

'You think I'm an animal don't you? It was your Government that brought me here to keep your country in order. I'm no more of an animal than your people...'

'My people are not animals.'

'No? Then what do you call their behaviour in your precious Long Life bar?'

'Some are, but not the majority.'

'In Africa the minority rules and the majority doesn't count.'

This was what she disliked about him sometimes: his nasty tone and sarcastic comments. The unexpected shrill of the telephone interrupted their conversation. Chameleon got up and skipped to the phone. She could hear him talking loudly, and although she couldn't hear what he said he sounded excited. He appeared back at the veranda doors.

'We have been invited out to dinner at the Lighthouse. Get changed.'

'Am I a dog?'

Chameleon rolled his eyes, 'Are we back on that again?'

'Don't talk to me like that. Stop ordering me around with that nasty South African accent. I'm not one of your soldiers...'

'Oh? So my accent is nasty is it?'

They both looked at each other. Shalimar couldn't tell what was going through his mind but he looked slightly offended. She didn't care.

'Yes, it grates my ears. English and American accents sound better.'

Chameleon bellowed with laughter. This annoyed Shalimar. She had encouraged him without even realising it.

'I have done more for your country in four years than those idiots did in their 150 years of colonizing you people.'

Shalimar got up and walked past him. He moved out of her way, still laughing as she went. This infuriated her.

'I don't know what is so funny. You still act as though you are superior. Well you're not... those days are over!'

He smiled haughtily: 'Is that why blacks are running things so effectively in Africa? Huh? They are doing a good job around here chopping each other's limbs off, I can tell you that. You should read the papers and find out how well things are going in South Africa since...'

'Just shut up!'

He raised his hands in the air to surrender, clearly surprised at the degree of her irritation.

'Hey, I'm not trying to upset you. We are going to a nice place to eat tonight with an old friend of mine, and he too has been here for a while just like me. You'll like him.' He paused for effect. 'He is American.'

Shalimar glared at him.

'You can drop me off at my father's house. I know where he lives now.'

Chameleon straightened up in acknowledgment and asked, 'You spoke to him?'

'No, I said I know where he lives. So, you can take me there to meet him and then I can come back and pack my things.'

'Well if that's what you want, I can't stop you.'

Shalimar moved to the bedroom, wondering why she was still annoyed with him.

'So you're not going to come out to dinner with me for one last time?' Chameleon called after her.

Shalimar turned to face him. There was a twinkle in his eye as he smiled at her. He knew she wouldn't refuse him. He was arrogant and so sure of himself. Shalimar nodded and closed the bedroom door.

'Make sure you look good, heh?' Chameleon called. 'I don't hang around with ugly women! I have a reputation to uphold.'

Chapter 10

An enthused Shalimar hurriedly put on the classically tailored cerise dress. She couldn't believe she was going to meet her father for the first time, and it was important to appear smart and presentable. Although she procrastinated on many aspects of her life, she needed to take the reins this time and move forward. She could not sit around watching and waiting for the war to end. Her family needed her. Her sister needed her. Her father could be the key to help bringing her family back together again.

Shalimar could barely contain herself as she directed Chameleon to her father's house. Her nervous excitement manifested itself as non-stop chattering. Chameleon nodded in all the right places, aware that it would be pointless trying to add to the conversation. They got to the yellow house, which was surrounded by high white walls and a set of large black ornate gates. He hooted. Shalimar's heart pummelled when an old man appeared to open them. Chameleon drove inside and parked up.

'*Aftanoon, Sah.*' The old man's face appeared through the open window.

Chameleon switched off the engine and opened his door, but Shalimar grabbed his arm.

'No. I can go on my own.'

Chameleon leaned back into his seat.

'Are you sure?'

'Yes. I need to do this by myself,' Shalimar replied.

Chameleon pulled out a stainless steel flask from the compartment above her knees and took a swig. He offered it to Shalimar, but she declined.

The old man informed Shalimar that *Madam* was at home and asked her to wait at the entrance of the house. Shalimar felt her nerves getting the best of her and tried to compose herself as she told him her name.

The old man squinted and asked, '*You nah Pa Barrie im niece?*'

'Well not exactly but I am a relative...'

The old man entered the house without her. Shalimar stood on the pale blue tiles of the entrance door and peered around the dark hallway. The inside walls were stone washed white and dotted with photographs that she couldn't quite make out. Her palms became sweaty as she waited, but she dare not wipe them on her new dress. Would her father even accept her? Her mother's harsh words through the years had made her wish for acceptance elsewhere.

The second entrance door unbolted from the inside and the servant reappeared with a woman. He shoved the door open and left Shalimar face to face with a big, voluptuous old woman.

'Good Afternoon, Mah. My name is Shalimar. I thought I would pass by to say hello to you and Pa Barrie.'

'I know who you are.' Her voice was flat. She eyed Shalimar intensely as if deciphering her next move. Shalimar stammered. She did not anticipate a cold reception but understood that all might not welcome her presence.

'I just came to see my father. I live in Blama, but the Rebels attacked my village...'

'Where is your mother?' The woman's deadpan stares did not falter. Her cold eyes drawing out any positive energy Shalimar had left.

'I...I don't know. They attacked the village and I lost contact with my family.'

'So you thought you would come here. You want to claim this house..?'

Shalimar hesitated. She did not turn up to create conflict but this woman wanted to fight her. Her words and demeaning stares made Shalimar waver. It was pointless being nice. This woman wasn't interested.

'I'd like to speak to my father, please.'

'You are ten years too late, my dear.'

The sides of her mouth quivered slightly as she spoke. She stamped the cane on the floor as she shifted her body weight onto her other leg.

'He is dead.'

Shalimar's cheeks flushed with disappointment. The old lady slammed the cane repeatedly on the ground as she made efforts to turn away.

'Tell your peasant mother, she will never get this house and you are not welcome here either. Go crawl back under that hole that you came from. There is nothing for you here.'

The old lady continued to mutter as she shuffled away without looking back at her unwelcome guest.

Shalimar stood in the doorway, her mind racing with scattered thoughts and reactive responses. The old lady moved slowly away, stamping her cane for support and murmuring loudly about the inconvenience.

'What did I do to you?' The words fell out of her mouth as a shriek. The old woman stopped and slowly turned around.

'What did I do to you?' Shalimar repeated, 'I am just his child looking for my family! I have done nothing to you. What kind of woman are you?' Shalimar screamed at the old woman.

Ma Barrie continued to eye Shalimar suspiciously, but chose not to reply.

'You think I want your house? You stupid, lonely, miserable woman!'

Tears started rolling down Shalimar's cheeks, frustration taking over from her anger. All the years dreaming of meeting her father - the reunion played over in her mind many times - and now her dreams had been smashed.

'Stay and rot in your house!' Shalimar spat at the old woman.

'What kind of a woman was your mother? Ask yourself that. She almost ruined my marriage. She almost ruined my life.'

The woman started stamping her cane again; pounding the wooden flooring with such force Shalimar thought she would make a hole in her own sitting room. She marked out each syllable as she spoke, battering the floorboards relentlessly.

'Your mother tried to ruin my marriage after I took her in and gave her a roof over her head. I hope she came to the worst possible death and thought about my pain just before she entered the gates of hell!'

The old woman's words brought pain and exasperation. Shalimar turned away not wanting to hear anymore. Her father was dead and his wife still hated her and her mother after all these years. Shalimar had never imagined this type of hostility awaited her. She rubbed her sweaty palms together and inhaled deeply. Shalimar slowly gathered herself and walked away from the still open door, back to the Jeep. The pain and hatred still ran through the woman's veins as though the affair had happened yesterday. It made Shalimar realise just why her mother acted the way she did. Both women had been unable to put the past behind them and yet again she had borne the brunt of another's anger and frustration. Shalimar promised herself she would never have children under the same circumstances.

Chameleon lay back in his seat with his eyes closed. The sight of him made Shalimar want to burst into tears again, but she couldn't work out whether it was from relief or rejection. Chameleon opened his eyes as she closed the passenger door.

Shalimar stared out through the windscreen, unable to look at him. Her tongue stapled itself against her mouth. His questioning eyes trailed over her.

'You done?' He asked.

As much as she wanted to, she couldn't bring herself to answer or look at him.

'The food is really good at this restaurant.' He said.

'Let's go.'

*

The Lighthouse Restaurant was built on a rocky outcrop overlooking the 'man-of-war' bay. The open-air eating area overlooked the ocean with fantastic views. The waiters tottered about in black and white uniforms: Shalimar marvelled at the wealth of the restaurant's clients, all exquisitely and immaculately dressed in western styled clothes. Styles she hadn't yet seen in the late editions of Ebony and Essence Magazine or indeed any other magazine left lying around Long Life. Those wearing traditional African outfits were draped in the most expensive colourful embroidered cotton, all stitched to perfection.

The waiter ushered them to a table overlooking the Atlantic Ocean. Shalimar hesitated and Chameleon felt her pause. He looked at her questioningly as she stood her ground, realised the reason for her hesitation, and then moved past her to take the seat next to the barriers separating them from the water.

Chameleon's friends Marvin and Augusta arrived soon after. Chameleon greeted them both warmly, introducing Shalimar to them as his 'good friend' much to her annoyance.

Shalimar wondered if Marvin was partly deaf as his voice rose over everyone else's during conversation. She smirked. He was an uncouth as his good friend Chameleon.

Shalimar did her best to ignore the conversation; she was far more interested in the entertainers that sailed past the restaurant in canoes, juggling balls and breathing fire as they paddled. The restaurant clientele clapped and cheered as they dined. It all made the incident in her father's house seem like it had been imagined.

It was obvious Chameleon and Marvin had a lot in common. Augusta on the other hand behaved no different from other influential European women working in the country. She spoke slowly to get her meaning across and often paused, pursing her lips together in disagreement. Her taut features were enhanced by her black hair which was scraped back into a tight bun. A beautiful emerald necklace that contrasted with her magnificent blue eyes sat atop her pointy collarbone. She smiled at Shalimar and did her best to include her in the conversation. She told her that she was employed by a Canadian

99

Charity and had been in the country for three years. Shalimar told Augusta that she had only recently arrived in Freetown as a result of the RUF's invasion.

Augusta's face ran a mixture of awe and fascination as she recounted some of the stressful encounters with the rebels she had faced whilst working with the charity. Chameleon cut short the conversation.

'Don't worry Augusta. You will have secured a highly paid international job when you go back to cold Austria. Maybe you can establish some links for me, eh?'

Augusta did not answer. Her eyes darted in Marvin's direction before pushing her fork into a lone broccoli at the side of her plate.

'Hey man, you think I can get one of those jobs in the UN?' Marvin joined in the teasing, oblivious to his girlfriend's unease.

'Of course. That's the latest trend, isn't it? You form a charity and get some UN funding. Tell them you are 'grass roots' and visit us here three times a year. I tell you my friend, we are in the wrong job.'

Augusta's face reddened and Shalimar wondered why she did not answer back. Chameleon excused himself abruptly from the table upon recognising another diner.

'So what is a fine African woman like you doing with the white boy?' Marvin asked suddenly.

Shalimar stared at him surprise. What kind of man was this, asking her that kind of question in front of his girlfriend? Marvin leaned forward.

'Y'know I could introduce you to a brother, an American like me. You don't need to be with no Nazi Afrikaaner Boer Motherfucka...'

Marvin's words managed to aggravate Shalimar even more. This man was rude and presumptuous. He didn't know her well enough to talk to her in that manner. Marvin clearly did not even know the nationality of his so-called good friend. She recognised the word Nazi from her school days.

'He is not German and please don't question me about my private life. It's none of your business. You don't own me. Concentrate on the woman in front of you.'

The surprise on her recipient's face shocked her, but before Marvin had a chance to reply, Chameleon was pulling up his chair and sitting down again. The afternoon ordeal had changed her and she did not feel like being nice to anyone anymore.

'So what are we talking about?' Chameleon asked.

'I was just asking your friend what it was she saw in a blaggard like you,' Marvin answered.

'I'm sure that went down well.' Chameleon replied, obviously unconcerned with his reputation.

The gizzard melted in Shalimar's mouth allowing her to switch off, unimpressed with the company Chameleon managed to keep. She was not going to even make an effort anymore.

'He hasn't been asking you why you are with a white man by any chance?' Chameleon said out of the blue.

Shalimar stopped chewing in surprise. She looked at Chameleon, then over at Marvin. This must have been enough to confirm Chameleon's suspicions. Chameleon leant back on his chair, wagging his finger at Marvin.

'You always like to start trouble with that Black shit.'

'I don't know what she's doing with your punk cracker ass.' Marvin said in a quiet, even tone. Shalimar couldn't understand whether the two men were joking around or not.

'Cracker ass? Is that the new word now ...out there in the American Ghetto? You people having been using your imagination to move up from the word 'honkey', huh?'

Marvin leant over the table towards Chameleon wagging his finger at him.

'Jamie; you ain't nothing but white trash. Where I come from no black woman would EVER have your cracker ass on top of her. You have...'

Chameleon said nothing. He just sat back with a grin plastered on his face, clearly amused that Augusta had put a hand up to stop Marvin in mid-flow, and was now chastising him for taking the conversation in a direction that made her feel uncomfortable. Chameleon waited for Augusta to stop, and for Marvin to calm down. He tapped his finger on the table.

'You're just pissed off you didn't find her first? While you prune yourself in the city, hanging around hotels and complaining about mosquitoes and the lack of electricity, I am out in the bush. You are just a black man, but I'm African. This is my home.'

'Find me?' Shalimar interrupted, suddenly riled. Is that what women are to you people? Like bulls or cows, to be found and discovered?'

Augusta's chair scraped over the tiled floors as she stood up, looking directly at Shalimar who remained seated. She was not going anywhere. The conversation had just become interesting. Both men oozed with arrogance and talked about her as though she was not there. They were exposing themselves to her in a way they did not understand. Augusta excused herself to the ladies but neither man even noticed.

'Your home, huh?' Marvin continued; ignoring Shalimar's last comment. 'Keep telling yourself that and someday you might just believe it. You offer help with one hand and loot with the other.'

'My friend, I'm an African man with an African woman. Don't forget I'm more African than you could ever hope to be.'

'Oh yeah?'

'Fuck yeah.'

Marvin lifted the Star beer bottle to his lips and said, 'Man, fuck you. Yes, I am American and proud of it.'

'Glad they enslaved your people? Look at the state of this place. Now you definitely know you are better off, huh?'

Marvin sighed and put the beer bottle carefully on the table. He glanced briefly at Shalimar as though he felt sorry for her.

'How many other African women has he brought to you, Marvin?' Shalimar interjected.

'Don't listen to this idiot.' Chameleon answered. 'His bullshit is world class like his country.'

'You better pipe down before I knock you out, motherfucka.' Marvin answered leaning over the table.

Chameleon did not answer; instead he waved at the waiter for the bill and gulped down the rest of his beer.

'Time for us to go. Always a pleasure, Marvin.' He added with a grin.

*

The drive home was a short one. Chameleon parked up in front of the hotel instead of going to the usual parking place.

'I'm at the Casino tonight. I'll see you later,' he said abruptly.

Shalimar stared at him in surprise. He handed her the keys without looking at her, revving the car, waiting for her to get out. A surge of growing resentment and hurt filled her. Why did he say nothing to her up till now? She had been left for over a week without company, with no one to talk to and now his intentions were to stay out all night. He didn't even ask her what happened in her father's house. She climbed out of the car and slammed the door as hard as she could.

Chameleon sped off unperturbed. She glowered after the car and then stormed into the hotel. It occurred to her he probably picked up prostitutes from the bars in the area and slept with them in other hotel rooms. He could even be meeting Miatta after she finished work. He was a nasty horrible person and the next time he touched her she would fight back. If he killed her then so be it, she couldn't spend the rest of her life like this.

The agonizing loneliness swallowing her up caused a painful ache in her heart. She recognised her need for comfort far surpassed the need for money. She needed some relief from the cruelty of war and family. Back home the constant company of others walking by the house, stopping for a chat or just joining in to sit around the fire at night was always a heart-warming experience. This silent hole stayed deserted most of the time during the week. How she missed her family. What if they were all dead? What if she truly was alone in this world?

A loud groan awoke Shalimar in the middle of the night. She blinked in the darkness to see Chameleon's arms and legs flailing as he gurgled from deep in his throat. Alarmed at the thought that he was choking, she tried to lift him up by his shoulders but his flailing arm hit her in the face. She yelped in pain and immediately let go of him. He continued thrashing wildly. Shalimar realised he was dreaming so called his name out softly. She raised her voice, tapping him forcefully on the shoulder at the same time. He awoke instantly unaware of his surroundings at first.

'Are you okay? It's me, Shalimar.'

He trembled uncontrollably and looked at her, unable to answer. Feeling sorry for him she gently stroked his arm.

'You had a nightmare, I think. A bad nightmare. It's all gone now. Go back to sleep.'

He sat up abruptly. 'I need to take a slash,' he said and hurried to the bathroom.

She could hear him emptying his bladder as she snuggled back into the sheets. The toilet seat fell noisily back down in its place. The bedroom door opened, he said nothing to her and walked past the bed into the front room.

Shalimar lay awake unable to sleep for what felt like hours, before deciding to find out why Chameleon was taking so long to come back to bed. The cold tiles were little comfort to her bare feet as she walked through the empty front room to the veranda. Chameleon sat drinking, just staring into the darkness. He looked up as she walked over.

'What are you doing?' she asked.

'I'm having a long talk with my friend.'

'What friend?'

'His name is Jack...Jack Daniels,'

'Is this what you're going to do for the rest of the night?'

He stared into the darkness without looking at her.

'It will be better for both of us if you go back to sleep and I stay out here.'

His behaviour frustrated her.

'Is this the way you live your life? Drinking when you can't sleep as if that is going to solve your problems?'

The black-labelled bottle was already at his lips. He paused in mid air as she spoke. He tilted it upwards and gulped the rest down before turning to face her.

She continued, 'You need to grow up and face your life. Every time there is a problem you drink and then when you are sober you're still in the same problem. Any idiot would have worked it out by now!'

His mouth lifted into a sneer as he slammed the bottle on the table making her jump.

'Since when did you become an expert in commenting on my life? I take you to a couple of restaurants and now you think you know me?'

'I don't want to know you. Who wants to know a drunkard?'

'You fucked a drunkard; what does that make you?'

His malicious response startled her. The sneer did not leave his face.

'What does it feel like to fuck a drunkard? Can a drunkard fuck you better than a village boy?'

His vile words mocked and belittled her. Baindu would have probably slapped his face. She crossed her arms against her body. Wounded by his words, her voice faltered as she spoke.

'With all the money that you have, you are still miserable. You are worse off than the poorest human being. No wonder you're still alone; no one can stand to be around you.'

She turned her back on him and moved towards the glass doors.

'Hey don't get so upset!' Chameleon called after her. 'I was just joking. You know you are my princess.'

Shalimar stopped and turned back to him. He was hanging off the side of his chair with the bottle flailing about as he tried unsuccessfully to put it back on the table. She realised he was even more drunk than she had first imagined. He tried to stand up but wobbled, falling straight back into his seat. His head tilted back as he ran his fingers through his hair. He chuckled.

'You are my main woman. You don't have to worry about other women. You are number one...'

His voice trailed off in the distance as she walked away, shaking her head.

Chapter 11

Shalimar searched under the mattress for the wad of money she had saved. When she had woken, the bed was still empty and there was no sign of Chameleon anywhere. Eight months had passed and she was desperate to leave. The way he spoke to her and treated her last night brought a worthless feeling to her soul. He had shown her no respect and she was a fool to believe he was capable of behaving any other way.

Frustrated on not feeling the banknotes, Shalimar flung back the mattress to reveal the wooden beams. The money was gone. She covered her mouth as her heart pounded like a drum. She tried to focus, but her mind went off in too many directions. When had he found the money? She willed herself to remember when she had last checked on her stash. How long had he know of her intentions? Now that he had found out, what would he do with her?

She decided to search all the rooms in the suite. She checked under the Chinese rug, behind and underneath the television set, and all the bedside table drawers. The drawers were full of men's clothes; underwear, socks, and vests, along with a few documents. The bathroom held no surprises. Shalimar slumped on the sofa, exhausted and frustrated. There was no money anywhere in the suite. Chameleon probably had a safe in the hotel.

The sound of keys twisting the lock made her realise she had not changed or had her shower yet. He would wonder what she had been doing all this time. Before she could dash to the bathroom, he was in front of her with some packages in his hand. Their eyes met, but there was no expression on his face. He put the packages on the empty coffee table and lifted the contents out, setting them on the table. The smell of food filled the air, Shalimar realised how hungry she was. He sat beside her on the sofa and dished out the food onto the plates.

'Time to eat, my beauty. Aren't you hungry?'

She nodded with a weak smile as he handed her a plate of sausages and eggs. She ate slowly, wondering when he would ask her about his money. Instead he put the radio on to Sierra Leone Broadcasting Service, occasionally commenting about the results of the Africa Nations Cup. He did not appear to be angry or even resentful. There was no sign that he even remembered last night's argument.

Chameleon stood up and threw something into Shalimar's lap. She looked down to see a photograph. An elderly man with a friendly smile stared back at her. He shared her eyes, nose and complexion. Shalimar gasped.

'Where did you get this?'

'That's all you need. The rest is an illusion.'

'What do you mean? How did you get this...did the wife give it to you?'

'You're not listening to me.' Chameleon sighed. 'You never needed that man.'

'That bitch gave this to you?' Shalimar asked, astonished.

'The childless bitch isn't worth thinking about.'

'What?'

'Just enjoy the picture for what it is. I need to take a shower...are you going first?' Chameleon replied, ignoring her question.

Shalimar didn't know what to say. Chameleon's gesture shocked her and now he stood before her, impatient and elusive. She excused herself to the bathroom. An explanation would have been appreciated but she knew him well enough to know he never gave any.

Her sweaty nightdress clung to her body as she peeled it off. She laid the picture upright against the sink so that she could stare at it while she changed. The shower spray hit her body like pellets and she yelped from the shock of the cold water. Chameleon stepped into the bathroom completely naked, his body glistening with sweat. He climbed into the shower to join her, grabbing the soap and loofah from the railings. Shalimar stared at him in surprise but he merely smirked in response. Why couldn't he just give her a minute to wash herself? The answer to that question came with the slapping of the soapy loofah onto her shoulders as he started to wash her.

'What's the matter...you never did this with your other boyfriends?' he asked in response to her obvious amazement.

She shook her head unsure whether the question was out of surprise or sarcasm.

'Boyfriends?'

The loofah moved across her body and around her breasts. Her nipples hardened at his touch while he carried on soaping her stomach and thighs. He finished by turning on the shower to rinse the soap from her.

'Do me now,' he said, holding out the loofah.

Shalimar scrubbed Chameleon hastily. It felt odd to wash a grown man. His skin turned red from the friction, leaving her confused as to whether he found it painful. She had to tip toe in order to reach his shoulders but Chameleon didn't budge. Instead he sneaked a kiss as she moved her hands across his shoulders.

Shalimar rinsed him off, then grabbed the bath towels to dry him. She reached out to start patting him down, but Chameleon pulled her towards him, pinning her against the wall. He smiled at her, loosened his grip on her arms, and leant in close to kiss her. His kisses reminded her of the loneliness she had felt when he left her alone, and how angry she had been when he drove off to the Casino unannounced. He had made love to her and left her cold and alone. An intense feeling of hunger consumed her as she took the initiative for the first time and pulled him closer. He kissed and touched her in places that made her body tingle then turned her around so that she faced the wall. His hot breath warmed the small of her back as he nibbled and kissed her moving up to her shoulder blades. The outside world didn't matter anymore. Her father's face disappeared from her memory. Shalimar winced with pleasure. She closed her eyes anticipating every kiss, the pleasure even more exhilarating than before. He turned her around to face him and cupped her face.

'Call me Jamie.'

She chuckled, repeating his name as if to reassure him. He kissed her, opening his eyes displaying a hint of green. Shalimar hesitated, remembering the rumour of his eyes changing colour. He saw her uncertainty and paused.

'Your eyes are green,' she exclaimed, unsure of what to think. He smiled. She waited for an explanation but he simply kissed her lips again. She allowed him to kiss and touch her but when she opened her eyes she felt uneasy. He sensed this, stopped and opened his eyes. Shalimar whimpered in desperate fear pushing him off and scrambled for her clothes.

'What is the matter? Did I hurt you?'

She ignored him and rushed to the door, but he was too fast. He blocked her getaway. A forgotten familiar feeling rose within her. Salia's story rung in her ears: the witch woman with green eyes who stole souls to make herself stronger. He could be the powerful woman that changed shape, or even a dead man living amongst the villagers. That would explain his disappearances in the night. He had made love to her once before. This meant she was his to take away and do with what he pleased as demons did with women. Chameleon interrupted her thoughts.

'What's going on Shalimar?'

She was too afraid to answer or touch him in case he decided to reveal his true self to her. Chameleon grabbed her arms forcing her to look at him. Shalimar squealed in fear.

'Shalimar, what is going on? What did I do?' Chameleon demanded.

'It's you. I know you!'

'What are you talking about?'

'Please, I beg you. Don't kill me. I've never done anything bad to anyone.' She shrieked. Chameleon grimaced.

'What is this about woman? What the hell are you talking about?'

'You are a witch woman that sucks out people's souls to give you power. That's why everyone calls you Chameleon. You have revealed yourself to me. I know you, and I remember you.'

Chameleon stared at her in disbelief as they stood naked on the cold tiled floor.

'Shalimar, you have that same look in your eyes that you did the first time I met you. You ran away from me as though I was a leper after giving me a helping hand. Do you remember doing that?' He touched her gently with imploring eyes, the blend of grey a little more visible. 'Do you remember running away from me?' He asked.

'I was afraid of your eyes.'

'I wanted to say thank you but you rushed out of the room.'

Shalimar said nothing. It was as though she was seeing him properly for the first time. He looked completely different. The bearded man with the Jesus Sandals who always looked old and tired had somehow transformed into this flamboyant young man in front of her. The grey in his eyes became clearer and more predominant.

'I am the dirty sick white man that you gave your bush medicine to. You tried to help me without wanting anything in return. That never happens in my world. Everyone always wants something from me. You saved my skin and fled from me before I could say thank you. You had such fear in your eyes as though I was a monster. It hurt my feelings.'

The green eyed monster that she had feared did come to claim her, only he was neither a witch nor a sorceress. The eyes that had given him the name Chameleon continued to change colour before her.

'Why do your eyes change colour?' she asked.

Chameleon shrugged,

'The sun changes the colour most of the time, but you will have to ask God for the remainder of the explanation. That's why the locals call me Chameleon, because of my eyes. I thought you knew this.' He sighed. 'There is always… something with you.'

'No wonder Mama Kaikai spat at you.'

'Lots of people spit at me. What was *her* problem?'

'You.'

'I'm always the problem, never the solution.'

He pulled her closer to him, brushing his mouth against her cheek and whispering into her ear.

'You are the woman that offered me a helping hand for no reason other than her good nature.'

'Is that why you helped me escape from the Rebels?'

He answered her with muffled kisses on her neck and forehead. She suddenly felt terrible for not trusting him. He had taken her away because he cared. He had confronted her father's wife. Guilt surged through her. All this time he had treated her with the respect she deserved.

'I'm sorry I took your money.'

'You don't need any money as long as you stay here. I will take care of you.'

Shalimar shut her eyes taking a deep breath wondering when her fears would finally come to an end. She tried to remember Chameleon as the bearded man in the stockroom. He did not speak to her, but his eyes had followed her every move. He had seemed surprised that the medicine she gave him worked. She wondered what happened to the other man with the cough.

Chameleon lifted her up, pushing such thoughts from her mind. He carried her to the bed and lay her down gently before lying beside her. They made love in the deep silence of the night. He woke her up with wandering hands, caressing, kneading and probing. The need for each other was becoming paramount. Each seemed to satisfy the others desire for tenderness, compassion and security. The intensity between them had the room teeming over with the aura of sweat and sex, nullifying the effectiveness of the air conditioner. For those moments it felt as though no one else was alive aside from them. Shalimar wondered was this what it felt like to be wanted? The overwhelming intensity that allowed you to forget that anybody else was remotely important, apart from the two of you.

She marvelled at the contrast in the colour of their skin, as she lay with her body intertwined with his. He had many years of sunburn leaving him permanently tanned, but still it was no match for her bronze complexion. She tried to look at his face as he slept but his arms lay across her body, and his grip on her remained strong even as he slept.

Chapter 12

The Government officials that represented the constituency that included Shalimar's town would occasionally visit the area with bags of rice for relatives and friends. The gesture had been deemed very generous by everyone in the town, who were grateful and happy to receive a bag of rice that was big enough to last for a month or so. Now Shalimar realised those bags of rice were a drop in the ocean, just miniature gestures compared to the way the Ministers were living in the city. She expressed her concern to Chameleon as they left a Minister's house one afternoon. Surprised by her comments he searched her face before responding.

'The problem with your people Shalimar is that they are only concerned with how much meat is in today's pot of stew.'

He leant over and kissed her as if continuing the conversation would hurt her feelings.

When Shalimar sat in the high street shops, or waited in a restaurant while Chameleon conducted his business, it was easy for her to spot the displaced peoples who had recently arrived in the city. Many were traders, selling ridiculous items such as matches or bottle openers, but most were beggars. Shalimar still harboured a desire to become a trader, but she was not sure what product she wished to sell. Fruit such as mangoes were seasonal and she needed to sell something all year round to bring in money. It seemed all the displaced people were traders in Freetown but she did not want to become a trader here. She wanted to become a trader in Bo, closer to home.

The number of amputees on the streets soared each week, with women and children amongst them. They were a reminder of the unresolved brutality that the RUF were capable of. The amputees sat on the roadside, their eyes vacant as they begged for food and money. Their children ran after the well-dressed city women. They flooded the open windows of Mercedes Benz and BMW's caught up in the endless traffic jams.

As the flow of refugees grew by the day, it dawned on Shalimar that she was lucky to be alive. The confirmation that God's fortune had been handed out in her direction was apparent when observing the swarming mayhem in the colourful crowded capital streets. Why did this happen to her? Was she the lucky one or was her sister living in a fancy cement house with servants, somewhere near Blama? Shalimar wondered whether Chameleon would be the one to help her find her family if their relationship continued to improve. He had shown her immense compassion by getting a photograph of her father. Since then his increasing affection had been comforting to Shalimar, and he had even been forthcoming with some details of his past.

On one particular morning, Shalimar was sat on the floor on the Chinese rug with a mirror propped up against a chair, carefully combing her hair. He had walked over, sat on the sofa and pulled her between his legs.

'I can do all that; watch me…give me the comb.'

Shalimar burst into fits of laughter as he yanked her hair with the comb. She held her stomach in hysterics while he tried to part her hair down the middle, but her laughter stopped when she felt the comb on her scalp neatly parting another section from ear to ear. Then he had proceeded to plait her hair into four bunches. She had stayed silent till he had finished. Shalimar ran to the bathroom to look into the mirror. Her hair was parted neatly although the four bunches were poorly done, still she was shocked that any man, especially a white Mercenary would have any idea how to plait hair. She had walked back into the front room to find Chameleon sitting smugly on the sofa. She asked him who had taught him how to plait hair. His answer surprised her.

He had a half black sister, named Martina. His father had left his mother when he was eight years old to work in Botswana. Six years later he arrived back on their doorstep with a four year old coloured girl. As if reading Shalimar's thoughts he told her his alcoholic mother had no choice but to let his father back into their home as she couldn't cope with the finances and pressure of being a single mother with a teenage boy.

'Where is your sister now?'

'She's dead.' Chameleon replied. His face set like stone as he continued to narrate the story, now avoiding eye contact.

'She was raped and murdered by some local men when she was only twelve years old.'

Shalimar hands had flown to her stomach. She was not sure she wanted to hear anymore. She had reached out and touched his arm in response. He had continued; motionless and vacant.

'That's what the country descended into when Apartheid was over. They called me up for National Service and I served in Angola, so I was not around. All the rich whites left for England and America pretending that they were against Apartheid because they did not want their sons to be called up for National Service. I operated in a pathetic war that served no purpose, except to massage the egos of the men who wished to force their utopian ideals on others. That war was a complete waste of my fucking life.'

Shalimar had taken the initiative by getting up from the floor to sit on his lap. The pain in his eyes had compelled her to give him a tight hug.

'When I went back home there was no more Apartheid and no more Martina. I left South Africa for good. She was the only person worth going home for. These days I just go where the money takes me.'

He had responded when she kissed him, making love to her on the cold tiled floor as though grateful to release some of the negative energy.

*

It was only a few weeks later when Chameleon announced that he had to go away for a couple of days. Shalimar marvelled at how different the situation was. She had never anticipated that a whole year would go by and their relationship would change so dramatically. This time he informed her that he had left enough money for her in the bedroom drawers. Chameleon asked her what she wanted him to bring back for her as a gift although he did not mention where he was going. This seemed a strange request, for he gave her everything and she wanted for nothing. Her only desire was to return home to find her sister and bring her back to the family, but of course she could not tell him this. Chameleon's eyebrows furrowed when she declined any gift. Shalimar leant forward brushing the first coat of pink nail polish onto her toes.

'What is it that you think I need?'

He shrugged his shoulders, 'A necklace? Or would you like a set?'

She looked at him as he zipped the small suitcase, pulling it upright. He did not know her or he would not ask what she wanted. She needed to find out what happened to her family. That was all.

'I do not want anything Chameleon. Just make sure *you* come back.'

'I told you to call me Jamie.'

Shalimar sauntered over and kissed him lightly on the cheek. This was the second time he was leaving. Perhaps she could leave too? Just to sort out things with the family. Chameleon stood silently watching her as she moved back onto the bed to apply the second coating of polish to her toes. She could feel his eyes on her; it was as though he was trying to read her thoughts, actions and words. She did not look up, afraid he would read her mind. He did not move or speak as she carefully covered each toe with the brush so as not to make any

112

smudges. He left quietly without closing the door behind him. Shalimar didn't look up for five minutes, feeling uneasy with the way he had left. He could be testing her and dawdling outside to see what she would do. He gave her money every day, money that she didn't need. It was as though he was giving her the money for her family indirectly. She decided not to leave the hotel that day as it could be too risky. She would leave tomorrow with the intention of bringing her family back to Freetown. She did not intend to leave him permanently this time.

That night she slept on Chameleon's side of the bed burying her head in his pillow to remember his scent. She had learned to appreciate just how much he had helped her, and she was grateful, but she still had to find her parents and her sister. No amount of time spent in a fancy hotel, drawers full of new clothes, or evenings spent in fine restaurants would ever take away the ache in her heart when she thought of her family.

Chameleon's musky odour flooded her nostrils as she inhaled the scent of the pillow. She thought about the way he made love to her. Sometimes he was gentle; caressing and stroking her as he made love tenderly. Other times he thrust into her violently, gripping her wrists and pounding into her like it was a form of punishment. She turned to lie on her front, wrapping herself in his aroma. Shalimar lost herself in his scent aware of how essential it had become to her. The extent of her feelings troubled her slightly because tomorrow she would leave. She thought how Chameleon would react if he knew. He was the type of man that would seek her out. But this time she would let him know that she would come back to him. Chameleon treated her as though she was valuable. He gave her a feeling of self-worth and leaving Chameleon permanently was no longer an option.

In the morning, Shalimar packed a few essential items into one of Chameleon's Puma Sports bags. Her plan was to head to her village, where hopefully she would find her parents. She would leave them some money then locate her sister. This shouldn't be hard or dangerous as Baindu was probably married to Ali by now, and living safely among the RUF. Baindu could be persuaded to come home, even if it would just be to talk to Mama to explain her situation properly. The money Shalimar had would help the family set up home again, repair any damage from the fighting, and allow them to survive for a while. She stashed the notes in her brassiere, bag and jeans pockets. It was not wise to keep the money in one place.

Shalimar wondered if Chameleon would find it in his heart to forgive her when she got back. She knew how to write letters; Mrs

Kemokai her primary school teacher beat it in to her. It was important that Chameleon knew how she felt and that they would always be together. She had a duty to her family and that was all it was. She explained everything as best she could and promised to return soon. Satisfied that he would understand, Shalimar signed her name at the bottom and left the letter on Chameleon's pillow.

There were two ways to go downtown. She decided not to walk down Lumley beach strip; instead she chose to take the shorter route over the Aberdeen Bridge. The sports bag was awkward to carry as the straps kept falling off her small shoulders. When she held the handles the bag knocked around her legs slowing her down.

Soon the huge steel bridge was in front of her. Shalimar eyed the massive structure with some trepidation. Although there was a walking path across it, the path was just metal grillwork, allowing an unobstructed view down to the sea. She stood there, trying to push aside the rising nausea she felt as she willed her legs to start moving. Pedestrians walked past her and onto the bridge casually. Some looked back sensing her unease. She wanted to walk with someone but still couldn't move. Maybe she should call to one of the boys playing football on the road to escort her across and pay them for their services. Her heart thudded against her chest and her breathing became laboured. Just thinking about it and looking at the bridge was making her sick. There was a small café on the side of the road where the bridge began. Shalimar decided to take a break and gather her courage inside.

Shalimar sat in the small dingy café, sipping on her bottle of Coke and watching the ears of the lazy guard dog flick in protest at the number of flies trying to settle on it. She closed her eyes trying to will herself the courage to walk over the bridge. She opened her eyes to find a young man hovering in front of her. He leant into her and whispered quietly.

'Drink done leh we go.'

Shalimar blinked with surprise, as she did not know or recognise him. He stood with an air of authority, waiting for her to stand. His expressionless face remained unfriendly as he eyed her over.

Shalimar asked indignantly, 'Do I know you?'

Another young man appeared from outside the café. He walked impatiently towards her. His eyes were bloodshot.

'Who are you? Leave me alone!' Shalimar barked at them angrily.

Now she was ready to leave and walk over the bridge. She grabbed her bag, but the red eyed monster snatched it from her. The other man spoke first.

'Mek we go back.'

'Back where? Gimme me bag now!'

Shalimar tried to grab the bag from the man but he moved away from her and towards the door. Another man sat in a brown Land Rover, right outside the entrance. He kept looking inside the café, like he was waiting for them.

'Take the bag. See how much money you will find. You Stupid idiot...' She stopped in mid sentence realising it was not the bag they were interested in, it was her.

The first young man moved in so close she could feel his breath on her cheek. He was extremely handsome, but his eyes were vacant and bloodshot. She could sense him weighing up whether to take matters into his own hands and force her into the Land Rover.

The first man stood in the doorway, looking at Shalimar, an evil grin turning up the corners of his mouth.

'We are watching you so just forget about running away. It's never going to happen.'

She knew these men had been on the frontline in the bush. They were well dressed, but their eyes gave everything away. The handsome one had a grip on her arm, and was looking at her as though she was naked. He spoke in a low tone so the others could not hear.

'You can choose to run away if you like. I can help you disappear. Nobody would ever find you.'

'I'm not that stupid and you will never be that lucky.' Shalimar spat at him.

The handsome one laughed as he pulled her towards him, spun her around and frogmarched her out the door.

Shalimar sat in the passenger seat and looked across the Aberdeen Bridge. Even in a vehicle, she couldn't shake the awful feeling she felt in the pit of her stomach. She closed her eyes and imagined driving onto the bridge - a huge hole opening up in front of them - and the Jeep crashing down into the sea. The Jeep pulled away from the café, stopped at the junction of the main road, and then swung to the left and away from the bridge. Shalimar opened her eyes and was surprised to see they were driving back towards the Hotel. So the men worked for Chameleon, and he still didn't trust her. The Jeep swung into the car park, sliding to a halt by the entrance.

'Get out.' The handsome man said. 'Don't try and leave again.'

Shalimar walked calmly to reception, desperately trying to maintain a cool facade. She took the key from the haughty receptionist, ignored the disdainful look she gave her, then took the stairs up to the suite.

Once inside, Shalimar burst into tears. She tore up the letter and flushed the pieces down the toilet. He didn't deserve to know the extent of her feelings if he didn't trust her.

Shalimar was half asleep when Chameleon returned the following morning. He slipped into the bed, kissing the back of her neck tenderly pulling her to him. She shut her eyes unsure of her feelings and recoiled from his touch. What kind of men did he have watching her? Dangerous, desperate, drug users who would gladly harm her if he was not around. She moved away from him and got out of bed. She walked to the bathroom, slamming the door behind her.

Shalimar spent the morning on the veranda watching the world go by whilst Chameleon slept. She flicked through the newspaper, looked through a couple of magazines, but found it hard to concentrate on anything. Why didn't he trust her? She thought they had grown closer, and were like a couple now.

'You want to go for a walk?' Chameleon said behind her, making her jump.

She turned to look at him. He was freshly showered, clean-shaven, and looked full of energy after his long sleep. His light grey eyes contrasted against his now burnt complexion making him appear refreshingly handsome. He would always behave as though nothing had happened, just like Mama. Shalimar realised she must confront him about the men in the café, but her heart was beginning to play havoc with her mind, and her resentment gradually subsided. She stood up not wanting to be confined to the hotel any longer.

*

Chameleon walked along the beachfront holding her hand. He did not attempt to cross the road to walk in the white sand that spread out before them. They stopped at some of the stalls, checking out the cheap jewellery, handicrafts and fake goods. After devouring some ice cream from one of the bars they continued to walk along the road, on the opposite side to the beach.

'Let's cross,' Chameleon said abruptly.

He was looking at her now, pulling her gently across the road and towards the beach.

'No!' She pulled her hand roughly away. He swung around surprised.

'No! Leff me! Ah nor deh cross obar!'

116

It was too late to cross over as a car was almost upon them. Shalimar turned to make a dash back to where they'd come, but Chameleon seized her just before a car going in the other direction ran her down. The car swerved, beeping its horn repeatedly. A roar shot out from inside the vehicle.

'*Ow bah you crais?!!*'

Chameleon held her with a vice-like grip and pulled her back to safety. They stood at the side of the road, Shalimar breathing rapidly, shaking from head to toe. He offered her his hand again.

'Come. Hold my hand and we won't cross until it is completely clear on both sides.'

'I can't.'

'You can. You don't have to walk near the ocean just in the sand.' He was smiling and nodding, his hand still outstretched.

'It is not the sea. I don't have to go near it, even when I walk on the beach.' She said angrily. 'This road so busy. So many cars. I am scared.'

'You have to learn to trust me Shalimar, please.'

His words surprised her; this arrogant man was pleading with her for something that would benefit her, not him. His eyes appeared much lighter under the sun as he smiled.

She took a deep breath allowing him to take the lead. He walked slowly encouraging her to gaze only at the sand and the mountains that engulfed the coastline ahead. She could hear the movement of the water, the rising and falling of the waves, children laughing as they struggled to beat the waves at their own game.

'I am here with you, nothing bad will happen. You just have to trust me.'

He interrupted her thoughts. She looked at him unsure; his grip was strong and warm. She watched the beads of sweat appear on his forehead as they walked under the overbearing sun.

'I want to go back to Blama.'

It blurted itself out. The words felt as though they were expressed by someone else. She wondered if she sounded ungrateful. He nodded his head without surprise, as though he expected her outburst. She felt lighter, quieter, and calmer.

'I have to find my sister and take her home. I have to go back home.'

He stopped and faced her, looking into her eyes as though looking for the invisible weight that had suddenly left her soul and disappeared into thin air.

'I understand,' he said after a brief silence.

The music from a nearby bar infiltrated their world. Chameleon took her hand again, smiled, and headed for the seats and tables on the sand. These were covered by large open umbrellas, providing some welcome shade. Shalimar sat under the umbrella wondering if her outburst had properly sunk in. Chameleon ambled inside the bar - unimpressed with the waiter service - and reappeared quickly with two bottles of Star beer. He pulled his chair close so they were sitting side-by-side, and placed his hand on her thigh caressing her affectionately.

'Are you still scared?'

'A little.'

'As long as you're with me you have nothing to fear.'

'What about when I go to Blama?'

He stared at the ocean without answering her. He did not want her to go, he never really intended for her to leave. She knew this now. He was being selfish at her expense.

'Being with you makes it difficult for me to do business now.'

This surprised and confused her. Was he responding to her request?

'I make it difficult for you to buy diamonds?'

'That's not the only thing I do business in. I also...'

'Hey, Jamie. My main man!'

They both turned to see Marvin coming towards their table; loud Hawaiian shirt and Star beer in hand. Marvin pulled a chair over and he and Chameleon started talking about money. Shalimar tuned out. This macho talk was boring. Instead, she chose to watch the local fishermen coming to shore with their early evening catches, stretching out their nets in the sand. Some fishermen were laying out fish to dry in the last hours of the sun, while others headed to the different restaurants on the strip to try and sell the best of their catch.

'Hey man let's get stuck in the best beer in the world. I've gotta head to the Ukraine in a few days, so I'm gonna miss this shit for a while. Shalimar you never answered my question. How come you're still with this drunk?'

'She understands me,' Chameleon answered for her. 'She doesn't try to change me like my own kind back home.'

Marvin laughed aloud, 'You mean the bored housewives? Or are you more of a glamour girl type of guy.'

Chameleon continued, ignoring the baiting.

'When they have you in their clutches they want to change you.' He paused. 'And the black South African women? Well they just straight up hate my kind with a passion. So I just find women outside of the country. Shalimar does not try to change me, she accepts me for who I am.'

'And in return, he speaks for me because I don't have a tongue,' Shalimar interjected glaring at him. Marvin snorted in amusement.

'Have you heard of Blama, Marvin? It is a small town in between Bo and Kenema.' Marvin shook his head, 'No, I can't say I have.'

'That is where I am from. I have to go back there.'

'That's a shame. It's kind of dangerous to travel to those parts, ain't it Jamie?'

Chameleon sucked on his Star beer without answering.

Chapter 13

'We are going to the Banquet next week. I should take you shopping and pick out a fancy dress.'

'What Banquet?'

'Haven't you heard everyone talking about it? It's at The Lagunda. They have one every year, and it's always full of the wealthiest, most important people in the country. Strictly invite only.'

Shalimar and Chameleon visited the plush Lagunda nightclub on occasion. The exorbitant cover charge meant it was always full of Lebanese, Chinese, bored Aid workers, mercenaries and local prostitutes. It was not one of Shalimar's favourite haunts, as prostitutes constantly visited their table to ask Chameleon for a dance. He would glance at Shalimar with a big grin on his face and politely decline the invitations, but she still felt humiliated. Shalimar told Chameleon that she didn't feel comfortable about attending the event, but he assured her that the banquet had nothing to do with the nightclub. This time the hotel would be full of the country's wealthiest and most influential people and the prostitutes would not be there.

Chameleon took her to an associate's house on Spur Road, one of the middle class residential spots in Freetown. A charming self-employed young man sold imported wholesale women's clothing and they were to have first pick of the latest arrivals. He led them to a bedroom where the clothes lay spread out, piled on top of each other in clear plastic coverings. Chameleon quickly picked out a blue shirt and pair of black trousers for himself. Shalimar changed into four different types of dresses before she lost her patience with his indecisiveness. She demanded that he buy both the white and soft pink evening dresses. He laughed at her annoyance when she threw one of the dresses down on the bed, declaring she would not try on anything else.

'You just want me to try dresses. You're not helping me decide at all. You're not listening to me. I've made up my mind.'

He lifted up his hands in defeat.

'Whatever gave you that idea? I just like to look at you. Is that a bad thing?!'

'Well you're wasting time!'

Chameleon couldn't help laughing at the petulant display.

'And to think you wouldn't accept the simplest of gifts not so long ago. Now you want two fancy dresses straight from the Milan catwalks. I've created a monster.'

She smiled at his comment. 'It is nearly a year now. You wear me down.'

Chameleon turned to his friend, told him they would take both dresses, along with the shirt and trousers.

*

The banquet evening was a night to die for; anybody who was anybody had been invited, and the luxury of the hall astounded Shalimar. It was like nothing she had ever seen, despite living the past year in a 5 star Hotel. The room glittered in pink and greys, with huge velvet drapes falling from the ceiling. Real fire had replaced the light bulbs, covered by bright gold shades hanging on the walls. Long tables stretched out with a magnificent array of French, Chinese, Lebanese and Sierra Leonean food. Lobsters, crab, bush meats, and fish spread evenly across the tables crowded with people filling their plates till they overflowed.

Upon arrival, they were escorted to a table occupied by a continental looking man. He was much darker than Chameleon with black hair tied back into a ponytail. He wore a long blue African Kaftan and stood up to greet them as they approached the table. They all shook hands before sitting down. His name was Angelo, an Italian who worked in the fishing business. The men talked about land, war and money while Shalimar sat silently observing the crowd, wondering if the people in this room were aware of what the RUF Rebels were doing in the countryside.

Chameleon excused himself. Shalimar watched the back of him saunter across the hall. She did not noticing Angelo get up immediately out of his seat to sit next to her and was surprised when he placed his hands on top of hers. She looked at him questioningly withdrawing her hands, but he pulled them to his chest.

'Are you out of your mind?' Shalimar said, aghast at his blatant behaviour. She could feel the shape of muscles underneath the Kaftan as he moved her hands against them.

'You are so beautiful. You should not be here...you should be in Italy working for me. I have a successful business there.' He kissed her hands, now cupped in his.

Shalimar yanked her hands away in disbelief and attempted to kick him unsuccessfully under the table. It was clear that he had the wrong impression just because she was with Chameleon.

'I have helped many other African women like yourself…too beautiful to be here, wasting your life away.'

'Let me go now otherwise you will be sorry. I will slap you so bad your face will be knocked up like the State House steps!'

He laughed at the challenge and leant forward with pursed lips and closed eyes. A hand fell on Angelo's shoulder; Chameleon spoke calmly.

'I think you better get off my chair Angelo, before I make you.'

Angelo instantly let go of Shalimar's hands, and held his up in the air as if to surrender. He stood up, moving back to the other side of the table. Chameleon slowly eyed Shalimar as he sat back down on his chair showing no emotion. She smiled faintly and went back to picking at her food, relieved he had returned in time. She still wasn't convinced that Lagunda was a nice place to be in.

'Ever had a fist shoved so far up your ass you choke from it coming out of your big mouth…Angelo?'

Angelo laughed nervously: 'You're a real joker sometimes Jamie.'

An older ginger-haired gentleman tapped Chameleon on the shoulder, breaking the tension that had arisen at the table. Chameleon turned and let out a big smile, jumped up, and greeted the man warmly. Others followed, approaching the table with plenty of shouting and clapping.

'Peter! Good to see you. Hey…Abdul, my man!' The men all hugged and it was clear they had not seen each other for a while.

Shalimar sat there, feeling overlooked. She turned towards the bright lights of the dance floor trying to ignore Angelo's lustful gaze, not wanting to create a scene. The ginger-haired man's roving eyes fell on her. He was a well spoken English man.

'What a beauty you have here, Jamie…do you mind if I take her to dance?'

Chameleon did not answer. He and Abdul were now deep in conversation.

'Come along, he won't miss you. This is all business for him. You on the other hand should be having fun.'

Nodding, she got up from her chair and followed the man to the dance floor. Keith Sweat's crooning RNB song faded into the background and was replaced immediately with the local hit single by Daddy Bongo '*Comot beyen me*'. People filled the floor, all gyrating and clapping along to the familiar song. Soon the dancefloor was packed tightly, not allowing much room to manoeuvre.

'What's your name Princess?'

'Shalimar.'

'What a lovely name…'

'Thank you.' She closed her eyes and lost herself to the rhythm, determined to capture the pleasure of the moment. They danced for a while until the music changed to a much slower Celine Dion track. Her dancing partner immediately grabbed her by the waist, pulling her close and rocking from side to side out of sync to the music. He sung loudly into her ear. Shalimar pulled away.

'I…I really must go and sit down…'

His face was a mixture of disappointment and confusion.

'What? Why? We just got here.'

'I should. I'm sorry.' She turned and pushed her way off the dance floor.

Chameleon was not in his seat. He had been standing just off the dancefloor, watching them the whole time. She was surprised to see him dragging on a cigarette; she had never seen him smoke before. He eyed her blankly and stubbed the cigarette out in the clear silver ashtray.

'You done?'

'Yes. What's wrong?'

'Get your things, it's time to go.'

He was curt, but she decided against arguing about the way he spoke to her at this point. She picked up her bag from the chair and followed him out of the huge hall. He said nothing to her on the short drive back to their hotel. Parking the Jeep in the same spot as always they climbed out and entered the hotel walking up to their room in silence.

Chameleon twisted the key and the door unlocked with a quick clicking sound. Shalimar followed him inside, tired and disappointed with the somewhat abrupt end to the evening. Her instincts never failed her about Lagunda. Whenever she graced the place with her presence she always left there with a dejected feeling. Chameleon put the keys on the table and immediately slapped Shalimar across the face, causing her lip to split open and bleed.

Shalimar stepped back in shock touching her mouth instinctively. There was fresh blood on her fingers. She stared at Chameleon dumbfounded. She could not believe that he had this in him.

'So now you're everybody's whore! What I do for you is not enough?'

Chameleon shouted: his face now the colour of beetroot. His eyes became slits as he moved towards her with bad intentions.

'What are you doing? Are you out of your mind?' Shalimar shrieked. 'Nobody can hit me except for my mother!'

The pain in her mouth turned into shooting pains around her body. The sides split further when she shouted. She trembled as an outpouring of hatred ran through her. Shalimar raised her fist to Chameleon's face. She had been right in her first impression of him. He was evil and now he was showing his true colours. She didn't know how fast she rushed towards him or how hard her punch was as it almost landed on the side of his face. Chameleon was a little slow in his response to protect himself from her blow. The force had both of them staggering backwards and falling to the floor. Blinded with fury, Shalimar pummelled and bit Chameleon on the arm. She heard him gasp as he tried to grab her arms and push her face away from his body

'Stop, Shalimar. Stop.'

She could hear the change in his tone, although his grip was strong he did not press onto her wrists to hurt her. She was not listening. She wanted to harm him. She insulted him vehemently while struggling to untangle herself from his clutch. Chameleon was speaking but she couldn't hear. The shouting bounced off the walls and reverberated around the room. They were as loud as her cries the day she had taken the cane from her mother and broken it into two clean pieces. The thick rough edged cane had dug into her back when swiped against her skin. That day darkness had covered her eyes as she had tried to grab the cane and fight against her mother. Papa had surfaced carrying her away and wiped the blood from her body while she had sobbed uncontrollably.

The pain in the side of Shalimar's face was becoming intolerable as her adrenaline dropped and her energy began to ebb with it. It hurt to move her lips. Chameleon was still talking. His words became clearer as he repeated himself.

'I'm sorry. I'm sorry. I'm sorry.'

Shalimar's head buzzed with the combined effects of the alcohol she had drunk and the anger that coursed through her veins. She was unresponsive to his apologies. When would she wake up from this nightmare? What had transpired in the past couple of minutes felt surreal. She wanted to die.

Chameleon let go off her wrists. She could feel his weight suddenly ease away from her body as he mouthed the words 'I'm sorry' and stepped away from her. The room swayed as she sat up.

'I never meant to hurt you. I don't know what came over me.'

Shalimar could not answer, her whole body remained unresponsive as she sat on the floor, bewildered and aching.

'I kept you here because Salia asked me to look after you. I never accepted his money. Salia sold Long Life to Barrow the day we arrived with the sickness. He knew the RUF would use it as an outpost, he just did not think you would be involved. He begged me to look after you. He wanted the money to marry you and take you to live with him in Bo.'

Shalimar covered her mouth as the emotion welled up inside her. She could not believe what she was hearing. Salia's betrayal was unthinkable. How could he sell Long Life? It was neither his property nor his right. Did he not know this would affect the village? Did he not care? She remembered Salia arguing with Barrow as she looked after the sick men. She could feel an invisible knife carving away in the depths of her heart. Her sluggish thought process intertwined with the throbbing that now pulsated from her head to her eyes. She closed them. Salia wanted to marry her? He loved her, and not her sister? He was going to take her away from Mama.

Chapter 14

Shalimar couldn't remember how long she screamed, or how long Chameleon tried to calm her. She saw his lips moving, but couldn't hear what he was saying. She screamed until her voice disappeared into the cool night air and then lay in silence refusing to speak to the number of persons that appeared around her. They all spoke in another language. She wanted to drift away and never come back. She wanted to join those who had gone before her. Why was God depriving her off permanent sleep? Why couldn't she be at peace like the rest of the villagers? She took all the medicine they gave her and dared death to visit. She was ready.

The sun's bright rays snaked through the room from the crack of the half open bedroom door. Shalimar slowly opened her eyes, and yawned. The pain in her jaw made her wince. A buzzing sound whizzed past her ears as she lifted the sheet off her face. Her ears tuned to the sound; her eyes wandered around the room. There was no way of telling how long she had been in bed but she could smell her own sweat distinctively, soaked through the bed linen. Her tangled hair stuck against her damp neck and pillow case. She pulled herself up and gasped at the pain in her jaw. A huge black fly blotted the white wall in front of her. It flew off the wall and buzzed around the room landing on Chameleon's pillow. Shalimar grabbed onto the bed post and hauled herself out of bed slowly in case her head spun. Her body was screaming for a cold shower.

When she entered the bathroom she headed straight for the cabinet mirror to see herself, unsurprised to see her face marred by swollen lips and matted hair. Different voices were whirling around her in her head. Salia had loved her in that way and had kept it from her. He had made plans to surprise her. She wondered if Baindu knew of this. She wondered if her sister really loved her or had tried to sabotage her future. What Shalimar was most confused about was how Salia could contribute towards the destruction of Long Life without contemplating the fate of the village? She remembered Chameleon's words 'The problem with your people Shalimar is that they are only concerned with how much meat is in today's stew.' She struggled to turn the shower taps on unable to focus through the tears that now flowed easily down her cheeks.

She glanced at her reflection in the mirror again. There were dark circles around her sunken eyes, and she looked like she had lost weight since arriving in Freetown. The veranda doors clicked shut loudly:

Chameleon must have been outside all this time. She heard his movements but he did not attempt to come into the bathroom. He was no different from Mama, controlling her and abusing her.

When Shalimar eventually left the bedroom, Chameleon was sat with a few local newspapers open around him on the sofa. He closed the one on his lap when she entered the room. He stood up but she raised her hand for him to stop. There were visible bags beneath his dull grey eyes which made it look like he had not slept. The rims surrounding his eyes were slightly red as though he had been rubbing them all night. He looked a little afraid when she moved closer but he did not flinch.

'I'm sorry for what...'

Shalimar raised her hand again to stop him talking, and he obeyed. She did not feel sorry for him but the hatred that had consumed her last night was no longer there. She felt herself trembling slightly but it was not from fear. She did not know why her body was reacting towards him in this manner.

'I threw the whisky out. I will never drink again.'

To this she found her voice: 'A monkey cannot deny its black hand.'

'Okay. I didn't want to tell you all this, but I have no choice now. You think everything is so black and white here, but there are no defined lines. Everyone looks out for themselves, including your sister, and your friend Salia.'

Chameleon straightened up on the sofa as he gesticulated to emphasise the drama that unfolded around their lives bringing them into contact. Chameleon likened Salia to a snake as he described his attempt to sell what was not his - the Long Life Bar - to Barrow. He knew the RUF were on their way and informed no one. Instead he made his own plans to sell the bar, and then leave with Shalimar. He would have enough money to make her his wife and give them a new life in Bo. However, a double-crosser is nearly always double-crossed, and Salia not been prepared for the RUF's direct involvement in his proposed transaction. It was the worst possible scenario for him when Rambo made his grand entrance, taking a shine to Shalimar, and then murdering Mrs Foday. Salia knew then that his plan was doomed to failure. Chameleon knew what was happening, and stepped in to take Shalimar out of the immediate peril that threatened to end her life. She had offered him a helping hand when he needed it most, and that was something he did not forget. In his world, people only took what they could get from him. Her warmth and smell that day had stayed with him, and he could not leave her to die.

Shalimar wondered whether resentment for Salia would replace the void that she was feeling as Chameleon relayed the story to her. She flinched when he told her that he cared for her and knew that she would take it upon herself to travel back to Blama. The roads were not secure and she had no one to protect her. Shalimar was trying to process the overload of information and did not realise Chameleon was now upon her, pulling her towards him. She yelped and drew back at the touch of his warm hands against her back. A loud knock at the door made Shalimar jump.

The elderly man who had tried to calm her down in the taxi stood before her with a smile. He greeted them both and asked after her health after yesterday's drama. Shalimar rushed towards him to get away from Chameleon.

'Take me away from here. I never want to see him again.' Shalimar grabbed the elderly man's hands and tried to lead him away. He resisted.

'Madam, I came up here to see how you and Mr Jamie were doing...'

'It's okay Mohammed. You can take her with you,' Chameleon said defeated.

Shalimar did not look at him; she opened the door and remained outside as the two men spoke.

Chapter 15

Mohammed ushered Shalimar through the hallway.

'You and me we know what love is... he does not know, Madam. He does not know what love is.'

Outside the hotel the security guards stood around talking and laughing with one another, oblivious to the incidences that transpired in the hotel above them. Shalimar was led through an opening in the fence at the back of the hotel, and across the road to an array of corrugated shacks. A collection of women sat in front of their wares selling fresh and fried fish. They stared at Shalimar walking past them. Mohammed explained that the shacks were the habitat of most of the staff during the night depending on their shifts. Some lived there permanently with their families, their wives selling their wares to make extra money.

He led her to a rickety old shack made of corrugated iron; chickens scampered aimlessly and half naked children ran around barefoot in the yard. They stepped inside. There was no electricity attached to the shack, just a kerosene lamp in the corner of the room to light up the area. Along the wall was a mat with two folded sheets placed neatly on top.

'You will stay here until I speak to this man to sort out the problem. It will be in your favour I promise.'

Shalimar nodded, weary with emotion.

'You must decide what you want to do. If you don't want to stay with that man you must begin to think seriously about where you are going to go.'

'I don't need to think. I want to go home. I want to go back to Blama.'

Mohammed nodded as if expecting that reaction. He spoke in a comforting manner to defend the man who was tipping him generously for taking care of her.

'That man cares about you, he just does not know how to show it. He is not an ordinary man. You are both alike and do not have an ordinary lives.'

'I'm not like him! I will never be like him!'

Shalimar did not appreciate the comparison. Mohammed nodded, patting Shalimar on the arm.

'Don't worry, there is a solution to every problem. I believe God will always find a way.'

Shalimar said nothing. She was in charge of her own destiny from now on. Mohammed left her with some reassurance of his intentions to help her. Shalimar quietly observed her surroundings. The door closed behind Mohammed, leaving Shalimar alone in the dim light. It was now she realised how much luxury she had been immersed in. Here there was no electricity, no private shower and no mosquito net. The noise from outside filtered into the room. Nothing was making her feel any better. Nausea suddenly racked through her whole body and she ran outside to throw up. Mohammed passed through to check up on her in the morning, bringing her some breakfast. Shalimar was comforted to see him again. Shalimar stayed around the shacks for fear of bumping into Chameleon on the road. She did not want to see him again, and still couldn't believe he had hit her. She had allowed him to be intimate with her and now felt humiliated. It was this feeling that had nausea whirling uncontrollably around her insides from her stomach up to her throat. Mohammed had given her some ginger the evening before, and now she chewed on it to curb the nausea. Chameleon had taken everything from her including her dignity and Salia it seemed had betrayed the people of Blama for love or money, or both. This she did not know for sure, and probably would never find out. Those that were closest to her hurt her the most. She did not know how she was supposed to survive this. Every time she closed her eyes, she prayed for death.

*

When Shalimar finally had the courage to walk along the beach front, she found it cleared her thoughts and calmed her. The crashing waves appeared beautiful yet brutal to Shalimar, in many ways mirroring her life. Worn out with the uncertainty of life in Freetown, she longed for the familiarity of home.

The walk by the ocean allowed her to clear her head. When Mohammed passed through to begin his shift, Shalimar told him her plan.

'My decision has not changed. I am going back to Blama. I am not staying here any longer than I have to.'

'I expected as much, he said softly. 'I am in negotiation with Mr Jamie. Don't worry, I will make sure you go to Blama and you are secure, I think that is the least he can do.'

Shalimar nodded, thanking the old man for all his help.

'If you change your mind the hotel has a few vacancies for waitresses in the restaurant. They will pay you good money. It's not a bad job.'

'No, it has been four days and I'm not going to change my mind. I need to go home and see if my family are okay.'

'I understand. I believe that Mr Jamie understands too. Everything will be fine tomorrow, don't worry.'

It was difficult to fall asleep, mosquitoes bit her legs and arms through the sheets despite her effort of hauling it over her head in the unbearable heat. The dream of travelling back to Blama was now becoming real. She could almost smell the town, the chickens, the soil after the rain, the bark from the trees, the burning of firewood to cook the food. She wondered if Baindu had returned home without her.

In the morning, Mohammed dutifully turned up with breakfast informing her as she ate that Chameleon was waiting for her. The idea of him waiting for her in the room filled her with anxiety. She was no longer indebted to him. She didn't care how she got to Blama, with or without his help she was leaving - today. She told Mohammed she was not afraid of Chameleon.

'Maybe he is afraid of you.' Mohammed chuckled.

Shalimar did not know how to react to that, but anger and hurt swelled within her just thinking about him. She knew that to keep her sanity she needed to get away from him. She thanked Mohammed for his care and concern and made her way towards the hotel. Her heart pummelled against her chest as she walked along the corridor towards the suite.

She entered without knocking. Chameleon sat quietly on the sofa in a red Manchester United T-shirt. His eyes flickered momentarily at the sight of her. He got up and reached out to touch what was left of the bruise on her face. Shalimar jerked back startling him.

'Don't touch me,' She hissed. 'Go and find another woman to lock up in a cage and beat. Obviously you can't get a woman that's why you have to steal them and hide them away.'

He stared at her in silence, choosing his words before answering.

'I can get women. I can have any woman I want.' His voice faded slightly. 'But not a woman like you.'

He turned without waiting for a response and picked up a brown envelope that was lying on the sofa. He held her gaze for a few seconds, and then held out his hand, offering the packet to her.

'Here...this is for you.'

She looked at him questioningly accepting the packet.

'You don't have to count it: it's $2000. American.'

Her eyes widened in shock as she opened the envelope. She had never seen so much money before, and certainly not foreign money.

'Get yourself set up; find a place to live, get a job... or start a business.'

He paused as she stared at the brown package in her hand and then at him.

'Just like you Shalimar, society has forgotten me. I fought in a war in Angola nobody cares about anymore. I watched my friends lose their lives for what? The scars that I bear everyday have no significance in history.'

Shalimar sneered at him. 'If you have a family you are never forgotten!'

Chameleon paused. 'I never meant to hurt you. I spent all this time trying to protect you.'

'Protect me?' She guffawed.

'The nights I spent at the casino were because I didn't want to scare you with the night terrors that I have.'

She remembered the disappointment that had consumed her when he had abandoned her on many occasions to go to the casino in the evening.

'That's strange. I thought you were visiting prostitutes.'

'I was trying to protect you.' He repeated in a defeated tone

'Do you think I'm stupid?'

'No, you're not stupid.'

She let out a loud sigh letting him know she was fed up and no longer wished continue the conversation. Shalimar followed Chameleon's eyes to a small black suitcase propped up against the wall next to the entrance door. He had packed her clothes.

'I'm sorry for what I did...what with the drinking I lost control. I just couldn't stand to see you with other men. For what it's worth I didn't mean to hurt you.'

She said nothing slightly taken aback by his honesty. He continued to talk not waiting for a response.

'Goodbye Shalimar. I'm sorry I wasn't capable of making you happy.'

She didn't know why she was rooted to the spot, but she was. She had no intention of feeling sorry for him. That was the tactic with these people used, once they laid a hand on you. They would try to make you feel sorry for them so you would take them back. He stood silent for a while as if waiting for her to say something. But she didn't.

'Goodbye Shalimar.'

He turned his back to her and walked away, sliding the veranda door closed behind him. The click of the veranda doors brought her down to earth. Half of her yearned to follow him outside and comfort him.

Inside the brown envelope the bundle of dollar bills had been separated by elastic bands. Shalimar could not contain her amazement. She managed to pull out two $10 dollar bills and stuffed them in the back pocket of her jeans. Now she could become a true business woman. She would have to find somewhere to change the money slowly and discreetly otherwise she would be robbed in the first instance. Without looking back she picked up the suitcase walked out of the hotel room.

The light case caused little strain pulling it down the hill towards the beach front. Thankfully she hadn't managed to build up a large collection of clothes and this made the walk bearable. There were no trees at the bottom of the hill by the junction, sweat dripped off her body as the sun burned rapidly through her clothes. Many cars sped past and all the taxis already appeared to be full of passengers. Chameleon wandered back into her mind as she waited. This money would change her life and give her the independence she craved. She would prove to Mama she was not a worthless child. She would give her family enough money to rebuild their home and then she would leave. Shalimar went over Chameleon's apology repeatedly. It sounded genuine but why did he have to strike her in the first place? He was a confused man who did not know how to treat people. He was better off alone.

A taxi stopped in front of her and hooted, making her jump. The taxi driver waited for instruction. Shalimar pushed her head through the open window.

'Bus station for go up country.'

He nodded and pointed to the back seat. Shalimar got in and began to barter. The fare agreed, the taxi drove down the five-kilometre stretch of Lumley Beach and past the extravagant suburban houses that lined the roads surrounding the well-off area. As the taxi drove uphill, Shalimar looked out of the window at the splendour of the mountains now far away from the hotel and Chameleon. Her home was behind those mountains and would soon be within sight. The taxi turned into the notoriously steep Hill Court Road, an extremely narrow winding road on a cliff top overlooking the entire city. As the taxi snaked down slowly the picture postcard view set against the ocean was breathtaking. Water seemed to be everywhere in this city, there was no escaping it. This was what she had wanted for nearly a year, but why did she feel so empty. Why was there a hole in her heart? Things could have worked out differently if he hadn't tried to hurt her. He had sealed his fate by laying his hand on her. She took a deep breath as the taxi spun down toward the city.

There was a stark difference in noise level in the city from the tranquillity of the hotel on Lumley Beach and it suddenly became overwhelming. She took for granted the peaceful meditation like feel of the Aberdeen area. Here people swarmed in the streets like ants and there was a constant sound of car horns blowing needlessly in frustration. Music blared out from the bars on the street corners and the commotion was endless. She cowered into the seat whilst the taxi stood still in traffic. Beggars clustered around the vehicle, hands thrusting through the top of the window in the hope of a few Leones. The young taxi driver hurled abuse at them.

As Shalimar watched the endless stream of people all around her, it struck her just how easy it would be for RUF Rebels to be amongst them; blending in, spying and taking their time before attacking the capital city. Stuck in a traffic jam, sweating in the stifling heat, and thinking about the rebels just brought all Shalimar's worst fears to the surface. What if she got to Blama and there was no one there? The memory of the smoke-filled towns and rotting corpses on the journey away from Blama alarmed her. Now she felt more vulnerable than she had ever been. In panic she tried to open the door with the broken handle.

'Hey, hey! You haven't paid me!' The taxi drivers face contorted in anger. His shouting brought her back to the present.

'It's okay. I thought we were there.' Shalimar lied. She sat back in the seat, clutched her case to her chest and closed her eyes.

'You don't know me do you? I can run fast no matter how quick you think you are,' he responded angrily.

Shalimar didn't hear the man. Her mind was in another place, forcing herself to take deep breathes.

The bus station was in Lightfoot Boston Street - a large space swarming with traders and travellers. There were only three small buses in the terminal when the taxi pulled up. This surprised Shalimar as she had imagined many buses stopped at this depot. Shalimar paid the driver, including a decent tip. She got out the car trying to look as if she knew what she was doing. She was aware that her small suitcase was a little expensive looking and her chicken heel slippers were not ideal for travelling in this situation. She bought some plantain chips and a bottle of water from one of the trader's seated next to the first bus, which was already half full. Men, women and children sat looking through the open windows with vacant stares. The words 'God is Great' spread out along the side of the bus. A tall young man stood at the entrance, his hand full of notes. He nodded at her as he noticed her studying the different buses.

'Makeni?'

She shook her head. 'Bo or Kenema?'

A passer-by pointed to the other side of the depot upon hearing her mention Bo.

'You need the bus that leaves from over there,' he said. 'You travel alone? You need help?'

'No, thank you sir. I'm meeting my brothers,' she said, to discourage the man from taking any further interest in her. She moved quickly with her suitcase banging into people as she went, swerving around sellers who shouted at the top of their voices desperate for a sale. She could feel sweat sticking to the back of her clothes and drops trickling down her thighs as she struggled through the crowd.

Two young men stood collecting tickets and counting money. Shalimar looked into the vehicle and saw that it was almost full. Other potential passengers informed her there would not be another bus for a number of days as there were only two buses in operation due to the ambushes taking place in that area. There was already a queue of ten people waiting to pay their fare. The old man in front of her informed her that the bus did not go quite as far as Bo anymore, and she would have to find other means of transport once they got to the final destination. This was not a concern. Her dreams were finally coming true and nothing would be too difficult with the amount of money she had. The two men were talking amongst themselves, taking their time. The driver of the vehicle swaggered slowly over, devouring a mango as he walked, before entering into deep discussion with the men. She realised they were working out how many more passengers they could take. She peered into the bus and saw there were only three seats left. She called out and beckoned to the men.

'*Ah get for go pan dis bus yah teday.* How much do you want?'

'Twenty thousand.'

She rummaged around in her pocket for the money, pulling out US dollars that more than covered the price.

'I need to go today,' she said, ignoring the angry stares of the people in front of her in the queue.

'Shalimar!'

135

The sound of her name made her jump. Chameleon appeared beside her. He looked fretful and uneasy, his clothes damp with sweat. She froze, wondering what he was doing there. She looked past him to see another man behind Chameleon, watching them both closely.

'Don't go, please.'

She still felt the smarting in her jaw when she answered him angrily.

'Leave me alone. I am going now and you are not going to stop me!'

She pulled away from Chameleon and rammed the dollar bills into the surprised attendant's hand.

'Cam nuh Madam. Cam siddown inside.'

The attendant beckoned, shoving the dollars immediately into his own pocket. Shalimar ignored Chameleon and walked past the queue to the door of the bus. Chameleon followed, grabbing her arm.

'I can't let you walk back into certain death.'

Shalimar turned to face him. He looked troubled but his earnest words agitated her greatly.

'You nor go leff de 'oman if e wan go?'

The young attendant voiced his opinion in her defence. She had already paid him.

'I am leaving and there is nothing you can do about it. You can't stop me this time. Not you or your stupid Rebel friends.'

'Please Shalimar. This bus isn't even going where you need it to go. It's dangerous. You have to believe me.'

'This is my country! I will find my way from there. It is not a problem. Now take your hands off me. Don't touch me anymore.' She punched his hand so that he would loosen his grip.

He let go of her and she climbed the steps into the vehicle. The other passengers pointed for her to sit next to the window - this was her privilege for paying in dollars. She rubbed around her eyes under the sunglasses and sighed. Chameleon appeared at the window almost instantly. The attendant was with him and now spoke in a matter of fact tone.

'Dis man say you wan go Bo? Notto now for go dem place deh. Rebel nain deh run dem area dem right now.'

'That's where I was born. I am not stupid. I know how to get home from there.'

'Shalimar, I am begging you don't go.' Chameleon pleaded, leaning through the part-open window.

A voice from behind shouted. 'Some people have all the luck and love!' The other passengers laughed. 'Tell the white man to get on the bus with us and go with you.' They laughed again.

An excited voice called out, 'What kind of cassava leaves did you feed him?' Passengers were laughing and clapping, they were no longer concerned with their own problems. She was becoming a spectacle.

A woman's voice cried out. 'Take me. I can cook for you, you won't regret it!'

Chameleon smiled, and nodded in response to acknowledge the jokes. He turned his attention back to Shalimar.

'I don't know what else to say. I'm sorry Shalimar for everything. I'm sorry. Let me make it up to you. I will take you back myself. You'll be safer with me than with a bus full of people.' He moved back and looked at the bus.

'This thing is a walking target. You cannot leave with them.'

Her clothes were saturated through with sweat. Beads trickled down her face and around her sunglasses. The young man who was in charge now climbed into the bus counting the passengers.

'Please Shalimar I will take you there myself. I swear...'

The older woman sitting next to her rearranged her baskets in order to lean over.

'He looks like he means it. Make him swear on his mother's life.'

Shalimar looked at him. She did not want to feel sorry for him after all the things he had put her through but something was pulling at her heart watching him plead through the window of the bus. She was reminded of his vulnerability the times she had woke him up from his recurring nightmares, how he trembled in her arms sweating and scared. He wasn't such a strong, tough man as people would like to imagine. She had gotten to know him more than anyone else. She was probably the only person in the world who knew and understood his demons. He knew hers and he owed her. He would have to face the fact that she needed to go home to make sure her family was okay.

'Swear then. Swear you will take me back to Blama. Swear you will help me find Baindu. I know you know those Rebels and you do business with them. Swear on your mother's life.'

The woman handling the baskets nodded in approval. Chameleon pulled back from the window, glancing at the crowd moving past him. A young boy replaced his position quickly, trying to sell ice through the window. He managed to sell five melting packets before being told to move on by the attendants.

'I can't swear on a mother that I never really had. I swear on my sister's grave I *will* take you back to Blama. I will help you find your sister and bring her home. I swear on Martina's grave.'

*

The Jeep turned into the familiar surroundings of the hotel car park. Chameleon carried the suitcase behind her as they walked through the hotel in silence. He stopped briefly at reception, asking for some snacks and sandwiches to be sent up to the room along with some fresh water. When they entered the suite, Shalimar noticed the change in Chameleon's appearance. He was as pale as a ghost and moved awkwardly, not knowing what to say or do. She sighed. At last she was able to read this cool allusive man. It was clear to her why he had tried to keep her with him for so long. He was unhappy and lonely with no real friends despite his wealth. He needed her. The only friend he had was the bottle. And now, although he towered over her, she no longer felt small. The tables had turned. When he finally spoke he sounded like a man who had lost his voice.

'I promise I will take you to Blama myself. I will not allow anything to happen to you.'

He moved towards her taking her into his arms and squeezing her whole body tightly. His warm breath made her tingle as he spoke quietly into her ear. She stiffened just a little this time.

'It's going to be dangerous. The RUF are making their way down here to Freetown. You must understand this...please don't feel disappointed if we find that Blama is gone.'

She nodded. 'I just need to know, one way or another.'

He cupped her face, 'Shalimar I will never hurt you again...I promise. I lost my cool because I know the type of men that are around here and what goes on in their minds when they see you...'

She turned her face away unable to look at him.

'I was angry because Angelo has many women working for him in Italy as prostitutes. He had the cheek to try to make a move on you as soon as my back was turned. I just want to keep you away from harm ...if I had left you in Blama those soldiers would have killed you.'

She could smell the whisky on his breath, the friend he so famously declared abandoned.

'You don't understand what it means to wake up from my night terrors and see a beautiful woman lying next to me asking me if I am alright.'

She did not answer or turn her head. He whispered into her ear.

'I'm sorry Shalimar, I'm sorry, I'm sorry, I'm so sorry.'

'You hurt me,' she responded. She tried to continue but a lump formed in her throat and her words faltered.

'I know.'

She stabbed his chest with her index finger.

'No you don't know. You hurt me. My mother hurt me…'

Chameleon tried to hug her but she pushed him away and pummelled him with her fists.

'How…could…you? You…hurt ….me!' She hit him harder with her fists. 'Why…did …you …hurt me? Why!'

Chameleon grabbed her. She struggled aimlessly. His arms tighten around her as he continued to repeat the words, 'I'm sorry' softly in her ear.

She allowed the words to seep into her perforated heart. She could not loath him. She longed for his touch. She needed to be loved by this man. Chameleon waited for her anger to subside a little before letting go.

'There is something you must know Shalimar. I will be going to Cape Town soon. I've been hanging around this country for too long. My time here is almost done.'

This was unexpected news to her. She accepted the tissue he handed her and blew her nose. All this time she was the one that wanted to leave. She was the one who had a home to go to. She had no idea that he wished to depart from Sierra Leone. Shalimar did not know what to say. He could not leave. She would have no one.

'You should come with me.'

He was looking into her eyes now as though he was able to read her thoughts.

'We can live peacefully on a farm.'

Shalimar stared at him unable to respond. How could she leave Blama, Sierra Leone...her home? Being in Freetown was the furthest she had ever been.

'I have just finished building a house in Cape Town. This place is no good for me. I need to retire and get out of this game.'

This was an unexpected bombshell. It had always been about her. There was always the notion that he would go away but only for business, and certainly not forever. Everyone she loved had betrayed her in some way. How was she supposed to trust anyone? She intended to live in Bo on her own but had always assumed he would be around. Now he was revealing otherwise.

'I have to go to Blama first!' she blurted out, not sure whether he was deliberately trying to pull her off course again.

139

Chameleon nodded. 'As you wish. If your family is alive then I will leave you there. That is your home and I wouldn't expect you to leave it behind. But if there is no Blama will you come with me?'

Everyone dreamed of leaving Sierra Leone, this godforsaken country where the government did nothing but fleece its own citizens, steal any aid handed to them generously by others and allow the mentality of bribery and greed to filter down through all levels of society. Everyone wanted to leave, but Shalimar was not so sure. She couldn't think beyond tomorrow. She did not answer him.

That night Chameleon spoke of his younger half sister's tears when it was time for him to leave for war. She slept in his bed on the last night offering her crucifix as protection. The necklace worked for him and kept him protected as he watched most of his friends die gruesome deaths in the bush. He returned home alive, but the pointlessness of the war left him angry and bitter. He recalled his parent's faces upon return when he asked for his sister. His mother appeared unmoved as his father gave him the news. They took him to her unmarked grave and left him there. He went home, stayed just one night and then left. That was the last time he had seen his parents.

Shalimar listened in silence as he opened up to her. She knew this was a rare occasion of sharing for him and that he had been forced into this position with the prospect of her leaving him for good. She wondered why fate had brought them together. Why God had allowed her to survive at the mercy of this man? His actions throughout his whole life had been ungodly, yet he had saved her life, feeding and clothing her, taking her to places she had only ever dreamt of after a night of palm wine with the farmers. The way he spoke affectionately about his sister made her wonder if she reminded him of her.

Fatigue crept up on her. It seemed the day's events - the morning confrontation with Chameleon, the shock of the money he gave her, the taxi ride to the bus station, the bustle of the busy depot and Chameleons surprise appearance - had finally caught up with her.

'Please, I want to lie down for a while. So much has happened today. Come lay with me. Just hold me.'

Nausea set in as they lay together. Shalimar broke away from Chameleon's tight grip and ran to the bathroom. She dropped to her knees over the toilet bowl just in time for the day's food to spew out. Chameleon appeared behind her rubbing her back as the force of the vomit caused her body to heave. Her eyes and nose watered. She hadn't eaten much - just a hotel sandwich - so she threw up mostly bile. The trauma left her sobbing in between heaves.

140

Chameleon helped her to her feet and washed her face in the sink before taking her back to bed. Agitated, he blamed her sickness on the hotel food. She heard him swearing over the phone at the receptionist and threatening to tell the rest of the hotel about dodgy meat. When he got off the phone he gave her a glass of water to sip on. He left the room to answer the knock at the door. Shalimar closed her eyes, tired but famished. Chameleon came back in with some bread and a bottle of water. He explained the water was like medicine. She should drink as much as she could to manage her dehydration, and the plain bread was to settle her stomach. She sat up and ate slowly, finishing the bread and drinking the medicine water. He climbed into bed caressing her back as she drifted off to sleep. He kissed her lips. Tired and weak she was unable to respond as his face brushed hers. Drifting off she dreamt he whispered 'I love you' but she was too far-gone in slumber to reply.

Chapter 16

Thunder from the heavens sounded like God was dragging furniture around again. The pelting rain showered down from the grey skies onto the corrugated rooftops with echoes of a disorganised orchestra reaching its climax. When it rained in Blama, the children rushed out of their houses naked, laughing, skipping and cheering as the raindrops broke on their bare skin. The older children surfaced with *Soda Soap* to wash themselves. Shalimar and Baindu would watch from the door of their house, caught up in the simple pleasures of the town and thankful for the relief of a cool breeze to cut through the humidity. Sometimes the rain stopped suddenly causing the children to scurry to the outside washrooms to finish up. Watching the storm from the hotel veranda in Freetown didn't serve up such happy, simple scenes. All Shalimar could see was the rain pelting the rooftops, palm trees swaying and bending to ridiculous angles in the ferocious wind, and a grey, angry sea in the distance.

The rains poured down endlessly for days. When they ventured into town the gutters had turned into mini streams and overflowing pot holes in the road widened and deepened becoming ten times more obstructive. Garbage from the gutter flowed onto the pavement; the smells compounded with the humidity left people suffocating in silence as they carried on with their daily activities. The city centre swelled up in numbers. Refugees from neighbouring Liberia fitted in unceremoniously, beggar children from Niger in torn clothes with straight long black hair stood out like a sore thumb, many of the displaced from the countryside now made the streets their home, each calling and begging for money with a story to tell. They accosted her frequently, Chameleon handed out money at random; his gesture purely on the basis that they, like her, were from the countryside. He called beggars gangsters and the street children organized Mafia.

Shalimar noticed the trip to Blama being put on the back burner as Chameleon's business deals became paramount. She reminded him of his promise; he listened only to repeat that the timing was misplaced.

Shalimar confronted him on their way back to the hotel from an afternoon spent at the Aqua Sports Club.

Chameleon's eyes remained on the road. They were crossing the Aberdeen Bridge which usually caused Shalimar to cower in her seat holding her breath as the vastness of the water lay out on either side of the road. Today she almost didn't care. She fumed whilst gripping the sides of her seat.

'Shalimar, I've told you a million times: I *will* take you to Blama.'

'Well I've been waiting a million years. It's a four hour journey...that's all it takes four hours.'

'It's not the right time.'

'It's never going to be the right time! The war is never going to end. People are still travelling....that's life.'

Shalimar would not let the subject go. It was not clear to her whether he was stalling because of the danger, or because he believed she would be gone for good.

'You're a very impatient woman.'

'I want to see if my family is still alive...is that so bad? Not knowing is killing me!'

Shalimar could see from her outburst that Chameleon was unable to conceal his emotions the way he used to. Her demands continued as they entered the hotel room.

'Jamie, I will do anything you want me to do. I will go with you anywhere you want me to go. I will go with you to South Africa...to Cape Town, but I have to try to see my family. I have to know if Baindu is alright.'

Chameleon stared at her silently as she tiptoed barefoot to look him full in the face. It was clear she had an undeniable impact on him, as when she moved in closer she could feel him harden against her. He turned away to swig on his half full glass.

'Fine then, I'm going without you!'

'Okay then. I'll take you tomorrow,' he replied without turning to face her.

Shalimar pulled the glass out of his hand and kissed him.

'Why do you always have to be so difficult Mr Chameleon?'

*

Shalimar climbed into the passenger seat of the silver Jeep and gave Chameleon a peck on the cheek as he eyed the large black garbage bags in the back seat.

'What do you need all those bags for?'

'My family will need these clothes more than me.'

Pot-holes riddled the roads leading out from the city, turning them into obstacle courses. Chameleon had used his full concentration to avoid clattering the Jeep into a large hole and damaging the vehicle. As they edged through the outskirts they saw the extent of the influx of displaced persons, all vying for a piece of land in this designated area.

A disarray of shacks spoiled the untamed view of the land. Those that had been there the longest had started to build cement houses. Most had only 2 or 3 walls and a temporary roof in place, as everyone struggle to make the money to finish the building. Women walked along the road side carrying large round enamel pans filled with bananas, mangoes, and colourful vegetables. Children wobbled hauling heavy buckets of water. Colourful clothes swayed on washing lines, and children played in the filthy streets, chasing around after half-inflated footballs. Shalimar dozed off intermittently encouraged by the cool wind that picked up around them. They had travelled this same road before when she was terrorised and afraid. She marvelled at the difference and thought their predicament was strange. She wondered if it ever crossed his mind. Shalimar's thoughts passed on to Mama and an overwhelming feeling of sadness came over her. Mama would be happy and relieved to see her but for how long? If she did manage to bring Baindu home, how long would it be before the blame of something else was placed upon her? The road stretched out in front of her would take her back to familiarity and family. Shalimar moved about in her seat and leant back to gaze at the shapeless clouds.

Shalimar glanced at Chameleon who seemed tense, his jaw line clenched as they swerved around the never-ending pot- holes. He remained silent throughout the whole journey. He was taking her back knowing he could lose her but willing to take the risk, and his knuckles were pale from gripping the steering wheel so tightly. Shalimar moved towards Chameleon and caressed his thigh affectionately.

'Stop,' he said abruptly without looking at her, his eyes never leaving the road. She leant forward and nibbled his ear. He glanced at her quickly and slowed the vehicle down. Shalimar repeatedly kissed him lightly on the cheek, excited about the possible outcome of the journey.

'Soon I will introduce you to my parents. They will thank you for all that you have done. My parents are good people, you will see. Maybe Baindu has even gone home and they have made peace again. Baindu will ask you all sorts of questions. She is not afraid of anything, she is quite cheeky.'

She giggled at the idea of Baindu meeting Chameleon; it would certainly be something to behold - two outspoken fiery people, unlike her. She was sure they would get on. Baindu would take to him instantly. Her sister liked arrogant men. Her family would hear about his deeds and give him the best welcome ever.

144

'Maybe even Salia is still about? We could have a reunion at my house with some sober palm wine. Do you think he will be jealous?'

Chameleon slowed the vehicle down even further, almost to a standstill. He caught her eye briefly.

'I want to take you out of this. You don't have to deal with anything. Just remember I am here for you.'

Shalimar stopped her nibbling and sat back into her seat, saying nothing. Sometimes he could really kill the mood. Why did he have to say it like that? He had no proof that anything bad had happened to them. The villagers could easily have gone back to Blama to rebuild their homes. Chameleon's hand slipped under her dress, she had not noticed the Jeep had stopped. He leant forward and kissed her as he caressed her upper thighs. His other hand travelled over her breast.

'Jamie stop! Not here. Not for people to see.'

Chameleon stopped and looked around. There was no one in sight apart from the mountains that seemed to hunch over them in a protective way. He continued his caressing, and tried to kiss her but she pushed him away.

'Let's go. Let's not waste any more time.'

Four long hours passed before they slowly drove past the blackened burnt out shell of Long Life. The pit of her stomach began to gnaw as she covered her mouth in distress. Chameleon rubbed her back gently with one hand as if to reassure her.

'Are you okay?'

She nodded slowly unable to speak. His hand went straight back to the wheel as they drove along the familiar stretch of red dusty road toward Blama. Now she was uncertain about what lay ahead of her. They passed what appeared to be a pair of bloated legs sticking out from the bushes. The atmosphere in the air altered; she could no longer hear the birds or crickets singing. The land looked unoccupied and desolate.

'We can't stay here too long.' Chameleon interrupted her thoughts.

She pointed to the familiar site down past the grassy knoll. Her humble home appeared uninhabited and austere, with no neighbours to greet them. Chameleon drove slowly down the small track to the house, and parked up.

'It's not safe to leave the Jeep here. I'm allowing us five minutes Shalimar…then we are out.'

She suddenly noticed the pistol on his lap. He cocked a round inside the chamber. When she climbed out of the Jeep, Chameleon was immediately by her side, the gun posted next to his leg. Without speaking he pushed her forward - his hand on her back while he aimed the gun from left to right. His movements alarmed Shalimar as she swiftly realised the seriousness of the situation they were in. This was Chameleon in soldier mode and he was handling her as though she were someone else. They moved toward the hut promptly, once inside he pulled her behind him, aiming the gun from left to right again.

The front room was without life, and the furniture lay shattered and spread over the floor. She climbed over the broken pieces, following Chameleon's voice into her parent's bedroom. He stood at the window looking out.

'There is no one here,' he said coldly. He studied the nearby area through the window.

'There's no one anywhere.'

Shalimar gazed out of the window and saw the stool her parents used to sit on smashed to pieces. The money! The money would answer all her questions. She bolted for the door and ran outside towards the stool. She could hear Chameleon shouting her name, clearly annoyed with her behaviour. She kicked away the remains of the stool and began digging up the area with her bare hands as fast as she could. The money flew out of her ploughing hands. Shalimar slumped on the ground. This was not what she expected. Her breathing became short as her chest tightened. She tried to compose herself by exhaling deeply. Trembling, she looked around and caught sight of a dog lying by the Mango tree, a few metres away. The dog moved slightly. Shalimar rose up heading towards it but stopped in her tracks from the rotting smell that seeped into her opened mouth. She bent over and coughed violently trying to regain her composure. She sunk to the ground doubled up and coughing. It was not the neighbour's dog she had seen. What lay before her was a limbless blackened body.

'Lord have mercy!'

Shalimar held her nose. Her eyes continued to water, but she willed herself to keep moving forward. Although she recognized the dress, she couldn't place it. The blue and white zebra print shape dress very unusual for these parts. A flicker of recognition caused her to let out a loud cry. She fell to her knees screaming. She turned at the sound of gunfire, struggling to get up off the ground. Now weakened with trauma, her body heaved as she gagged. She raised her head briefly when she heard the familiar shattering of twigs. It was too late; the butt of a gun hit her across the face and she fell into darkness.

Chapter 17

A splash of cold water brought Shalimar back to consciousness. The sound of male laughter filled the air. Her vision was blurry making her unable to focus. She blinked repeatedly, trying to clear her vision. The throbbing in her head felt like the grinding of groundnuts between the glass jar and the chopping board. The uneven muddy floor teemed with black boots and bare feet. Shalimar blinked again trying to sit up. Her head felt as though it had been split in half with a machete. A young boy sprinkled water over her with a cupped hand.

Shalimar slowly made out the three men talking and watching her as she gradually took stock of her surroundings. Searing pain suddenly racked through her body like electric shocks, causing her to double up and hold her stomach. It was then that she noticed her dress had been ripped to shreds, her breasts improperly exposed. A burning sensation rose between her legs as she tried to shift on the floor. The pain escalated with every move, bloody scratch marks savaged her body as though she had been mauled by a cheetah. A pair of black boots marched towards her.

'Put the lapa on, we are leaving.'

She followed his eyes, grabbing the country cloth from the floor quickly to cover up. It was hard to mask the pain that consumed her whilst dragging herself up to lean against the cold damp wall. The young men were clearly visible now, unwashed with sooty complexions and red eyes. The one that spoke had a small round protruding pot belly. He hauled her up off the wall and yanked her out of the hut, where she tried to shield her eyes from the sunlight. The podgy Rebel let go of her arm unexpectedly. Her legs buckled and she fell, putting her hands out just in time to protect herself. Tasting the earth, her eyes met with another's that remained vacant and dead, mouth open in horrific anticipation. Shalimar yelped, bolting backwards almost immediately. The podgy Rebel pulled her up roughly and shoved her ahead of him.

'Move.'

There were at least six other women situated outside the hut. None looked up when Shalimar crawled over towards them. She curled up into a foetal position hoping to stifle the painful spasms moving up and down her body. The Rebels surrounding them argued with each other about logistics. Shalimar was in too much agony to care. A few hours passed before the Rebels rounded the women up to move on. Shalimar struggled to follow the group of men and women moving effortlessly through the forest. Trees towered over them shutting out the sunlight intermittently, only allowing reams to peek through from time to time. The ground remained uneven, twigs, branches, small scratchy bushes and long grass all hampered what seemed like an arduous journey through the bush. She gasped with every step from the pain of the surging fire in her loins. She moaned and whimpered when climbing over fallen trees while trying to keep in line. They reached an open stretch of land filled with thatched roof mud huts. An abandoned village with smoke still filtering from a three stone fire left behind. Shalimar's breathing remained short and hampered, dull throbbing now replaced the agonizing sharp pains that had besieged her body. The women were made to stand and wait while the Rebels checked inside each of the huts emerging with food items, demanding the women cook what they found. Two of the women were pulled away to prepare the food. Shalimar counted ten Rebels as they moved around talking amongst each other. The weapons hanging off their shoulders filled her with dread as did the bayonets some of them chose to wield aimlessly around.

Shalimar's stomach growled as the familiar smell filled the air. The women emerged with a huge bowl of rice and *bittas*. The Rebels were served first before ushering the women over to eat. Shalimar joined them pushing and shoving for a place, hands flew into the bowl unceremoniously scooping up the rice and stew. One woman fell during the scuffle only to rise up and ram into her opponent. Shalimar secured four handfuls of rice in the chaotic rush and moved immediately away from the physical scrapping.

Two young men moved forward and grabbed one of the younger women as she cleaned out the empty bowl with her fingers. They tugged her plaits backwards causing her to fall on her bottom. Realising her fate, she wailed melodiously as if humming a melancholy tune whilst being led away into the bush behind the huts. Silent terror gripped the group. Shalimar looked at the women in turn. A look of terror was frozen on each face. No one was eating now. The woman to her left had a trickle of urine running down her leg, whilst most of the others sobbed quietly. The sweeping sensation of nausea crept up on her; she turned her head away as the stew churned out of her mouth.

As dusk fell, the women huddled together, swiping away the humming mosquitoes that plagued their exposed bodies. Shalimar curled up against moist skin desperately hoping she could sleep off the continuous ache that consumed her. She was not as fearful as the other women at being taken away in the middle of the night. The men had no use for her in that way anymore. Shalimar concentrated on the weird and wonderful noises of the forest encircling them, hoping it would lessen the pain. None of the women slept. Each anticipated their abduction that night but the Rebels were either too tired or too busy playing cards to bother with them.

The Rebels moved the women on at the first hint of daylight and they were made to carry the spoils of war. Upon approaching a small stream deep inside the forest the men signalled amongst themselves, separating Shalimar and another from the group. Her blood ran cold and her heart jumped inside its ribcage. The women stole brief sympathetic glances as they parted company and steered off to walk across the stream. The Rebels pulled Shalimar away. Her body jerked with fright, unable to formulate words as she whined like a dog in pain. The podgy soldier shoved his AK47 into the small of her back cutting her grief short. Shalimar struggled to walk, consumed with terror of what was in store for her. The sounds of twigs cracking under the weight of their feet and the distant croaking of frogs were all that could be heard for miles. They ambled all day without rest, the three Rebels continuously whispered amongst each other as they walked. Shalimar couldn't hear what they were saying, but they seemed to be in disagreement about something. The other woman never spoke or made eye contact with Shalimar the whole day. Then suddenly without warning two of the Rebels branched off pulling the other woman along with them. She screamed, but a slap across the face cut it short. The absence of tears did nothing to assist the burning in Shalimar's eyes as she watched them slide away through the trees.

It was already dark when they approached a tiny clearing. An unfinished cement house stood next to a shack. The Rebels took the lead towards the veranda of the cement house. Two young men sat on chairs playing cards on a large table. They looked up as the group climbed the stairs, shoving Shalimar forward.

'We brought you something Boss. We found her hanging around in Blama.'

The man he addressed wore a green beret to complement his green army uniform, and dark glasses covered his eyes as he looked up slowly. He smirked. This man was a lot younger than her, lean, with a smooth copper complexion. He sat back in his chair silently eyeing her behind the shades.

'Well...we have a full house. What is your name?'

'Shalimar.' It came out as a whisper.

'What were you doing in Blama?'

Shalimar trembled. 'Looking for my mother…'

'A mercenary was snooping around...' The podgy soldier interjected. The Boss remained motionless.

'The snake is no longer amongst us, Commander.' The leader smiled at the news.

'Take her to Jeneba,' he said, waving the group away.

The soldiers nodded and frogmarched Shalimar inside the house through to the back yard. The unfinished front room was a shell with no furniture or linoleum to cover the cold floor. In the back yard a young woman around the same age as Shalimar bent over a three stone fire fanning a boiling pot. She looked up; a wave of surprise ran through her face when she laid eyes on Shalimar. The podgy Rebel spoke.

'Commander says we should leave her with you. She is here to help you.'

They let go of her arms and disappeared back into the house. The young woman immediately followed behind them and shut the door loudly. She turned to Shalimar and smiled warmly.

'What is your name?'

Shalimar answered warily, still unsure of the situation that was unfolding in front of her. The attractive young woman's neat corn-rowed hair resembled smooth car tracks down to the nape of her back. She was very dark-skinned with wide eyes, full lips, and a pear-shaped body outlined against her wrapper. She introduced herself as Jeneba and told Shalimar she had been living at the camp for six months. The Rebels looted her village and murdered everyone in sight. The Commander took a liking to her, spared her life and brought her back to camp. Jeneba touched Shalimar's arm noticing the unsightly scratches marred with dried blood.

'Don't worry. You are safer with the Commander than with the soldiers. All I do is cook and clean. The Commander is away most of the time and nobody bothers me. The others can't touch you if you are under the Commander.'

Jeneba helped Shalimar over to the outside bathroom, which was fenced off with makeshift branches from fallen trees. Shalimar slowly washed off the smell of men, dirt, grime and vomit that had plagued her for the last three days. She winced in agony from the stings of her open wounds. Silent tears rolled down her face. Shalimar dried off in the small shack at the back of the house, listening to Jeneba's excitable chatter. When she rejoined Jeneba, the woman gave her a couple of wrappers that had been brought by the Rebels from looted villages. She explained that the Commander was territorial, and extremely fussy about appearance, expecting Jeneba to look presentable at all times even when she was cooking.

'Before you put one of those on,' Jeneba said, 'let me apply some herbal medicine to your wounds.'

Shalimar stood naked in front of Jeneba as the woman applied the poultice to her numerous cuts and abrasions. The cooling effect was almost instant. Jeneba then helped her into the wrapper, and gave Shalimar some painkillers.

'The herbs will heal your body, but the tablets will help you rest. Don't worry; the worst is over, as long as you do as you're told and pray for this war to end.'

As far as Jeneba was concerned, only God knew the reason why they were both still alive. Shalimar thanked this generous soul for her comfort. Shalimar's thoughts of what could or should have been were now damned. She had come home but home did not exist anymore.

'Commander asked me two months ago what I wanted. I told him I wanted a friend. I did not think that he would do this. I can't believe that God has sent me someone to talk to. I still can't believe it!'

.

*

Chameleon entered her thoughts. She wondered was he dead? Did they really overpower and kill him? He always seemed so invincible. She couldn't bear to think of him lifeless. He had been her only hope, her only real chance of escaping the war and even poverty. Now he was taken just like the rest of her family and she had nothing. Shalimar blamed herself for Chameleon's death knowing deep down inside it was her own fault that she had been captured. In her heart she felt she should not have harassed him to take her back to Blama instead she should have accepted her fate and left the country with him, for a better life with a man who clearly found her desirable. She now knew it would be better to imagine your family is safe and happy, than to know the truth. How could she ever forget the sight of Baindu, her brave and strong sister, lying hacked to pieces outside the family home. Her street smart had failed her at the most vital time of her life. If she had not met that man Ali, she might still be alive.

That night Shalimar wept until the stabbing pains in her stomach made her dizzy. Her eyes throbbed: swollen and raw as the tears dried up and her vision altered. She shook with grief until exhaustion claimed her as its victim.

The dutiful sound of the cock crowing awoke the two women in the early hours of the morning. Shalimar was astonished to find Jeneba sleeping beside her on the mat. She told Shalimar the Commander never allowed her to sleep with him through the night. He didn't trust anyone, let alone a woman that he was holding captive. The Commander was known by another name - Predator. He was notorious for wiping out small villages. Unlike the other RUF Commanders he did not see the point of maiming civilians by cutting off their limbs. It was his duty to put them out of their misery for good.

Shalimar listened to Jeneba's stories throughout the day somewhat distracted. The smarting between her legs surged through her body like electric shocks limiting her movements. She stood at the entrance of the shack peering over the tall grass beyond the cooking area surrounded by thick bushes, curious as to what lay behind it. Jeneba talked non-stop about nothing in particular. Her eyes shone as she laughed at her own observations and jokes. Shalimar spent most of the day throwing up in a small plastic tub kindly handed to her by her new friend. Her nausea only increased the aching around her body and she longed for more painkillers. Jeneba's kind gestures brought little comfort to Shalimar. Her newfound friend clearly preferred to exist without fuss or expectation. Shalimar promised herself that she would not do the same.

Chapter 18

The Commander was absent from the camp for several days. This was difficult to deal with as Shalimar anticipated his arrival every second. This increased the dread that already filled her being with thoughts of what he planned to do with her. Her body healed slowly. When she managed to leave the shack, she still hobbled around the yard in an undignified manner - to keep up the illusion that she was injured whilst familiarising herself with both the camp and the day-to-day activities. The irony behind this was that there was not much to do. Most days were filled with shared stories of the lives once lived before the war.

Jeneba had witnessed the execution of her whole family by a boy soldier barely twelve years old. He had fired at the unfortunates lined up in front of him and on everything around them while Predator had held her head up so she did not miss a thing. He had told her that she was to become his wife but if she closed her eyes or screamed in any way she would join her family. She watched her mother and little brother being unnecessarily riddled with bullets even when they were dead. It was as though the Rebels wanted to rid everyone, even dead bodies, of any kind of dignity.

Shalimar listened wide-eyed with sadness, wondering if she was better off not knowing what had happened to her parents. There was no hint of emotion in Jeneba's voice as she spoke of her ordeal. She did not say that she missed her mother, father or little brother. She did not choke over her words as she detailed the moment death befell them. Instead she put the wooden spoon back into the pot to stir the stew mumbling that nobody could ever accuse her of not cooking and serving a tasty dish.

The women hardly ever left the back of the house. The Rebels stayed in and around the clearing, collecting firewood for the cooking and sometimes providing bush meat. Shalimar never spoke or looked up when they were in her presence. The forest lay in abundance beyond the clearing and anything could transpire within its seemingly endless mass. Jeneba was not afraid or resentful of the soldiers and she conversed with them as though they were her friends. Shalimar ventured in and around the forest briefly to check on the firewood suppliers with Jeneba. The podgy soldier from her ambush often checked to make sure they were 'not doing anything suspicious like planning to run away'. He reminded them that the Rebels owned the area. If they were lucky and behaved themselves, when the war was won they may even be rewarded with a diamond each for their troubles.

He spat on the ground as he spoke, assuring them they were not all bad but there was no reason why they should not enjoy the country's mineral wealth just like the Lebanese and all the thieves in Government. Shalimar hated the way the podgy one looked at her. He always tried to catch her eye with a lingering smile, deliberately licking his lips as if he savoured the memory of their little secret.

*

A slight tap on the cheek in the middle of the night startled Shalimar out of her sleep. A Rebel hovered over her.

'Go to the Predator's room now.'

The insides of Shalimar's stomach tightened. Jeneba stirred against her. Forcing a smile, she patted Shalimar on the back.

'The first time is always the worst, after this it won't mean anything. You will be fine.'

Shalimar walked carefully over the stones as the stars in the sky threw light to aid her walk to hell, unaware of the plight she was going through. Predator laid on a king size bed waiting for her. His army uniform scattered over the cold floor highlighted the colourless bare cement room.

'Come.' He said, patting the space beside him.

Shalimar hesitated, wondering if this would be her last night alive. His hungry eyes wandered over her physique. She could see now why he wore sunglasses during the day. His eyes bulged out of their sockets like a frog, and he was not an attractive man. He sat up naked with his hands behind his head. His manhood stood up like a gun pointing towards the ceiling. He smiled at her uncertainty.

'Aah yellow woman...take the wrapper off,'

She obeyed instantly folding her arms as if to shield her body.

'You have put on weight since arriving. Good, I don't like bony women, there is never anything to hold, no ass to grab. Come here and lie down.'

He patted the empty spot next to him again. Shalimar limped slowly over to the bed trying to swallow her fears, but an impatient Predator grabbed her by the arms and pulled her across him onto the empty space. The musky smell of sweat overwhelmed her as he squeezed her breasts gleefully rubbing his face in them. His fingers ran along her body to her woman hood still raw and tender. She winced and yelped in pain. Her reaction brought another broad smile to his face as he climbed on top of her and sunk his teeth into her shoulder. The scream filled the campsite.

Jeneba was awake when Shalimar returned. She was waiting for her with two cups of palm wine.

'I heard you. He did this to me also, but only the once. I think he is just marking his territory.' Jeneba handed Shalimar the cup. 'I got this from the boys. I knew you would need it.'

The familiar smell of fermented alcohol was a great source of comfort. Shalimar sipped slowly, closing her eyes to visualise a colourful Blama; free from terror and destruction. She prayed the magic of palm wine would melt her existence into oblivion, that it would answer her prayers for a painless world filled with darkness and solitude. It was the closest existence to death and peace. Jeneba's finger pushed into Shalimar's wound.

'The skin is broken, you must have excited him.'

She rubbed a white mixture into Shalimar's wound vigorously as though her life depended on it. Shalimar's eyelids grew heavy and hazy as she drank the palm wine. The painful throbs dimmed into slight twinges. Sleep beckoned to her like an evil witch in search of a victim. Shalimar emptied the last drop of liquid pleasure onto her tongue that would allow her to numb her heart and soul.

Predator surprised the women the next morning whilst they set about lighting the three stone fire. They stood up immediately as if being inspected. He was a tall man against the five soldiers that followed him. Predator pulled Jeneba away from the fire and squeezed her breasts playfully. Jeneba did not seem to mind, and laughed as though it was nothing. His hands trailed to her bottom before resting his eyes on Shalimar.

'We have taken Freetown.'

Shalimar stared in despair at the news. The Predator moved towards the boiling of food and carefully lifted the lid of the pot. His nostrils flared following the steam that dissipated into the air, inhaling deeply to savour the lingering sweet smell that engulfed the back of the house.

'Get me a plate when you finish cooking. We are the rulers of Sierra Leone now. We have taken the capital city. They thought we couldn't do it, but we are the victors! The president has run away like the headless chicken that he is and Freetown is ours.'

'Does that mean we are going to get a diamond each?' Jeneba asked chuckling. This question tickled the Predator and he let out a loud laugh without answering, before walking off to the front of the house.

Shalimar watched them leave with a sinking feeling. If they had captured Freetown that meant the war was over. What were they going to do with them?

'Did you hear what he said?' Shalimar asked Jeneba.

'Shhh, let's wait until he has gone. We cannot talk about it now.'

'But did you hear what he said?'

'Yes, I heard what he said.'

Jeneba was too calm and carefree. She asked for a diamond even though this man had brutally gunned down her whole family. Shalimar stayed quiet for the rest of the day. If Chameleon were still alive he would have been in Freetown. She shrugged her shoulders wondering why she was kidding herself. Chameleon's body was probably rotting away in a ditch somewhere in her village. She needed to accept this although it hurt like hell. Whenever she thought of him she could feel the outline of the hole in her heart. She would never see him again. The war had taken away everyone and anyone who cared for her.

Shalimar ate alone in the evening while Predator called for Jeneba's services in the cement house. She cringed at the constant moaning and groaning that came from inside the house and ate hastily to get away from the noise. When Jeneba returned to the room in the middle of the night, Shalimar kept her face to the wall pretending to sleep.

'Shalimar. I know you are angry with me...' Jeneba whispered earnestly.

Shalimar did not answer. Her blood boiled from the day's events. Jeneba annoyed Shalimar by tapping her several times on the shoulder. Shalimar slapped her hand away shouting.

'Don't try to cover up the fact that you enjoy this. You don't even care that the whole country is now in Rebel hands! You don't even care about your own family being murdered by that animal. All you care about is a diamond? You want a diamond. You are the same as the Rebels, greedy and selfish...'

Jeneba burst into tears.

'It's not true Shalimar. I care... of course I care.'

'Your concern is for money.' Shalimar replied.

'What am I supposed to do? I cannot show my true feelings. I have to pretend all the time. Predator knows me and is watching me. What do you want me to do? Please don't be angry with me. I will do anything for you, I am your friend. Have I not been good to you all this time?'

Shalimar paused. The physical demands on her body still left her feeling delicate. It was true Jeneba had been good to her, but her reaction to the Predator's news left a deep distaste in Shalimar's mouth.

Jeneba continued to plead, 'Shalimar, I am so grateful that you are here. Every day I have to forget that I had a family. Every day I have to pretend that this is my family. Please try to understand. Can you understand?'

'I'm trying,' Shalimar replied. Nobody was going to fool her.

'I am just trying to stay alive and believe me I have not given up hope of escaping from here. I will one day, even if it kills me.'

Escape. The word rang in Shalimar's ears like the local church bells in the early hours of Sunday mornings. Notions that rapidly swirled around her head since arriving suddenly became clearer. They needed to find out what lay beyond the forest without the Rebels realising. A clear decisive plan could be thought out if they worked together.

'We *can* escape if we plan it properly.' Shalimar said.

Jeneba gasped.

'What are you talking about? How would we escape? This is Rebel country now.'

'We have to escape. There must be a way.'

*

Their situation in the camp had become less clear with the news of the capture of Freetown. The Commander would probably head to Freetown, and he had no reason to take the women with him. In Shalimar's reasoning, they had to get out quickly. With luck the soldiers would not waste too long looking for them; the lure of Freetown being too strong to delay them. Jeneba had developed a good relationship with some of the lower ranked soldiers and might be able to acquire some information from them. Shalimar outlined the advantages of this arrangement to her friend and witnessed her hesitation. Jeneba was used to her life here and preferred to only dream about the possibilities of freedom. Shalimar felt it important to give Jeneba a sober reminder of the precariousness of their situation.

'Soon the Predator will have no use for us. When all this is over they will kill us!' Jeneba's silence exposed her fear but Shalimar did not care. She reminded Jeneba of the life she once had - one of simplicity and happiness. There had to be a way out of this situation and both women at this point had nothing to lose.

Chapter 19

Shalimar decided she must take immediate advantage of the newly relaxed atmosphere and general disorganisation in the camp. Under the pretext of gathering herbs and roots, she scoured the surrounding area. She memorised every tree stump, rock and branch that lay in her way. She gazed beyond the trees wondering how far the forest stretched out. Was there a thriving village or a town unaware of their existence? The broken twigs and sticks pierced her bare feet and she stumbled around in agony. Back at the shack she purposely stayed away from the men. To her they were dangerous animals, and given the slightest opportunity she believed they would pounce on her again. The memory of her capture, and subsequent treatment proved too much for her to encourage any kind of conversation.

One Rebel in particular indulged in long conversations with Jeneba. He was barely twenty years old with a little stubble around his chin. He took every opportunity to hang around the cooking pot, with more interest in the food than in his duties. This was the man Shalimar wanted Jeneba to carefully glean information from. Whenever he turned up, Shalimar would find something to do away from Jeneba. She hoped the man would be comfortable enough around his friend to carelessly divulge some little facts that the two women could find useful.

'Anything might be useful.' Shalimar told her. 'Some idea of where we are, or which direction to the nearest town or village. If we just run off we may get lost and go around in circles until we starve.'

Later that morning the man ambled over to the cooking pot, asking what treat the women were serving up for lunch. Shalimar held Jeneba's gaze for a second, then wandered off to wash out some pots. She sat by herself in the corner, and turned on the battery-operated radio that Predator had given them from one of his looting sprees. She wanted to appear busy in her work, allowing the man to relax with Jeneba. Hopefully in a relaxed frame of mind, he would loosen his tongue.

He left fairly quickly, Shalimar hurried over to see what Jeneba had found out.

'I couldn't get him to talk about anything, Shalimar. I tried, I promise. All he would say was how excited he was to go to Freetown.'

'That's not good,' Shalimar replied. 'If they are talking of leaving, we haven't got much time.'

'You should talk with him too. He's not so bad, you know.'

158

Shalimar shuddered at the thought of chatting casually with these animals. Too often she had secretly observed them in the forest sniffing *brown brown*. This was some type of drug they took before going on their murderous looting sprees. Shalimar had seen what they were capable of once high and out of their minds.

*

A couple of days later, Predator left the camp. The women speculated that he was in a hurry to enjoy himself in Freetown, and couldn't wait for orders. The remaining Rebels grew sullen in contrast to their excitement of the early days of Freetown's capture. Some of them wanted a piece of the action in the capital but had been left holding the fort in the middle of nowhere. The campsite was important because it remained undiscovered. It was extremely unusual for RUF to remain in one area for longer than a couple of days and this camp had been occupied for many months. The young soldier had even told Jeneba that other RUF Combatants were unaware of the camp's existence.

The days passed, and still no orders came to move out. The men grew restless, the frustration of their situation causing arguments and backbiting. The women kept the soldiers well fed, and Jeneba continued to encourage gossip with them.

*

The rainy season arrived with little notice, battering the building with strong winds and forceful rain. The women moved their sleeping mats to the centre of the room away from the growing trickles of water seeping through the cracks on the sidewalls. The weather was much cooler than it was in Freetown, and Shalimar did not remember it being so cool in Blama during the rainy season. The women prepared pepper soup for breakfast; anything to stop the chill entering their bones. The steaming hot pepper soup produced watery eyes and warmed the soul bringing relief from the damp shack and thin cotton covers at their disposal.

Shalimar's nausea had ebbed over the past eight weeks, but there were moments when it reared its ugly head in full force just to remind Shalimar of her predicament. At first she had thought her queasiness was caused by the stress of their captivity, but over the weeks she had observed the skin tightening around her stomach as it grew. She scratched the surface and pushed her stomach in with flat palms to no avail.

She deliberated daily that the fact she was alive was really a curse. Why must all this happen to her? Did she deserve it? Maybe she was paying for Mama's sins. Her father was a married man and they should not have had an affair. But in her heart Shalimar knew it did not warrant this kind of affliction.

The possibility of death inched closer and closer with every cock-crow that sounded in the morning. The only saving grace was that Predator had not returned. The fluttery feeling that surfaced to the pit of her throat made her stop what she was doing to take deep breaths. She counted four months since her abduction. The hunger pangs gnawed at her insides constantly and she was forced to eat the scraps from the soldier's unwashed bowls. Whenever the alien kicked inside her, she chewed on raw pepper hoping to feel a flush between her legs in the middle of the night. The expanding invader within her was all the more confirmation that she should leave the camp before Predator returned and noticed the change.

On a cold cloudy morning, music and gunshots filled the air. The women awoke to the sound of the chaos and scrambled to put on their clothes. Predator had finally arrived after a whole month and a half away and the front of the house swarmed with RUF Soldiers. They sat around smoking and drinking in the grass, on the steps and veranda, oblivious to their presence. There was a pile of electrical devices dumped on the veranda - a television, VHS Player and a few tape recorders. Shalimar couldn't help wondering what use the television was when there was no electricity supply to the house.

Predator stood on the steps sporting a clean t-shirt, blue jeans and brilliant white sneakers. He looked healthy and wealthy behind his sunglasses. He smiled while reaching behind him to produce some wrappers. He threw them out to the women not waiting to see if they could catch the items.

The women gathered up the items expressing their gratitude, but were abruptly commanded to stop as they turned to leave. A young girl barely past puberty was pulled out from behind Predator and shoved toward them. She stood naked from the waist up with smooth dark skin and short cropped hair. Her plum breasts shook as she sobbed softly. Predator chuckled as he spoke.

'Don't cry. I have two big sisters for you...they will treat you well. Just do as they say.'

The young girl tearfully glanced over at the two women. Jeneba forced a friendly smile to her lips and beckoned the girl over to her.

'She is a mute,' Predator called out after them as he turned back to join his men.

Chapter 20

They decided to name the young girl Musu. Her story proved difficult to extract as she was illiterate and the women could only try so many gestures with their hands, faces and bodies. They ascertained she was just fourteen, and had been captured while selling oranges along the road side. This was as far as they got before the young girl shut down, rocking herself back and forth.

Predator provided Musu with her own mat and a couple of wraps. Jeneba gave the girl palm wine during the first few days to aid her sleep. The Predator did not call for Musu in the beginning - it appeared there was an unspoken rule of thumb that the new girl settles in before being mauled.

Musu found solace through cooking. She absorbed herself into any one single activity, enjoying mundane tasks such as grinding the onions and pepper or picking the greens from the stem. Shalimar and Jeneba allowed her to do as she pleased for a while if only for the single pleasure of hearing the young girl's laughter on occasion.

Shalimar was summoned a few nights later. She felt like she lost a piece of her soul every time she entered Predator's room, though it happened less often these days. His waning interest showed when he collapsed on top of her like a useless dead dog thrown on the rubbish tip, swearing under his breath. It was ironic that to lengthen her chances of survival she had to spend time with Predator, face down on the mattress, barely able to breathe. Shalimar picked up her wrapper and scurried back to her mat, relieved that it was only the scar on her shoulder he had examined closely. It wouldn't be too long before his desires for Musu became paramount, then hopefully Shalimar would be left alone.

It didn't take long for the Predator's thirst for new pastures to take hold. Jeneba was summoned to the Predator's bedroom, but reappeared minutes later with a vacant look in her eyes. Shalimar awoke to a dazed woman unable to settle down to sleep.

'What happened?'

'He wants the mute today, not me.' Jeneba said indignantly.

Musu sat up wide-eyed as though she had been anticipating this moment for a long time. She was instantly aware of what lay before her.

'I tried to plead with him. I said she is young and he should wait. He yelled at me to get out and watch my mouth. He has never raised his voice to me before.' Jeneba slumped onto the mat.

Shalimar put her arms around her friend, unable to understand the extent of her distraught. Her relief was far greater than that of Jeneba's. The Predator's desires would lie with Musu for a longer period of time. Shalimar knew better than to disclose this to her friend. Musu did not wait to be called. She had left the room.

'Did she just run away?' Jeneba said in a panic.

'No, she can lip read. I think she just went to Predator's room. That girl acts older than her age.'

The women awoke in the morning to find an empty mat in the corner of the room. They quickly threw on their wrappers and headed outside to discover Predator taming burning firewood as Musu prepared the food.

'Musu is cooking. Make a plate for me when she is finished. Don't give Shalimar too much to eat or she will get even fatter.'

Shalimar cringed at the Predator's remark. She had allowed too much time to pass. This was a rude reminder that the women needed to talk about their future.

The women ate breakfast in silence, with Jeneba clearly disturbed by the Predator's favouring behaviour. Shalimar took an extra helping, unable to hide her hunger and past the point of caring. When asked where she slept, Musu responded with deep bellowing sounds pointing to the Predator's room. Shalimar watched Jeneba stiffen. Her 'first wife' role was becoming more and more insignificant. Shalimar knew she had to step up the escape plan, so continued to map out the surrounding areas when nobody was paying any attention to her, crouching down in the long grass to remain invisible when the soldiers roamed around.

*

Shalimar welcomed the fresh spring water as she rubbed her hands over what was left of the soda soap. Jeneba burst into the outhouse interrupting Shalimar's shower.

'What's happened?'

'Musu has disappeared. I can't find her anywhere!'

'She must be in the forest getting some firewood. She is fine, Jeneba. She can handle herself.' Shalimar was getting tired of Jeneba's weird obsession with the girl.

'No. I checked, and nobody has seen her for a couple of hours.'

'Well let me finish here and we can look for her together.'

Shalimar suddenly became conscious that Jeneba was gaping at her stomach. She quickly threw the last of the cold water over her body to finish off.

'Shalimar; when was the last time you had your period?'

Shalimar's hands trembled as she tied the towel round her chest.

'Shalimar! When was the last time...?'

'I heard you the first time!' Shalimar snapped. 'I don't have periods...'

'What do you mean you don't have periods? Every woman has periods. What are you talking about?'

'Well mine have always been irregular!'

Shalimar stormed back into the empty shack with Jeneba close behind.

'What do you want now? Why don't you go and look for your adopted child?'

'Shalimar, you are pregnant aren't you?'

Shalimar did not answer. She dried herself off shoving Jeneba out of the way to look for a wrapper.

'Shalimar, why are you denying it? It is becoming very obvious...you've been sick ever since you arrived here and you are always eating.'

Jeneba's words were too much to bear. This predicament was not her fault.

'Do you know what the Rebels did to me?' Shalimar screeched. She collapsed on the mat unable to control her sobs.

'I don't want it. Help me get rid of it, Jeneba please!'

Shalimar's distress was short-lived as the relief at being found out was much greater. The weight had suddenly lifted off her shoulders.

'I cannot do that...I wouldn't even know how.' Jeneba replied.

'You must know something. Please Jeneba, I'm begging you. I can't have it!'

'Wear the gowns Predator gave me, that will hide the bump for now.'

Jeneba moved to the corner of the room to pull out a bundle of clothes piled up next to Musu's mat. She sifted through them, found what she was looking for, and passed it to Shalimar. She took the gown and pulled it over her head. It flowed perfectly over her now large voluptuous figure. Both women worked out that her pregnancy must be now around five to six months. It was unnerving to calculate how much time she had left to live. There was no mirror to see her reflection so all she could rely on was Jeneba's appraisal.

Shalimar decided it was time to tell her friend about her exploration around the forest area, how deep she had walked into the bush studying every curve, tree and path she came across. She told Jeneba about all the markings she had engraved into the trees with the razor blades they had used to slice onions and plassas. Jeneba listened in amazement.

'We have to leave this place or they will kill us eventually,' Shalimar tried to justify her movements.

'Shalimar, it is dangerous. They will come after us and they know this area better than we do.'

'I will not stay here just waiting to die. They will definitely get rid of me, so I have to leave.'

'Then they will certainly kill us all.'

'I would rather die than allow these demons to touch me again.'

Jeneba took a deep breath, 'I need to think Shalimar, what you're suggesting might cost us our lives. We need to sit down and plan it, but for now let's just make sure Musu is alright.'

They searched the immediate clearings in the forest even though they were not supposed to. The search became increasingly frustrating as they were unable to call out for her because she was deaf. The women returned for food and rest before embarking to the other side of the camp. This was even more dangerous as it was the area where the Rebels practised their shooting. Shalimar had sworn never to venture there unless forced to, but now Jeneba assured her the men wouldn't dare make a move on them. They were too afraid of Predator.

The Rebels were surprised to see the women walking around so boldly, but none of them knew where Musu was. Shalimar recognised the small cave in the corner of a hill where she had seen the Rebels disappear to before taking their brown brown. They waded through the grassy plains towards curious noises coming from inside the cave. The women halted in their tracks. Their eyes fell upon an unexpected sight leaving them stunned and horrified. Men with trousers to their ankles waiting as Musu, with her legs in the air, moved in motion with one of the soldiers on top of her. The commotion stopped with the arrival of unexpected guests. Shalimar recognized the familiar rush to her throat and turned away to heave but she was not too late to miss Musu mouth the words, 'Fuck off from here'. Shalimar fell on her knees throwing up, her body jerking amid the confusion surrounding them. The women were dragged out of the cave, and one of the Rebels kicked Shalimar hard in the groin.

'One word from you about this and we cut out your womb. You understand?'

Jeneba pleaded in agreement with the Rebel, who used his gun to push and knock her about. Shalimar remained on the ground trying to catch her breath from her ordeal. This was the final slap in the face. She coughed. Her lungs filled with fire from the force of the kick.

Musu appeared above her. She sneered at them both before brushing an open palm against Shalimar's stomach. She then led the Rebel away without looking back at her forlorn friends. They disappeared back into the cave.

Jeneba wept with anger as they struggled back to the shack. This was the sign Shalimar had been waiting for. It was time to take charge of their lives. Musu was dangerous.

'That evil witch! She is a witch. I tell you; that is why she is a mute. Shalimar, we have to get rid of her,' Jeneba screeched.

'Now do you understand when I say we have to get out of here? I am leaving with or without you.' Shalimar asserted.

'Did you see that? She will turn everyone against us. I know what her plan is - she wants everyone to favour her over us. If we don't act soon she will have the Predator get rid of us. You saw how he kept her in the room all night. He never did that with me. I have been here longer than anyone. She is trouble Shalimar. We have serious trouble on our hands.'

Shalimar pointed past the trees leading into the forest revealing a little detail of her whereabouts over the past couple of months. The time had come for Jeneba to take her seriously. Jeneba listened this time and did not argue with Shalimar. A mischievous smile grew across Jeneba's face.

'I will take care of things from now on. If anyone knows this place it's me.'

Chapter 21

The sharp twinge on her right side stopped Shalimar in her tracks as she walked to the washhouse. It wrenched around her stomach to the small of her back. She gasped. She tried to take a step forward but buckled under the pain. Shalimar heard a movement and looked up. Musu appeared from the front of the house. Shalimar gritted her teeth. She could not allow Musu to see her like this. Things had not been the same since the Rebel kicked her in the stomach on that horrendous day. Musu hardly slept with the girls in the shack. She spent her time canoodling with the Rebels only cooking with the women when necessary. Shalimar pushed forward. The pain had gotten worse over the past week but she couldn't share this with Jeneba, it would hamper the mood of their escape. Musu bellowed. She had one of the pots in her hand and needed something. Shalimar proceeded towards the washhouse ignoring her.

It was difficult to get comfortable in order to sleep. When Shalimar did manage it she had terrible dreams. Dreams of her limbless sister chasing her through the forest enraged that she was the one that had cheated death. Dreams of Chameleon handing her over to the Rebels, declaring that she was of no use to him anymore. She would wake up shaking in fear or weeping for the loss of those who had touched her life, remembering the way Chameleon had trembled in her arms. She longed to tell him that she knew what he felt but it was all too late now. Now that she that realised she loved him. If only in his memory would she try to make it out of here alive. He had been right all along to insist they stay in Freetown.

There was still the problem of the young Rebel who hung around Jeneba like a young schoolboy with a crush on his teacher. Shalimar watched the way his eyes followed her friend around when she cooked and washed clothes. Shalimar brought up her concerns with her friend. Jeneba's response to her anxiety was to describe the Rebel as one of the good men.

'He is just like us and can't wait for all of this to be over. He tells me that E.C.O.M.O.G is fighting the RUF in Freetown.'

Shalimar half listened determined not to be put off by any more betrayals. She travelled deeper and deeper into the forest every day, marking the route to freedom. The pain in her side surfaced periodically with an intensity that alarmed and frustrated her. The curse wouldn't go away no matter what she ate and now it wanted to sabotage her escape. The anxiety that emerged with every twinge left Shalimar hurting and exhausted. Jeneba had insisted she replace her at one point but Shalimar refused. If you wanted something done you had to do it yourself. She had learnt much about trusting and relying on those closest to you. They never meant to let you down, but they always did.

Shalimar was cutting onions by the pot when the Predator returned from a couple of days away. The familiar sound and smell of the men filled the air. Their constant gibbering and laughter irritated her. Although Predator hardly required her services, his arrival always made her nervous. A Rebel appeared almost instantly to summon her to the front of the house. The Predator sat on the veranda talking and laughing with his men. He sported new sunglasses and his men had new jeans and t-shirts. He smiled at Shalimar, and asked if Musu was being looked after properly.

'Take her inside. There are gifts in the house waiting for you. Let Musu pick out some things for you women.'

Musu sat inside the cement house surrounded by the spoils of war. She guffawed at the sight of Shalimar who tried desperately to contain her anger. Musu handpicked the spoils for Shalimar, making silly grunting noises. Shalimar pointed at items only for Musu to shake her head. She lifted up simple wrappers and then threw them aside. It was insulting enough that a minor was now determining what she could receive as a gift let alone showing her such contempt. Musu formed a stomach outline with her hands and giggled. An infuriated Shalimar could not believe that this teenager was threatening and goading her with regards to her condition. She promised herself she would not give in to the confrontation that Musu wanted. She gathered her new belongings quietly and left the room.

Jeneba was nowhere to be seen. The firewood lay unused and it was time to cook. Shalimar rubbed her stinging eyes as she continued to peel and ground the onions. Simple menial tasks were becoming more arduous and energy sapping by the day. Shalimar entered the shack to pick up the pots. She found the young Rebel inside, canoodling with Jeneba. Her astonishment turned into fury.

'Are you out of your mind?'

'Shhhhhhhhhh!' Jeneba retorted quickly.

Shalimar stepped back in disbelief. This woman was playing with her life and telling her to be quiet?

'What the hell are you doing?' Shalimar asked angrily.

'I'm sorting things out!'

'In here? When the Predator is back?'

'Go and cook. Don't worry about us….just let me do what I do, okay?'

Shalimar stormed out without noticing the man who had kicked her in the groin standing with Musu as she beat peppers fiercely in the mortar. For some reason the haughty receptionist at the hotel sprung to mind. She hoped the bitch was dead. Loud bellowing noises from Musu interrupted Shalimar's thoughts. She walked back slowly holding her throbbing head. Musu stood scraping the ground onions and pepper into an enamel plate; she needed the pot to start the cooking. Shalimar walked past Musu back into the shack to find Jeneba alone.

Shalimar listened to Jeneba's disclosure about Lahai, the young Rebel. He was promising to provide assistance in helping them escape from the camp. Shalimar remained unconvinced. It was not part of the plan to involve a Rebel. As far as she was concerned Lahai could be plotting their death.

'Why can't you trust me or believe me, when I say I can get us out of here?'

'But Jeneba, what is in it for him?' Shalimar asked.

'What do you mean what is in it for him? Nothing!' Jeneba replied frustrated.

'What if he is scheming with Musu?'

Jeneba scowled, swearing at the mention of the mute's name.

'He has nothing to do with that devil bitch, trust me.'

'How do you know he hasn't had her? We don't know who has or hasn't.'

'He wouldn't touch that bitch in a million years.'

'Why?'

'Because he loves me!'

Shalimar gasped at her friend and laughed aloud. It did not seem as if Jeneba was in control anymore. How could she be in love with a Rebel? Especially a mere boy who was barely twenty years old. His whole adult experience was one of violence and destruction. How could she possibly find such a person attractive? Both women gathered their thoughts amidst the uncomfortable silence in the room. Jeneba's face revealed she was genuinely hurt by Shalimar's reaction. Shalimar wondered why her life continued to be met with people she could not trust.

'He loves me and wants us to be safe. He will do anything to achieve this, including risking his own life.' Jeneba insisted.

Her enthusiasm frightened Shalimar. Jeneba should never have included anyone in the plan. Everything was falling apart.

'You must trust me Shalimar. The reason why I have not spoken to you about this is because of your condition. You're not in good health…you do know this don't you?'

'No.' Shalimar replied adamantly. Now her friend was pushing the boundaries.

'You have headaches and dizzy spells because you spend half your time in the forest. You're in pain now. I can see it. You will have no energy left when it is time to escape.'

Shalimar had no idea her actions had been noted and surprise overtook the slow anger welling inside her. The throbbing in her head crept around to the front. She needed to shut her eyes and lie down.

'For once in this place I have found a little bit of happiness,' Jeneba gushed. 'I don't care if I die tomorrow, at least I am happy. Lahai told me there is a village at the end of the forest. He will make the contact for us. You lie down and rest. I will get you later.'

Jeneba's hands gently rested on Shalimar's shoulders, pushing her towards the mat. Shalimar conceded defeat, curling up on the mat, trying to force away the pain. The smarting made gradual progression to the rest of her body.

A tap on the shoulder caused Shalimar to leap up from the mat disorientated.

'Jeneba is in the forest waiting for you. I followed your markings and made some myself. Soon I will take you to the village; there you can get transport to take you away from here.' Lahai said smiling as he moved towards the entrance without waiting for her acknowledgement.

'Take the footpath behind the wash room. I will wait for you there. You must be quick; nobody should notice that we are gone. I have put a pot on the fire so they will think you are cooking.'

Shalimar shook her head to clear her mind. 'This is it' she said to herself. Do or die. She hurried over to the washhouse, stepped around and behind it to find the pathway Lahai spoke of. It was so thin only one person at a time could walk it. Jeneba was nowhere to be seen.

Lahai moved swiftly, darting through the bushes like a deer on the run. Shalimar struggled to keep up the pace - never quite catching up with him, but always making sure he was within sight. Although she knew the path well, walking at a swift pace was proving difficult. The familiar twinge sought its way once again to both her sides. Shalimar ignored it and moved forward. A short sharp pain shot up from her groin causing her to drop to the floor. Shalimar lamented. Of all the times why did this have to happen now? She would not allow Jeneba's concerns to ring true. She could not miscarry now. If the Rebels found her in the forest they would shoot her down and leave her body to rot.

Jeneba appeared from behind the trees without warning.

'I knew you would come. Please, help me up.' Shalimar said. 'We can all do this together.'

They were only halfway through the markings Shalimar had made. Now was the time to show Jeneba just how far she had managed to go.

'We have just walked halfway to freedom. Do you realise this Jeneba?'

'I really want this to work. Do you think it will work?' Jeneba asked excitedly.

'It has to work now or I am a dead woman. Let's go.'

'No,' Jeneba said. 'We can't go now! What's the matter with you?'

'What do you mean? This is it. We are escaping.'

'No, not now. Lahai is showing us the way, but today is not the right time to go.'

Shalimar couldn't believe it. Once again this woman was stalling and all because of a man?

'Jeneba, don't make me angry. I am not even having this conversation with you...'

Shalimar looked ahead at the markings and moved forward. No more waiting to die. It was time to leave. She ignored Jeneba's calls to stop. The broken twigs sliced at the soles of her feet as she stumbled through. Just ahead the markings merged from Shalimar's to Lahai's. Shalimar trod from the obvious beaten track through a thick batch of bush. The sting on her legs and arms from red ant bites were barely noticeable as she went. Jeneba's voice drifted off and disappeared in the thick of the forest. The grass was so long it was hard to push away without a machete. It slapped back ferociously into Shalimar's face and body as she forced her way through. She stopped to catch her breath, sweating and exhausted from the arduous journey. She straightened up, stretching her back, but a stabbing pain in her stomach made her shriek and fall to the ground. No longer concentrated in one area the stabbing pains filtered through her stomach and chest. She heard the rustling and slapping of palms nearby, and a thud of footsteps moved towards her. Lahai lifted her off the ground.

'Fighter woman. You cannot leave today.' He joked.

'Where is Jeneba?' Shalimar asked. He jolted as he carried her causing growing nausea within her.

'I told her to go back. You cannot be away for too long without someone noticing. She is upset with you.'

Shalimar said nothing. Jeneba was in the shack waiting for them. She glared at Shalimar as Lahai helped her sit back on the mat, providing old clothes for support. He left the room to let the girls talk over what had transpired. Shalimar watched her friend dish out her food. She accepted the plate and ate. Her back ached and her swollen feet were bleeding.

'Lahai and I will be together, far away from this place. We are going to go to the refugee camps in Guinea and start a new life. I love this man, Shalimar.'

Jeneba's words struck a note in Shalimar's heart. She remembered on occasion how she had felt when Chameleon had revealed his inner most secrets to her. She had fallen in love with him for his courage at that moment. To love was to be alive and the light in Jeneba's eyes and glowing of her complexion told the story of hope.

'You deserve so much Jeneba. You have looked after me and protected me. I hope that you make it to Guinea with Lahai. Then maybe we will find each other when the war is over.'

Shalimar's throat blocked because she meant every word. She thought about the moment she would say goodbye to her friend then have to face her own fate.

'You don't listen, Shalimar. You just make up your mind and run off like a mad woman? You're lucky Lahai could bring you back!'

'I'm sorry. I didn't think.' Shalimar replied ashamed. They had switched sides. She was now the thorn in Jeneba's side.

'By the grace of God Shalimar, we will all get out of this alive. We just have to have faith and pray.'

Jeneba attempted to clean the blood off Shalimar's feet. The pain in her chest and side subdued a little. Shalimar realised her friend had no intention of leaving her behind. Jeneba's determination for a successful escape included all of them. She wouldn't be able to run for a few days and had to conquer the stabbing pains. If these were symptoms of a miscarriage then she would pray for its demise. Jeneba interrupted Shalimar's thoughts.

'We must pray. Pray for success. God must not forget us. He must not.'

The two friends clasped their hands together. They leant their heads together in unison, eyes closed tightly in prayer.

Chapter 22

Shalimar found that the best thing to do was to ignore Musu. No contact with the girl was the only way forward. Only Jeneba chose to converse with the mute, eager to find out how she was spending her time. Musu would cleverly toy with her pretending she did not understand Jeneba. Shalimar couldn't understand her friend's obsession with the mute.

To Shalimar and Jeneba's surprise, Musu found herself sleeping once again in the shack after Predator returned - he obviously had other things on his mind. Shalimar watched her carefully as she helped with the cooking as though nothing had happened between them. Her childlike behaviour did nothing to change Shalimar's feelings. It was frightening to know that someone of her age could be so dangerously scheming without caring about consequence.

Shalimar slept alone in the afternoons leaving the others to prepare the food. The wood crackling under the fire alongside the rhythmic thuds of the pestle and mortar failed to wake her most days.

Shalimar had left them to take a nap and when she awoke there was no one around. She assumed the women had gone to look for firewood with the men or were in the front of the cement house. When she left the shack she found the firewood lying around unused and wet with no sign of either woman. One of the Rebels appeared at the door making her jump. Predator had summoned her. Shalimar checked that her gown was flowing well around her stomach. The Predator hadn't seen her for a while.

He was playing cards in the veranda area with other soldiers but stopped slapping them on the table when she approached. Sunglasses intact, he leant back into his chair and rubbed his hands together.

'Shalimar....how are you today?'

'I'm fine, Predator.'

'I've not had you in my bed for a while. Do you know why?'

Shalimar froze, trying not to show her fear at this unexpected situation.

'No...I don't know.'

He laughed and turned to the men playing cards with him.

'She doesn't know...'

They laughed in turn, the insides of their mouths red with pink tongues. One of the men hacked and spat out toward the clearing.

'I don't have sex with pregnant women.'

She didn't know why she felt so cold on such a muggy day, or why her body suddenly felt alien to her. She couldn't feel anything. This was the moment she had been dreading. She wondered if her friend had known this was about to happen and had made a run for it without telling her. Lahai must have known something was wrong, and that was why she had not seen anyone all morning.

'Do you know whose baby it is? It isn't mine...'

'I...I...' she stammered.

'This is no place for a baby; we are in the middle of a war...'

Shalimar blinked the tears away, took a deep breath and closed her eyes. This was it. Soon she would join Chameleon.

'There is no priest here to marry you, no Imam to marry you. Where is Jeneba?'

Her eyes flew open, startled at the mention of her friends' name. Predator slammed a card on the table.

'We will wait for Jeneba.'

The men ignored her while she stood alone observing the skyline and mountains that stood out before her like giant ant hills. She had forgotten how beautiful the natural surroundings were. A trail of ants carrying half a cockroach caught her attention as she waited, desperate to make a run for it. There were too many men around and she was too heavy. The alien kicked inside her as if it knew something was wrong. She anxiously tried to steady her breathing, taking measured deep breaths while wiping her clammy hands on her wrapper. A noise made her turn around. Jeneba appeared rearranging her lapa.

'I am here. Did you miss me?' she asked, stealing a secret a wink at Shalimar.

Predator stood up, pistol in hand. He smiled and threw all his cards on the table.

'Jeneba, my queen. You are here.'

'I was using the toilet, that's why I took so long.'

He nodded, stepping carefully down the veranda steps as though he were counting them. He stopped on the third. The crunching of dry earth made Shalimar turn again to see Lahai following close behind Jeneba.

Predator lifted his hand and fired the pistol.

The women shrieked in surprise, and in a split second Lahai lay motionless on the ground. Jeneba's piercing screams seared across the plains stinging the ears of everyone in the camp. Disturbed birds flapped their wings and the treetops rustled as they took flight leaving the area in haste. Predator walked to where Lahai lay. He kicked the body to see if there was any life left before plugging four more bullets into the corpse.

He turned to his audience sneering, 'This man was an adulterer. The ten commandments say 'thou must not commit adultery' but this man thought he could sleep with my wife.'

Jeneba made the sounds of an angry wild pig. Shalimar's hands were on her stomach as the alien pulled and pushed wildly inside her, warm fluid trickled down her legs. Predator turned to the women.

'There is no place for a baby here. So now, in this camp, we have fornicators and adulterers. There are sinners that live amongst us who will sway us in the path of the Devil.'

Jeneba dropped to the ground, writhing on the floor, pulling her hair out. She banged her head onto the ground as though she had lost her mind. Shalimar bent down to console her but was wrenched away, backwards on to the dusty ground. Musu appeared from inside the house and onto the veranda, the merest hint of a smile on her face. Jeneba roared at the sight of her like an angry lion desperate to finish its feed. She ran and jumped on her victim sinking her teeth into her face.

Predator laughed loudly in excitement as though the drama couldn't get any better. This was the icing on the cake for his tales in the future. A blood-curling scream left Musu's lips. Jeneba lifted her head and spat something bloody into the bush then buried her head into Musu's neck. Musu tried unsuccessfully to fight Jeneba off. Her child-like screams of pain struck the core of those around them.

Shalimar fell to her knees unable to stand anymore. She moaned frantically to block out the noise. It took five men to pull Jeneba off a bloody Musu who ran screaming like a terrorized child into the forest surrounding them.

Predator took charge by grabbing Jeneba by the hair. He whispered something in her ear. His brows furrowed in earnest as his face grew sullen. Jeneba listened. Her wild eyes darted about with no focus. The pistol appeared at the side of her head and fired.

Everything happened in slow motion when Shalimar screamed. Her friends expressionless eyes centred on her before slumping to the ground. Blood and brains sprayed those still sitting at the table, watching the bloody show before them and laughing wildly.

Shalimar couldn't hear herself scream. She couldn't hear the Predator talking as he strutted towards her waving the pistol around. She was seized and dragged to the veranda, where the cards were swiped off the table. There was fire in his eyes when he slapped her full across the face; the sting rang through her whole body, only magnifying the terror inside her. Its abruptness brought sound back to her ears. Predator continued speaking whilst the other men held her down on the table.

'We are performing a live abortion here today. I am doing you a favour, girl. You will thank me when you are with your maker.'

Shalimar begged for her life, choking as the vomit hit her throat. The cold steel violently tore inside her causing her to scream in agony. The Predator sniffed and licked the weapon only to thrust it inside her again.

An explosion went off in her ears and the world suddenly turned silent. The Predator stood motionless. His sunglasses slowly slid off his face to reveal an open hole in the middle of his forehead. He slumped on top of her. Shalimar shoved the body away screaming as a frenzy of bullets now whizzed past her. She fell off the table and scrambled across the floor to find cover.

The deafening noise of explosives was more than she could bear as she continued to scream. She squeezed her eyes shut, covered her ears, and prayed for what seemed like forever.

Someone grabbed her arm. Shrieking in terror, she lunged out blindly and retreated back into the corner, cowering like a frightened animal. The voice in her ear sounded like Barrow's. She opened her eyes to see a Nigerian soldier in E.C.O.M.O.G uniform. She continued to whimper as he spoke to her in broken Krio. He was trying to explain that he was not with the RUF and was here to help her. She quietened down but was still trembling uncontrollably. Behind the Nigerian soldier she could see the dead body of the Predator and his soldiers in full view, blood seeping from them and trailing along the veranda onto the stairs.

The Nigerian soldier beckoned for her to stand up as he held her arm. Shalimar whimpered like a woman out of her mind. He suddenly noticed her stomach and shouted out for assistance. Another uniformed man made his way hastily towards them. He spoke perfect Krio informing her that they were taking her to the hospital as she needed immediate treatment. Shalimar looked down and saw the blood oozing from her stomach and from between her legs. Shalimar remembered her friend and scanned the area shouting Jeneba's name.

'Who is Jeneba?' The Nigerian soldier asked.

'My friend, she was shot.' Shalimar pointed to the area of death now swarming with E.C.O.M.O.G soldiers.

The soldier carried her over to a small lorry full of civilians and soldiers. Shalimar could feel many hands on her body lifting, shouting, and negotiating the appropriate place to lie her down in the back. Their exclamations of urgency heightened when they witnessed her bleeding. A man squeezed her hand and pleaded.

'Hold on. Hold on. Nor sleep oh! De hospital nor deh far.'

Shalimar shook her head.

'No...I don't want to hold on anymore. It's time to die. I want to die.'

The man's voice faded and so did his face.

Chapter 23

A blur of people filled every corner of the room lying on raffia mats, rubbing against each other moaning, choking and crying. Groans of pain and desperation filled the room. Mothers wandered about with newborns against their chests. Young boys stared into space whilst others yelled out as they thrashed around sporadically as if fighting exorcisms. Shalimar leant back onto the soft pillow for support, her groans alerting a smiling nurse to her side. The strong smell of starch filled Shalimar's nostrils bringing back memories of a squeaking chalkboard and the commotion of repetitive nursery rhymes.

'You're awake. This is good news! You have been slipping in and out of consciousness all week. How are you feeling?'

Shalimar squinted at her carer. The pulsating in her head made it difficult for her to distinguish the features of the one who spoke. The woman thrust a glass to her lips. Shalimar struggled to sip the cool water that revived her parched mouth.

A tugging sensation from her arms made her recoil; she saw what looked like plastic tubes stuck into her veins that pricked and pulled inside her. The Nurse's stiff light blue uniform brushed against her arms as she pulled the glass away, murmuring.

'Sleep now...Sleep'

Shalimar closed her eyes and drifted off.

When she awoke again the room was teeming with people. Survival outweighed dignity in the race for life as the wounded lay on mats all over the room. Swarming flies buzzed over the blood stained bandages tightly covering the limbs of men, women and children. Soldiers stood at the entrance with weapons on display, a reminder of their predicament. The same nurse appeared smiling.

'Would you like some more water?'

Shalimar nodded suddenly realizing she felt different. What was it? She felt... much lighter? Her hands immediately flew to the flat of her empty stomach. She panicked, wailing as she writhed against the tubes to look around the room.

'The baby is fine. You must calm down. You are not helping yourself by losing control like this,' the Nurse said.

Shalimar tried to catch her breath and ignore the pain in her arms. She stared at the splattered dark stained ceilings ...*the baby is fine*...those words resounded in her head. She did not want to hear those words. She wanted to be free and disappear without a trace.

'We had to perform a Caesarean otherwise you both would have died.'

The solemnity of the nurse's voice did not compliment her smile as the vulgarity of Shalimar's unconscious childbirth spilled from her lips. The detail of unnatural delivery coinciding with near death left Shalimar lifeless and morose.

'You have a healthy baby girl. She is underweight, but it is you we are worried about.'

The nurse continued to discuss the effects on her health, introducing herself as nurse Kadi. Shalimar tried to listen, but very little stayed with her. Her mind wandered to the forest and the sting of the bushes as she pursued her freedom with stabbing pains in her stomach.

'We will bring the baby...'

'No,' Shalimar interrupted.

Nurse Kadi stopped mid-sentence, surprised by her outburst.

'No baby...I don't want the baby.'

'She is a lovely little baby, a fighter just like her mother.'

'No! I don't want the baby...you keep her...I don't want it!' She raised her voice in earnest trying to sit up, but Nurse Kadi repeatedly pushed her down.

Shalimar slumped back into the pillows still weak from her trauma. The thought of seeing the baby filled her with trepidation. It represented and reminded her of the terrible day when Chameleon had been taken from her, and she had been gang-raped by who knows how many rebel soldiers.

The Nurses were never clear when handing out any information. Whenever Shalimar enquired about how long she had been in the hospital, they merely shook their heads and repeated 'a couple of weeks'. Nurse Kadi did not mention the baby for a while as she fussed around her inserting needles into her arm and fiddling with the drips that sucked the energy out of her. Nurse Kadi continued to emphasise the importance of maintaining her health for she had lost a lot of blood.

'Is the war over?' Shalimar dared to ask Nurse Kadi as she fiddled with the tubes. She had to know there was nothing to fear anymore.

'By the grace of God it will all be over pretty soon.'

Not much solace was to be found in this ward. The staff spent much of their time consoling families and feeding hungry babies left to cry alone. The night shift told its own story; Shalimar watched as Nurses rushed in to carry a woman out with blood seeping from underneath her lapa. That woman never came back. Officials arrived during the day to claim children with no parents or relatives. What was the difference?

Shalimar wondered. Would a child have a better life as an orphan? Which was worse, a rape baby with a resentful mother? Or an orphan with no family?

Shalimar soon showed signs of improvement by wobbling around the ward without help. The stitches no longer pulled at her flesh and the plastic tubes were removed. Nurse Kadi sensed Shalimar's relief that she was improving and assured her she would soon leave the hospital to begin her new life. This was the next hurdle that troubled her greatly. A new life of uncertainty surrounded by strangers.

'What about the father of the baby?'

Shalimar turned her face away as Nurse Kadi held her arm up and squeezed her wrist to check her pulse. Nurse Kadi spoke softly, unperturbed by Shalimar's reaction.

'Someone is looking after the baby now, but all children need their mothers. That baby did not ask to be born and neither did you. A baby is a blessing; you never know what joy it can bring into your life. In the white man's country they are always stealing babies because they can't have them.'

'Well let the white doctors take the baby then.'

Nurse Kadi paused. 'At least see her, just once before we give her away. One of the helpers is looking after her and giving her the bottle. But you know that breast is best for the baby. Cow milk is expensive and unnecessary. I'm sure your mother didn't give you cow milk.'

Shalimar did not respond, instead she turned to face the wall waiting for Nurse Kadi to give up and leave. But Nurse Kadi would not give up without a fight, for the very next day she appeared without warning carrying the baby. Shalimar heard a distant gurgle before spotting the Nurse and the local doctor approaching her bed. It was like a bad dream. She cursed aloud, jumping out of the bed in a state of panic forgetting that movement was not one of her strong points. She doubled up from the sharp stinging pains that swayed over the lower half of her stomach

'We didn't come to give you the baby; we just want you to meet her.'

'I don't want to know...I don't care...Leave me ALONE!' Her words turned into a shrill scream that frightened the baby.

Nurse Kadi remained indignant to her protest.

'Miss Shalimar, today you will look at this little girl. Just this once. Then we will take her away and you don't have to deal with her again. The lady who is looking after her is quite old, but she is coping and enjoying it. Why don't you hold this child for the first and last time, then we will give her to the authorities.'

Shalimar closed her eyes and trembled with anger. They had no right to subject her to this. She made herself perfectly clear and they chose to ignore her, wishing and hoping she would change her mind. They were in for a surprise. She would not give in. She could feel the eyes of the ward watching her with baited anticipation.

'That baby is not mine.' Shalimar responded, her eyes still closed.

'Just once, let it be that you held this child in your arms, and then I will sign the forms so that they take her away tomorrow. I will find a good home for her myself. Inshalah!'

Shalimar opened her eyes to see the Nurse peering down at her questioningly as the ward looked on in silence. Shalimar sat up to receive the child, blank-faced and completely unemotional. She wanted this charade over with so she could get on with her life. The Nurse placed the baby in her arms carefully. Sudden fear arose within her just to take a glimpse at the ugly reminder of the past. The worst kind of keepsake a woman could ever have thrown upon her for the rest of her life lay in her arms. Nurse Kadi tapped her shoulders urging her to take a peek. Shalimar took a deep breath.

Slowly she looked down, pulling the tattered wrapper gently from the babies face. The baby was not asleep and stared back at her. Her heart missed a beat as she pulled off the wrapper to check the rest of the baby's body. Astonished, she lifted up the light cotton pink dress and checked for the correct amount of toes and fingers. She turned the baby over, her fingers lightly trailed over the small of the back to the towelling nappy, then tugged at the wispy hair softly turning the baby to her bosom again. This was not the baby she thought she was going to have. This baby was different, with light golden curls and faded green eyes. Shalimar sobbed into the tattered wrapper as the Nurse, Doctor, and almost everyone in the room watched her.

Chapter 24

The elderly woman who had looked after the baby introduced herself as Miss Mariama. She was small, frail and darkest black just like Mama. She assisted with caring for infants when the hospital needed her. It was clear she was fond of children and longed for the company of others. Although she resembled Mama, she did not possess her hard exterior. Miss Mariama's consideration and soft manner brought comfort to Shalimar's anxious existence, as she sat at the side of Shalimar's bed, gently rocking the baby back and forth.

'Such a beautiful girl,' she said to no one in particular. 'What are we going to call you? What name is fitting for a princess like you?'

But Shalimar had known what the name should be from the moment she laid eyes on her daughter. It had jumped into her mind instantly and was not open for negotiation.

'Her name is Martina.'

*

Martina's tiny body clung to her mother, spreading warmth through Shalimar's body as she lay beside her. These unanticipated events unfolding were truly a blessing. Now Shalimar felt she had reason to hope as she whispered into her daughter's ear 'Martina' repeatedly.

Nothing could prepare Shalimar for Martina's need to feed all hours of the day and night. She still found it difficult to move around and longed to venture out in order to gain a sense of where she was. Freetown had punished her for running away from its hypnotic chaos and now it had drawn her back into its bosom cradling and caressing her to prepare her for the future.

Shalimar impressed the nurses with the ease at which she fell into breastfeeding. It was not the same for others who complained of soreness around the nipples. Breastfeeding provided an overwhelming sensation of closeness and comfort. She had been unable to provide her daughter with any respite or calmness for most of the pregnancy, which saddened her greatly. Trailing the tiny stubby toes that curled and brushed against her waist, Shalimar promised herself Martina would not be exposed to such deprivation ever again.

Gaining independence with Martina proved challenging. Shalimar wished to undertake all of her responsibilities despite the offering of assistance by the Nurses who were more concerned for her health. It proved tricky washing the screaming child under instruction, and her emotions got the better of her most days. Shalimar was unable to come to terms with Martina's hungry cries; it felt as though she howled for all the violations that had distressed her in the womb. As soon as Martina let out a shrill cry Shalimar raised her top immediately to feed and cradle Martina with comforting murmurs.

*

The time drew near to leave those who had shown her charity and kindness in the ward. Amongst the patients the anticipation of someone leaving was always met with shadows of doubt. Shalimar, like most of them, had nowhere to go. The very thought of having to feed another human being in a strange city with little education and no money was daunting. What was a person to do? But Shalimar was not afraid. She did not know why the fear of the unknown had left her but she was now ready for anything. To fight, borrow, beg or steal if she had to. Martina gurgled happily in her mother's arms, sensing another's presence as Shalimar looked up to see Nurse Kadi approach her bed. Her progress and health pleased Nurse Kadi and she was full of praise.

'You have done well, Shalimar. You just have to be careful for your own health. Don't push it.'

'I know, I know. I will take it easy for now.' Shalimar nodded in agreement. Nurse Kadi's eyes darted between Shalimar and Martina.

Was the father white?'

Shalimar nodded, it was only a matter of time before the questions started.

'Did he know that you were pregnant?'

She shook her head unable to find her voice. To speak of him would result in raw emotions rising within her. Emotions she was not yet ready to face.

'You must have faith; I have dealt with many women not as lucky as you. Pregnant from rape and having to give birth to the child then carry it back home. You are one of the lucky ones.'

Shalimar nodded, hugging Martina closer to her bosom. She recognised the value of Nurse Kadi's words.

'Did you know the father well?'

'Yes. We were together a year before...before he left.' Shalimar said sadly.

A steady stinging in her chest rose to the surface. It was proving to be a painful moment for her.

Nurse Kadi continued, 'Do you know where he is?'

'He is dead.'

*

Shalimar sipped on the *pap* rice pudding that Miss Mariama brought in late that afternoon. The old lady changed Martina's nappy as Shalimar looked on, tired and in need of some sleep.

'You know that the hospital is going to have to let you go soon. Have you decided where you are going?'

Shalimar didn't know how to answer the old lady who busied herself wiping talcum powder over Martina's soft bottom. She flipped the sliding strap from her arm back onto her shoulder.

'My twins died five days after they were born. I buried them alone with my bare hands. My husband left me long ago because of my drinking. You may have nowhere to go, but a young woman like you will be fine. You can find work.'

Shalimar raised her eyebrows. She wasn't sure where this was going and wanted to tread carefully with the old lady who had shown much kindness to her and Martina.

'I am over seventy years old,' Mariama continued, 'so I only help out from time to time. I wash the bedclothes and clean out the pans whenever they need me. I sell cassava and potato leaves in the market when I am not here. I don't mind, but walking around can be difficult.' She lifted her wrapper to show Shalimar a caved-in knee surrounded with purple bruises.

'What happened?' Shalimar wrinkled her nose at the still heavily swollen and discoloured joint.

'I fell on the road last month. They looked after me here, the doctor checked me out and gave me free medicine but *aiy*! I am slowing down. I have a spare room for you and your child; you are welcome to find work and pay me rent. Then I don't have to come here anymore and I can look after Martina.'

The offer staggered Shalimar and she did not know how to respond. Miss Mariama nattered on without waiting for a response.

'A baby is a blessing no matter how it is conceived. If you had said no to this baby I would have taken her home.' She chuckled showing black gums with no front teeth.

'Everybody would think I stole the baby.'

'*Yes mah, tenki mah. God go bless you, mah.*' Shalimar stumbled over her words.

184

*

Shalimar's poignant farewell from the hospital left others discussing their own prospects, all unsure of the future that lay ahead of them. Shalimar knew to survive and overcome the war with Martina was a sign that many good things were possible. Now she would live for those whose lives were brutally cut short by those depraved thugs. She would not let them or herself down for she would live every day as though it was the first day of her life…her new life.

Miss Mariama lived downtown in a yard full of makeshift *pan bodies,* just like the ones behind the Hotel in Lumley Beach. Children played, women cooked, a scabby dog scratched its ear before running toward a group of girls playing *Jump Rope*. The people watched and greeted her with smiles and nods as she walked past them. Once inside the seclusion of her own room Shalimar rolled out her new *mattah* mentally exhausted and overcome with relief. Today was the first day of the rest of her life.

The very next day, Miss Mariama took Shalimar to see Mrs Jones, a *Krio* who worked with a local NGO dealing with the crisis of the displaced amputees in Freetown. They walked along a road with large colonial houses on either side, eventually stopping at a set of open gates.

'This is it, Shalimar. Mrs Jones is a very busy lady. She works all day and sometimes late into the night. She needs someone to look after the house, do some cleaning and washing, have a meal ready for when she comes home. You want to do this?'

Shalimar smiled. 'It is a beautiful house. I hope Mrs Jones wants me.

The two women walked up the driveway slowly, Shalimar helping the old lady who still struggled to walk.

'It will be good for me too, if she likes you. I can rest up and let my knee heal properly.'

The door opened before they even reached it, a tall dark, smartly dressed woman waited for them.

'Good morning, Mrs Jones,' the old woman said. 'This is Shalimar.'

'How do you do, Shalimar. Miss Mariama and Nurse Kadi told me all about you. I am so happy you are able to start at such short notice. My other girl leaves for Guinea next week, so I was starting to get a bit anxious.'

Mrs Jones gave Shalimar a quick tour of the house, explaining what she needed doing, and how much she was offering as wages. The expected chores were not as daunting as she had feared. The clothes were to be washed three times a week and the house swept in the morning. Shalimar could not believe her good luck. Somewhere to live, a willing babysitter and a job, all within two days of leaving hospital. A taxi pulled up in front of the house as the women said their goodbyes, and Mrs Jones excused herself, saying she had to rush off, and she would see Shalimar on Monday morning.

Miss Mariama waved her hands to the sky as they walked along the open stretch of pavement passing the brilliant yellow and pink colonial houses that rose and fell like jagged tips of mountain tops.

'Everything is working out for you, Shalimar. God is good.'

Martina slept soundly on her mother's back, completely oblivious to the stifling heat that sucked sweat from her mother's body they walked along the Congo Cross bridge.

Chapter 25

The familiar sights of Freetown seemed somewhat distorted second time around. The heavy heat and constant din of traffic echoed around her when she explored the area. It was nothing like the secluded glossy feel of Lumley Beach. She still found herself doing a double take whenever she heard conversations in *Mende*. There was a different sense of loneliness this time. She was no longer running away from anything or anybody. It felt surreal trying to imagine how desperate she had been to leave the capital in such dangerous times. At night, Shalimar's thoughts wandered to Lumley - the place that changed her life was only two miles away from where she lived. Shalimar wondered if the hotel staff would recognise her. The distant memory of the lifestyle Chameleon had introduced to her - five star hotels, fancy banquets, bars and restaurants seemed to exist in another lifetime. Sometimes it felt as though it had never happened until she looked at Martina. A peculiar love between two people that blazed and shred the pieces of their heart lay evident in her daughter's eyes. She knew what she had to do to stop her deliberations driving her crazy. She borrowed money from Miss Mariama, promising to pay her back with the first month's wages.

Forceful warm air blew through rear window of the taxi against the five sweaty bodies pressed together in the back. It was a relief to jump out at the end of Aberdeen Bridge; she used the wrapper to wipe away the sweat of others off her arms. Shalimar savoured the familiar fresh smell of salt from the ocean as she walked down the hill. Prickles rose on the back of her neck at the sight of the deserted road that led towards the place that had changed her life forever. The familiar sights caught her breath as she trundled over the stones and gravel towards the hotel entrance.

The hotel that was once home was now little more than a pile of rubble and cement. The few standing walls were riddled with bullet holes forming chaotic patterns. Pieces of cloth flickered in the wind stuck between debris; white dust covered a lone black patent high heel shoe. Shalimar caught her breath, the wind around her picked up speed as though encouraging her to move on and away from the lonely desolate spot. She rubbed the goose bumps on her arms and took a deep breath. This confirmation that she sought and longed for revealed there was nothing to show of her time with Chameleon, only memories.

*

She had survived against all the odds and because of this she was determined to take the wheel of life and steer it in her direction. She no longer wanted to serve others, she still dreamed of being a businesswoman. Shalimar still did not know what her exact trade would be, but she would help Miss Mariama in hers until she decided. As kind as Mrs Jones was, Shalimar did not want to work for anyone anymore. Her days of servitude were over.

Miss Mariama listened as she chewed on a cleaning stick spitting into a plastic cup intermittently. Shalimar had decided to ask Miss Mariama for advice about trading, aware that she must make money quickly to pay her rent. Miss Mariama's experience of the city and past history would help immensely although she did not want her to think that she would ever take advantage of her frailty. It came as a surprise when Miss Mariama suggested Shalimar take over her spot and sell plassas in the local market for her. The offer staggered Shalimar as Miss Mariama had a decent business already in place.

'You pay the rent and give me twenty percent until later. Maybe after six months you buy me out.'

'Miss Mariama...I don't know what to say?' Shalimar was dumbstruck by the old woman's generosity.

'I am getting too old to be carrying all that weight from the market. If you pay the rent, and I get a little money for the business, that is enough for me. Wait a minute; I have something to show you.'

Shalimar squeezed her body together in anticipation as the old lady disappeared into her bedroom, and reappeared with a black plastic bag.

The old lady chewed on her remaining stick, revealing crushed white sediments with a smile.

'God give me the brains to make money but nobody to leave it with.'

'Yes Mah.'

'Business nah small small.'

'Yes Mah.'

'Martina will be able to go to school...even secondary school!'

The old woman unwrapped the black bag and pulled out an envelope filled with colourful Leones.

'Count it.'

'Miss Mariama! Where...how...'

'I have no children and no grandchildren to spend it on. I make good business, and live a simple life. If you stay here, it will be like the little one is my grandchild, and I will love her and care for her as such.'

188

Tears formed in both women's eyes. Shalimar couldn't believe how fate had turned things around for her. She leapt at the old woman, hugging her tightly as the tears formed streams down her cheeks.

'Thank you, Miss Mariama. I am so happy; I will be here with you for as long as you want me to.'

'Bless you, child. Then that is settled. Oh, and if we are going to live like this, then Miss Mariama is too formal. Call me Mama.'

*

Shalimar decided to pay a last visit to Lumley Beach to search out her long lost friend, Miatta. It was hard to properly close the chapter after witnessing the destruction of the hotel. The scattered ruins resembled her life and picking up the pieces was all she had done since arriving back in the capital. Miatta may well be the only real evidence left of her former time here. Lumley beach was less daunting the second time around. Martina slept uninterrupted on Shalimar's back as the poda poda jolted to its final destination. Miatta was easy to find. Shalimar couldn't believe her eyes when she spotted the columns holding the thatched raised roof over the wine bar intact and unaffected by the war. Miatta's incessant screaming deafened Shalimar as they hugged each other tightly.

It felt like travelling back in time strolling through the golden sand that glimmered as far as the eye could see. The sounds of the hissing ocean went unnoticed this time as Shalimar looked out to sea remembering how it had once terrified her soul to the very core.

Miatta stopped in her tracks during Shalimar's abduction story signalling for her to stop.

'No more. I beg you. Ee do so!'

Their conversation took them into the evening as they reminisced about the afternoons on the beach, sharing a Fanta and laughing with the beach traders. Shalimar had never before told Miatta of the time when she had run away from the hotel in only a cotton shirt, treading on broken glass and ending up in hospital.

'That must have been a sight!' Miatta chuckled. 'So what happened to Chameleon?'

Shalimar knew the question would eventually arise and was prepared for it.

'He's dead.'

Miatta's eyes widened.

'Ayee God! How did this happen?'

189

The answer had been carefully worked out to maintain his dignity. Mercenaries died in combat and not at the hands of young boys while trying to save a woman. The story of an argument and a split appeared believable enough. The split allowed both to go their own way, with Chameleon disappearing, and an acquaintance informing her later of his demise.

'Plenty of Nigerians have also died for our freedom,' Miatta responded, acknowledging it was possible. It was a relief to hear there were no rumours about Chameleon's death.

'So what are you doing for money? Babysitting?' Miatta continued pointing at Martina.

'I sell cassava leaves and potato leaves in the market.'

'You should come and visit me one evening. I will show you a quick easy way to make some money,' Miatta said moving in to take a peek at Martina. What she saw had her step back in disbelief. '*Oh my God, You born for Chameleon? You been get belleh for am?*'

'Yes.'

Miatta took a deep breath, and pushed the faded wrapper away from Martina's face. She peered at her for several seconds before blowing out.

'Well I used to be jealous of you but now I am not. I can't imagine how it must feel for the father of your child to be dead.'

Shalimar's heart fell to the floor. She swallowed her emotions surprised at her own fragility.

'I just have to live with it. It is not at all easy for me.'

'Why don't you come with me, I am going to the Lagunda club. We will have a good time. You will see how easy it is.'

'How easy what is?'

'There are many foreigners working with all these NGO's and charity organisations. They are looking for women all the time.'

Miatta grinned as though she had just passed on the news that she would be starting a secretarial job at the President's office. The hairs stood up on the back of Shalimar's neck at the thought of Miatta selling her body to strange men.

'We go see how de makit go deh go'

Miatta laughed dismissively at Shalimar's awkwardness.

'No need to worry. Just come and see me when you're ready, of course. I can see you are a little shy right now. There is a lot of money to be made. You may need it, now you have the little one.'

It was depressing that Miatta was not ashamed to share this part of her life with her. It appeared to have no consequences for her friend who was in good spirits and wished to share the proceeds. As they said their goodbyes, Shalimar knew deep down she would never see Miatta again. The days of having a man forcing himself on her were over. Chameleon had been the connection and now he was gone. Being with a man was not something that had crossed Shalimar's mind since having Martina. Her one and only focus was to become a trader and feed the only family she had left. She ignored the men that spoke to her on her way home offering to take her out for a drink, begging for a date. It was not going to happen; it was never going to happen.

*

Shalimar was pleased with the choice of trade: cassava leaves, potato leaves and krane krane all worth the early morning hustle. A certain respect came naturally when running your own business, no matter how small. Money had people address you differently and pay attention to you when realising the success of your trade.

In the Early mornings as the city slept, the convoy of trucks arrived at Dove Court, bringing goods from the provinces for the traders to replenish their supplies. Shalimar and Miss Mariama would rise early and dress in silence anticipating the hard toil that awaited them. Paid labourers offered to carry their trading goods on the *omolanke* cart across town, but for Shalimar this was not necessary. Miss Mariama led the business venture bartering with the truck drivers during the first few weeks. Shalimar filled her basket with plasass and made her way to the market for the rest of the day. She walked leisurely through the streets with her wares on her head and Martina on her back, full of hope and excitement. Sometimes customers would call her into their houses having heard her cries from their balconies so she managed to sell half of the products by the time she set down to trade in the open market.

Martina enjoyed the freedom of her environment and occupied herself most of the time with the wares of other traders. Lunch consisted of raw cassava most of the time with the occasional luxurious coconut cake for Martina to snack on when she became restless.

The slow build-up of regular customers and the struggle to break even took its toll but Shalimar reminded herself that business was always precarious and there was nowhere else she would rather be than selling in the market. Miss Mariama's supportive streak continued as she offered to look after Martina some of the time. On these days Shalimar skipped lunch and only drank water, ignoring the pangs of hunger that drilled through her empty stomach. It didn't matter to

191

Shalimar - she had endured far more terrible things than hunger, and making money was more important. .

The children in the market yard could not resist picking Martina up and passing her around when she crawled around the stalls. Martina had an infectious laugh and showed no fear when other children pulled ugly faces. She played with rubbish left lying in the mud and picked out ants to put in her mouth. Her shrill screams filled the yard when the ants bit her fingers. Shalimar wondered whether Martina's wispy golden curls looked out of place against her bronze complexion. Her grey green eyes had soon been replaced with her mother's honeycomb colour. Shalimar still marvelled over the fact that she was a mother when she watched Martina toddle around in the midst of the market stalls. They would eat rich *olele* baked in banana leaves with Fula bread to mellow the appetite into the evening. Miss Mariama prepared Shalimar's favourite snacks in the evening; fried plantains, akara with peppered gravy and they would sit in the yard against the din of the rush hour savouring the food and discussing the possibilities of tomorrow.

Martina celebrated her first birthday with the neighbours. Shalimar purchased crates of various soft drinks and Star beer for the elders. Music blared out from a radio, and the children played games and danced. Martina glowed in her white lace birthday dress; she was as beautiful as any child in a magazine. Shalimar took the opportunity to thank Miss Mariama for all her support but was unable to finish as the old lady snapped at her and left the yard abruptly. The neighbours laughed at Shalimar's naivety accusing her of making Miss Mariama cry in public.

When the celebration was over and they retired to their sleeping mat, Shalimar thought about how close she was to losing Martina in the camp and how much her life had turned around. It was difficult to figure out whether this situation was permanent as nothing could ever be certain. Martina's deep breaths echoed in unison with the movement of her chest, her innocent face peaceful as she slept. She moved around to get comfortable and her chubby hands grazed against her mother's face. Shalimar could not imagine being without her. Miss Mariama had also benefited greatly from the newfound wealth of a family. The old lady deserved so much for providing a roof over their head and supporting them as though they were part of her flesh and blood. Shalimar had always longed to do something to show how grateful she was and she managed it gracefully.

Although the past lingered in her mind, life progressed so fast that it did not allow her to slow down. It was strange the way memories remained strong and emotional in the mind if you allowed them to. It still hurt that she had nothing physical to show of her family; it was almost as if they never existed except in her mind. Chameleon was evident in Martina, she chewed the sides of her mouth the way he did and squinted her eyes in his manner. Shalimar marvelled on how this could be possible when her daughter had never met him. Pleasure and pain moulded itself around her to witness these treasured moments alone. Not all reflections were as pleasant as she still suffered from flashes of Predator but Shalimar now had the ability to block them out almost effortlessly. Her nightmares turned into dreams that floated away bringing less and less emotion to her when she awoke from them. Time it seemed was healing some of the wounds.

Chapter 26

Shalimar showered the cold water onto a naked Martina, who squealed in dismay. She used the soft side of the loofah to wash off the mud and red dust from the market that had settled onto her delicate skin. Martina did not mind the soap but cried out when her mother's fingers moved around her face. It was amusing to see Martina struggle to stop her from washing her. She overturned the last cup of water over her before untying the towel from her waist to wrap around her daughter. Martina clung to her mother's soothing rubs and settled down.

'*Kooshe oh*, Shalimar.'

The voice rang familiar but she could not place it. Shalimar turned around sharply, standing tall before her was an extravagantly dressed Miatta. The mini skirt barely covered the beginning of her thighs and the long black wig resembled a horse's tail. Heads turned as Miatta sauntered towards Shalimar, though her high heels sunk into the soft earth causing her to topple as she strode through the yard. Shalimar could not hide her surprise at her long lost friend's transformation and entrance. There was something different about her friend's tone. She sounded somewhat detached.

'*You memba me tiday*? Long time no see,' Shalimar answered continuing to rub Martina gently.

'Finish with her, I will wait here,' Miatta said with authority looking around the yard slowly and then at her watch.

Shalimar stared questioningly at Miatta before leaving her alone in the yard. She wondered if Miatta had come with another proposal to join the prostitution ring that frequented the clubs at night. She was obviously making enough money to add a horse's tail to her scalp. Shalimar sniggered as she smoothed down the talcum powder over Martina's body and put on her soft cotton nightdress. Martina ran out of the bedroom straight into Miss Mariama's lap. Shalimar informed Miss Mariama of Miatta's arrival.

'What does she want?'

'I don't know. Maybe she is just passing.' Shalimar shrugged leaving the room.

Miatta stood in the same place with a faint leer in her eyes as she watched Shalimar approach. Shalimar could only put down this perplexing behaviour to the fact that Miatta now thought herself superior.

'I came to give you some news.' Miatta spoke fast and straight to the point.

'News?' Shalimar dared to think about Blama.

'Chameleon. You came here and told me that he was dead. Well, he is not.'

Shalimar stopped to catch her breath. She could feel a force within her tightening by the second, threatening to squeeze the life from her.

Miatta did not acknowledge her reaction, although a slight sneer came to her lips as she continued.

'He has been in Freetown for a while...but he is not the same man that he used to be.' She snorted. 'He has gone downhill if you ask me. Anyway I thought I would let you know as he doesn't know anything about you. '

Miatta's words sliced quick and sharp through Shalimar's body, like a machete cutting to her very core.

'So, if you want to find him, he is always in *Sonny Mac* on *Rodin Street*, hanging with lowlife and layabouts.' She paused as if coming up for air. Her frosty presence rejuvenated itself when she wrinkled her nose in disgust at her immediate surroundings. She turned ready to leave. 'Don't expect much when you see him.'

Something snapped in Shalimar as she watched her former friend walk away. Shalimar rushed to grab the horse's tail and pulled it towards the ground. The neighbours' exclamations of shock and disbelief reverberated around her. Shalimar continued to pull the hair as far as she could onto the ground, ignoring Miatta's roars.

'You knew he was alive and you purposely chose not to tell me?'

Miatta tried in vain to pull away Shalimar's fingers from the hair.

'You knew about Martina and you said nothing? You are evil!'

Miss Mariama's hands covered Shalimar's and removed them from Miatta's hair as she pleaded for calm. Shalimar obeyed, letting go of the tail. She wiped her teary eyes with the back of her hand, explaining the reason for the altercation.

Miss Mariama looked at Miatta with disgust, and then slapped her round the face.

'Get away from here, prostitute. You're not welcome.'

She grabbed Miatta, ripping her shirt as she pushed her away. Miatta toppled on her heels, falling to the ground leaving the mob of neighbours in hysterics. Shalimar watched from the doorway with Martina at her side, grateful for the support of others who shared her anger at such despicable behaviour.

Once inside, Martina fell asleep almost immediately. It was past her usual hour and she had been caught up in the emotion of the evening. Shalimar lay down gazing at her daughter's peaceful sleeping state. Her heart was on fire with a blaze of emotions. The evening's revelations had stunned her. She had lived for almost two years believing Chameleon was dead, and now this. She remembered the longing in Miatta's eyes for Chameleon's attention. It had made her feel insecure and yet satisfied that Chameleon's eyes had only been for her. Her instincts were right all along about Miatta and she should never have doubted them.

'What are you doing here? I thought you would be dressed and going down to that bar. Sonny Mac?'

Miss Mariama's figure loomed in the darkness blocking out the light from the lantern.

'I can't go now. I'm not ready. Give me time to take it all in.'

'You need to go and find Martina's father. What is there to think about?'

'I'm not going there tonight. I need to deal with this. I can't just go there. Tomorrow will be better. By that time I would have gathered my thoughts and be ready for anything.'

Miss Mariama stood by the doorway in silence. Shalimar knew the old lady was already thinking of tomorrow and what should happen. She wanted to go to Sonny Mac's and see whether this was all real, was he really alive? She wanted to see him, touch him and hear his voice but she was afraid. Sadness and grief were engrained in her and she was afraid to let them go because it was partly comforting.

Miss Mariama mumbled under her breath before moving away. She did not believe Shalimar and could sense her fear.

'Tomorrow we will go together with Martina.'

Chapter 27

Miss Mariama was not impressed when Shalimar left in the early hours of the morning to go to market. Shalimar couldn't wait to get out of the house but she knew that Miss Mariama always rose before dawn to fill the water drums because of the water shortage so she left hurriedly to avoid any small talk.

The market was a welcome relief and Shalimar indulged in extra-long conversations with customers and traders to keep her mind off the obvious. This did not quench the seed of fear that grew and sprouted within her throughout the day. Part of her wished Miatta's visit to be full of spiteful lies, but deep down Shalimar knew there was no reason for Miatta to call on her and lie about such things. She watched Martina play around the other toddlers, totally unaware of the events unfolding that could shape her future. Shalimar hoped for the peace that reigned in the country to finally reign in her life and her heart. She had found much contentment in her vocation. The market was everything she had wished for, the customers, the banter, the independence and familiarity. It was all she had desired and more. The only thing she had to tackle was the gnawing fear that consumed her soul as she watched the sun go down.

*

Miss Mariama looked smart in her white cotton top and a long gara skirt as she waited by the entrance for Shalimar. She took Martina off Shalimar's hands as they hugged and pushed her towards the outhouse to have a shower. Shalimar took her time in the shower trying to calm herself in preparation for what was in store. It was doubtful that Chameleon was alive as she had heard the gun shots as she lay semi-conscious in the dirt in Blama. Miatta had deliberately been vague with her revelation and Shalimar suspected that there might be more nasty business on the way in the form of *Sonny Mac's* bar. She was not scared of any outcome or of Miatta; her fear only resided in hearing some more bad news about Chameleon. Miss Mariama shouted Shalimar's name impatiently several times. Shalimar stumbled out of the washhouse and ran to the bedroom.

'*Martina don eat? Try nuh!*' Miss Mariama called out as she entered the bedroom. She picked up the towel and laid out a clean wrapper on the bed. This was a very unsubtle way of telling Shalimar to hurry up.

Shalimar sighed. 'I think I better go alone.'

Miss Mariama stopped shaking the towel with a questioning look. Shalimar faced her surrogate mother and spoke softly.

'It will be better that I go alone and find out what is going on.'

'Shalimar, you will need us there. What if...?'

'I need to do this alone. It doesn't make sense for all of us to go. If what she says is true then it will be too much for us all to turn up in a bar with a baby. I have to do this by myself, Mama.'

Miss Mariama might have felt a little left out and upset but she didn't show it. She shook the towel vigorously one last time and hung it on the chair.

'Well try nuh, mek you go.'

*

When Shalimar turned the corner into Rodin Street, the bar stuck out like a sore thumb. Hoards of people stood around the entrance, drinking and talking. Traders here sold music CDs and popular local songs blared out of speakers. Colourful schoolbooks stacked on makeshift shelves also filled the path to the bar. The lack of streetlights made it hard to see as she stumbled over people and bottles in order to reach the entrance. Loud music and voices echoed throughout the vicinity. She moved towards the bar scouring the place; there were so many people it was hard to outline or identify anyone. An unsmiling woman nodded to acknowledge her presence, waiting for her order.

'Ah deh look for Chameleon.'

Shalimar felt herself shaking as she asked the question. The woman shook her head ever so slightly, then pointed to the corner of the bar.

'Maybe he's over there.'

Nausea hit her throat instantly. What did this mean? She stood still for a moment to collect herself.

'I'll have a small whiskey first.'

Shalimar knocked the fiery liquid back and felt it burn the back of her throat. Her heart pulsated in her chest. The music blaring around her dimmed in her ears as she pushed past the hoards of people. She forced her way around the end of the bar, and came to a large table of men, with women sitting on their laps. She did not see Chameleon, only a gathering of people in the middle of what appeared to be a celebration.

One of the women noticed Shalimar's interest in the gathering. She nudged the man whose lap she was sat on; when he looked up at her, the woman nodded in Shalimar's direction.

'Can I help you?' the man shouted above the loud music. He was not rude but neither was he friendly.

'Chameleon. I am looking for Chameleon.' Shalimar heard herself whisper as the lump in her throat blocked out her words. She cleared her throat and repeated herself hoping that her incessant shaking would not put them off. The man merely tapped the man sitting next to him and leant over to whisper something in his ear. The woman on his lap was blocking Shalimar's view. The woman suddenly stood up and wandered off leaving Shalimar staring straight into the grey green eyes of a ghost. The sight of him affected her breathing straight away. Sudden heat rose from her gut straight to her exploding head. She coughed and struggled to breathe as impulsive tears brimmed, stinging her eyelids.

Chameleon flew to his feet immediately, the look of incredulity on his face almost mirroring Shalimar's.

'Shalimar?'

He stood before her almost afraid to reach out and touch her. Shalimar nodded unable to speak. She knew if she opened her mouth she would crumble.

He continued to say her name in disbelief. His hands outlined her face and hairline. His fingers entangled her hair as he moved in to smell her. He was touching her as though she had come back from the dead. Shalimar held onto him pressing her hands through his clothes into his flesh. She had to make sure he was real. He was supposed to be dead. He had been dead all this time.

Chameleon pulled her away from the crowd to the back of the bar. A few drunken folk lay about on the grass while others peed indiscriminately on the surrounding walls.

'You're alive, Shalimar? What happened to you?' His hands shook as he took hers.

'I escaped.'

'You escaped?' Chameleon repeated in disbelief.

'Yes, I went looking for you at the hotel.'

'It was bombed out. There is nothing left there.'

'You're alive...' She touched Chameleon's face. 'Where did you go? The hotel was bombed. I searched for you, I thought you were dead.'

'How did you find me?' Chameleon interrupted her. Those familiar wild eyes searched her face for clues and answers.

'Miatta gave...'

'Miatta?' He sounded surprised.

Shalimar was past caring. She told Chameleon of Miatta's visit the day before, leaving Chameleon dumbfounded. He took a step back and lost his footing almost falling backwards. There was no gravel or large pebbles in the back yard and Shalimar realised Chameleon was slightly drunk. He waved his hand to brush off his unsteadiness and laughed.

'We have to celebrate with my friends,' he said and dragged her back into the bar announcing Shalimar as his long lost wife. He demanded a toast amidst the perplexed party. This was not what Shalimar had expected. He was drunk and surrounded by people who were drinking away his money.

'We have to go.' Shalimar cut short his celebration.

'What?' Chameleon could hardly hear her above the booming dance music in the bar.

'We have to go, now. I have something to show you.' Shalimar tugged at his shirt and pulled him away, towards the exit.

A bewildered Chameleon stood watching her. Shalimar beckoned him to follow and stepped out of the bar to hail a taxi. Chameleon trailed behind her.

The warm night air blew into the taxi as they drove through the city. Chameleon moved to kiss Shalimar, expressing his shock at the unfolding night's events. Shalimar closed her eyes allowing his hands to trail over her clothed body. The familiar taste of whiskey on her tongue caused water to hit her eyes. She gently pulled away. Chameleon lay back onto the seat mumbling and passed out. Shalimar wiped away the tears that slid easily down her cheeks. She wanted to be happy but instead was filled with sadness. Chameleon was not the one who had saved her. She had saved herself. All the memories she had held of him were now being smashed to pieces by harsh reality. She did not wake him until they reached their destination, hoping that he would be at least half sober to meet his daughter.

Chameleon seemed to sober up once they got out of the taxi. He rubbed his eyes and asked her if this was where she lived before following her inside. She led him to the sitting room and asked if he wanted some water. He shook his head and sat down. There were visible lines around his eyes. His hair was longer and lighter than the usual mousy brown it had always been.

'Shalimar.'

He repeated her name in earnest and squeezed her tightly, burying his face into her neck.

'I searched everywhere for you. I knew you were not dead. I never gave up on you. I need you to know Shalimar that I did not leave you to die. I was ambushed and overpowered by those RUF Gangsters.'

He placed a finger on the raised keloid that trailed lightly along his cheek.

'I got this trying to fight them off. By the time I got away you were gone. I never forgave myself. I vowed I would never stop looking for you.'

'I thought you were dead.' She did not know why her voice sounded so flat and cold. Her whispering words exposed her feelings. She was not sure he could hear her. He gazed over her.

'I'm too late aren't I? I know that look. I've been a soldier long enough to know that look. Oh God, I know what they did to you Shalimar. I can see it in your eyes.'

The slow realization that Chameleon had been searching for her all this time brought thunder to Shalimar's heart. His caress and kisses spread warmth throughout her soul. He had not forgotten her. This was the moment she thought she would never experience.

'Jamie, I survived. I am okay now. Come, I have something to show you.'

She took his hand and led him to the bedroom where Martina slept peacefully.

'Shh...' Shalimar put her fingers to her lips as they moved inside the room. She pulled him towards the bed so he could get a full view of their sleeping daughter.

The shock on Chameleon's face came as an unexpected reaction. It was as though he had woken up to find his nightmare happening around him. He trembled uncontrollably and stepped back almost losing his balance. The smile wiped from Shalimar's face in a matter of seconds. Something was dreadfully wrong.

'When did this happen?' Chameleon's voice shook as he spoke.

'I didn't know. I found out after we were ambushed.' Chameleon looked at her questioningly.

'And they didn't kill you?'

Shalimar flinched at his response.

'I ran away before they could.'

Chameleon crumbled on the floor and put his head in his hands. The silence between them screamed around the walls of the room, the alcohol clearly having an impact on his emotions. Shalimar cringed as she heard herself trying to sound positive.

'Her name is Martina. She is almost eighteen months.'

Chameleon raised his head sharply and gawped at her.

'What?'

Shalimar struggled to repeat herself. Her voice wavered. Chameleon stood up and moved towards her. Shalimar recognised those slitty eyes. His whole face wet, eyes and nose streaming. Confused, she was unable to understand his reaction towards Martina.

'Look at my hands!' Chameleon shoved his open palms into Shalimar's face.

She stared at him as though he had gone completely mad and pushed them away.

'Do you know what these hands have done? Do you? I have murdered people with these hands.'

Shalimar stepped back as Chameleon insisted on pushing his hands into her face.

She slapped them away a second time.

'What has this got to do with me?'

'Maybe some of my stories might make you understand why this is a bad, bad idea.' Chameleon said pointing at Martina angrily. 'Do you want to hear the story about the village that wasn't expecting us? How about the one about the father and his two daughters? The father begged us to spare the life of his daughters and take his. So you know what I did? I chose one of the girls and brought her out in front of her family...'

'Stop it.' Shalimar implored him.

'Her father started crying like a baby, crawling on his knees like a dog. I pushed her to her knees and...'

Shalimar screamed pushing Chameleon away.

'Stop it! I don't want to hear anymore!'

Chameleon sneered. 'Why? You don't like to hear what I am. You don't want to hear the truth about Chameleon and what he is capable of?'

'Stop. Just stop!' Shalimar let out a sob at his cruel cold words. She didn't deserve this treatment.

'I am a murderer, Shalimar. When will you get it into your head? I don't sleep because all those I have killed wait for me. They visit me in my dreams and bait me. I took lives ruthlessly and I didn't care. When will you stop pretending to not understand what I really am?'

Chameleon backed away and slumped on the chair with his head in his hands. Martina stirred and mumbled. The noise had disrupted her sleep so Shalimar covered her with the cotton sheet to calm her. She did not want Martina to wake up fully and find a stranger in the room. She wiped her eyes as she patted her daughter, lulling her back to sleep. Nothing had changed: neither his bitterness nor his selfishness.

'How can I be a father?' Chameleon sobbed. 'How can I? I am not fit to be a father.'

Her blood boiled at his words. Shalimar could not believe the pitiable excuse that she was hearing. All these years she had dealt with had been thrown at her, and now to hear this so-called man make a pathetic defence against fatherhood was pitiful.

'Yes you are right. You are not fit to be a father. You have never been worthy of being anyone's father.'

Chameleon looked up at her in surprise.

'Do you want to know why you are not fit to be *her* father? Because you are nothing but a drunk!'

Chameleon flinched at the truthful words.

'Now you can get out and go back to your drunken friends. We have survived so far without you. I am a survivor and I can get on with my life without you. So just get out!'

Shalimar spat at Chameleon then turned her back. She waited. Her heart raced as the adrenalin ran through her body. Chameleon reluctantly moved past her towards the door in silence. She listened to Chameleon's footsteps disappear then she climbed into bed next to Martina. She was done with him. It was over. After everything she had gone through, Shalimar told herself this was nothing. She closed her eyes purposely recalling the Predator's hands all over her body. It wasn't long before the whisky she had downed in the bar seeped around her bloodstream. She felt warm and sleepy. Martina's heavy breathing was all that could be heard in the stillness of the night.

The mattress lowered under the weight of another, interrupting Shalimar's halfway house of dreams. She sat up disorientated. Chameleon had not left the house after all.

'What are you doing?' She hissed. 'I told you to get out.'

Chameleon tried to kiss her but she pushed him away. She did not like the way his hands caused instant tremors to her body.

'Shalimar. Please just listen.'

'No! I'm not listening to you. I hate you!'

'I love you, Shalimar'

'Stay away from us!' Shalimar tried to catch her breath.

'I need you both in my life. I'm just scared. I don't know what to do. Tell me what you want me to do.'

'There is nothing that you can do to me that will break me, Chameleon. I am a survivor. I will not allow you to come into my life and hurt me. No one is ever going to hurt me ever again. Never AGAIN!'

'I need you both in my life. I cannot be without you, Shalimar. Not after all this time.'

'I despise everything about you.'

'No you don't.'

'You are no good even to yourself.'

'There was never a minute in a day that I didn't think about you.'

'You are a liar and a thief.'

'I know that you could feel me around you. I know that you never forgot me.'

'You steal from my country; you make money from my loss.'

'Don't tell me you never imagined me touching you. Don't tell me you didn't miss me. Don't tell me you didn't shed tears for the man you hate so much because you thought he was dead.'

'So what?'

'Whenever tears fell from your eyes, my spirit was there to wipe them from your face. No matter how far away I was from this place I could smell you. I could feel you...'

'You lie.'

'I know you are angry. I know that I did many bad things, but I love you with my soul and nothing can change that.'

Chameleon pulled her close to him, but she turned her face away. He brushed his mouth against her ear.

'Why do you keep trying to push me away?'

'You are of no importance to us,' Shalimar answered.

'You are my life, Shalimar. Martina is evidence of what we shared. You cannot deny that.'

He kissed her neck lightly; a familiar tingling sensation crept up her spine. Shalimar winced. He kissed her again on the other side of her neck. His hands moved around her waist.

'Say you love me Shalimar.'

'Stop.'

His hands continued to trail over her body. The weakness she had felt so long ago came rushing back. She closed her eyes and a warm surge swept over her.

'Tell me that you missed me.'

'I missed you.' Shalimar shook uncontrollably as he kissed her.

'Say you love me,' he repeated. His face was wet.

She touched his damp cheeks with her trembling hand. He covered his hand over hers. There was nothing to see in the dark, but emotions could not be masked. Martina's sighs grew louder as her sleep deepened amidst the confusion.

Shalimar kept Martina on her side to avoid being crushed by Chameleon who had the tendency to toss and turn in his sleep. He held her close to him squeezing her every so often, placing kisses in her hair and on her forehead. He outlined her scars with his fingers and put his lips tenderly against them as though they would heal from his touch.

She moved her face against his smooth burnt skin to remind herself of his scent. She had missed his smell so badly and now he was here, touching and kissing her gently, holding her and caressing her body. She ran her fingers through the hair she used to marvel at, the hair that gave no protection to his scalp, light and thin between her fingers. He kissed her on the lips again. Although they could not see each other, the wealth of emotion between them spoke its own language. The singing crickets and Martina's heavy breathing merged with the taste of shared love.

Shalimar put her arms around Chameleon so she could feel his breathing against her neck. There was nothing in the world that could express her feelings at this moment. Chameleon broke the silence.

'I lead a simple life from the money I have made and I stopped in time because of you.' He continued. 'There are lots of things I have done that I am not proud of. The only one of those things I can change is us, but I need your help.'

It hurt to know Chameleon had not been the one who had saved her. She had saved herself throughout the war but he had not managed to do the same. War had overpowered and controlled him long before their chance meeting. Chameleon stroked her hair, trailing his fingers softly across her scalp and around the plaits.

'I have come home to my family,' he whispered

Shalimar tasted salt as she kissed Chameleon's face. Her fingers flew up to his wet cheeks. She pulled back a little alarmed.

'What is wrong? I thought you were happy.'

'Karma,' Chameleon's voice broke.

'Karma?' Shalimar repeated, slightly confused.

His fingers outlined the blackened teeth marks left by Predator and trailed to the rest of her body touching on her scars again.

'I know what they did to you, Shalimar. I lived my whole life in war. It pains me that everything that I am responsible for came back to me... through you...'

'Hush...' Her fingers traced his lips and tapped them.

'You suffered my karma...' He broke off and choked.

'Hush, Jamie. I am here, Martina is here and you are here. We are your Karma'

She kissed him, to stop him speaking then nestled herself into his body.

'Cry for your friend, Jack Daniels because he is the one who is not welcome here anymore.'

Chameleon chuckled cautiously. The silence that followed emphasised the importance of Shalimar's intentions. He acknowledged her words.

'It's difficult to cut off a long life friend. Are you willing to help me... get rid of him? It won't be easy.'

Shalimar could feel his growing smile against her neck.

'I will help you show him the door but you have to open it.'

'I have come home to my real family.' Chameleon said holding her close as though he would never let her go. 'I don't need anything else in the world.'

Milton Keynes UK
Ingram Content Group UK Ltd.
UKHW011831270923
429496UK00002B/8